The Sycamore Centennial Parade

(Part I)

C.S. McGrail

Fintan and Turtle Publishing

Syracuse N.Y. USA

Praise for The Sycamore Centennial Parade

(Part I)

"McGrail's voice crackles with humor, clever turns of phrase, and old-school charm. The dialog sings—snappy, smart, and so natural you forget you're reading."

-Literary Titan

"A lively tale of men with Peter Pan syndrome, and a pleasantly humorous mystery."

-Kirkus Review

The Sycamore Centennial Parade

(PART I)

© 2025 Fintan and Turtle

ISBN 978-1-944360-06-1

This is a work of fiction. All characters are imaginary. They were invented for the purpose of telling this story. Any similarities between any of them and any person(s) living or dead is purely coincidental.

Please explore more fiction at https://www.fintanandturtle.com

To Joan Hanlon.

Enjoy.

Wherever you might be.

Chapter 1

Babylon Hurley stepped out of his truck and checked his watch. He was a few minutes ahead of schedule. That was out of character for him and would surprise his sister, Jericho. Might even make up for the tie he wasn't wearing.

"*Maybe.*" He thought, with a grin. He looked down at his sports jacket. She had just given it to him, the night before.

"*Ugly looking thing.*" He thought. But it seemed to fit alright. He smoothed the lapel with his hand. And looked himself over in the truck's elongated outside mirror.

His mother had thought he should be wearing his medals from the army. She kept bringing it up.

"Pin them to the breast pocket." She said. "Your Uncle Billy wore his medals on his interview. And he got the job."

"Uncle Billy didn't own a suit then, ma. It was 1945. He just got home. He wore his dress blues. Besides, this ain't an interview."

"Don't say ain't." Pearl wasn't going to win, so she used the reprimand to close the conversation.

Tilting the truck mirror up and down, Babylon could see himself in two sections. Fresh shave, new haircut, collared white shirt and pale grey jacket on top. Dark blue slacks, instead of jeans, and polished black shoes on the bottom. For an out of work, 34-year-old dock worker, he cleaned up pretty well.

He checked his watch again. Could he pass as the salesman he was supposed to be? His sister thought so. At least, she said she thought so.

"If you look the part, you'll feel the part. If you feel the part, you'll act the part. And if you act the part, you'll make the sale." Is how she explained both the new wardrobe and the sales mantra they were supposed to adopt.

"Awful lot of moving parts." Babylon's brother-in-law, Poodle, had whispered, one night, while they were both getting an earful. Jericho had spent the last 2 weeks giving them a crash course in salesmanship. They weren't any better for it. But they could recite an awful lot of tactical nonsense.

"Not Poodle," Babylon said out loud, correcting himself. "Hence forth and ever more, he shall be Clark. Clark of the Canderankles." He was making light of another of Jericho's directives. Her husband was now to be addressed by his given name. And her brother was no longer allowed to be the Milkman, at least during working hours. He was back to being Babylon.

So, as Babylon, he came around to the front of his truck. The air was still cool. And the building behind him was tall enough that his truck would sit in the shade most of the day. Picking your parking spot was the only advantage he could see about being downtown at 7 AM. No one was here. Even the bums were off doing something else.

The front bumper groaned when he rested against it.

"Easy now." He said, patting his truck's grill. It was a '44 DIVCO milk truck. Arrived on this planet the same year he did. The Mythical Milk Machine, as it came to be called.

During his senior year, back in 1962, Babylon had gone with his father to an auto auction. They were looking for a used car for his mother. When Babylon saw the truck, he showed his old man.

"You think your mother's going to drive that?" His father asked.

"No. For me." Babylon said.

Damascus Hurley scoffed at his son. And told him to pass. The truck needed quite a bit of work.

But Babylon bid on it anyway. And with no competition, he won. Then borrowing a hundred bucks from his less than pleased father, they brought it home.

By graduation it was on the road. And by mid-summer it had been christened by his friends. And he, in turn, had become The Milkman, pilot of said mythical machine.

He and his pals had a summer full of adventures. But all their foolish stunts and ridiculous late-night journeys were short lived. By early autumn, college, jobs and military inductions had taken priority. The nicknames, however, never faded. All these years later, people still called him Milkman. Or more often, Milk.

He liked being Milk. And he liked Poodle being Poodle. He was pretty sure Jericho liked it that way too. But starting today, things had to be different. At least for a while.

With a resigning smile, he pulled a deck of cards from his jacket. He'd make the most of his time and practice while he waited. He began cutting the deck with one hand. Every third or fourth cut, he'd lift the top card and without looking, called it out.

"Nine of Diamonds."

He'd flip it over to make sure he was right. He always was. Then he'd put it back on top and do it again.

"Queen of Spades." And on and on. Each time checking before continuing. Every now and again, with the flick of his wrist, he'd make the top card appear to disappear. Then with a snap of the fingers, he'd bring it back.

In front of young children, or drunken bar patrons, it was a clever trick. They were always impressed. And he was always happy to perform.

But it was a simple slight-of-hand. Something any first or second year magic student could master. But he liked doing it. And practiced to keep it crisp.

He glanced at his watch. *"They'll be here."* He told himself as he flopped the lower half of the deck onto the upper, then peeled away another top card. "Two of Clubs."

*****

A mile away, Clark and Jericho Canderankle were headed towards him at what Jericho considered a 'law frowning' speed. Technically speeding, but not quite reckless. The window to being early was closing. And to Poodle's wife, on time was as bad as being late.

Things could have been different if Clark knew how to tie a tie. But he didn't. He'd only ever worn a tie three times in his whole life. Twice, clip-ons had been provided. And on the last, the tie snapped in the back. With those options, Clark didn't understand why anyone would ever waste their time learning to tie one of those hangman's nooses. His wife, however, held a different view.

She made him keep at it the night before, until he created a tie with a tolerable knot and a reasonable length. Then he slipped it off, still tied, so he could put it back on in the morning.

But neither of them had considered his Fred Flintstone sized head. It was huge. As was the rest of him. And when he carelessly pulled it over his skull the next morning, it stretched, loosened, and came undone.

They lost their drive time margin while she was re-tying it for him. Now they were scrambling. At least, she was.

"Did you hear me?" Jericho asked, looking into her rear-view mirror. Trying to talk was the only thing she didn't like about her new car. It was a '73 Volkswagen Beetle. Only 5 years old. The newest she'd ever owned. It was still rust free and shiny.

But she always felt like she was yelling. And she often had to repeat herself. That was because her car had no front passenger seat. Everyone, besides the driver, rode in the back. So, if she needed to talk, she had to raise her voice, or say things a second time, and almost always, had to set the inside mirror to eye level.

It was annoying. And she was still getting used to it. But overall, a small and necessary concession. Otherwise, her husband would have never fit into her car. Clark was almost 6 feet 5 inches tall. And that was way too much human being for her little bug.

With the seat gone, he could sit in the back and extend his legs comfortably. It just made conversations awkward.

And as expected, he hadn't heard her. He was looking down, playing with his tie. She beeped the horn.

"Hello!"

He looked up. "Sorry. What?"

"First, stop fondling your tie. Second, what time is it?"

"I wasn't fondling it." Clark answered, shifting the loose watch on his wrist around so he could see it. "I was... playing with it. There's a difference."

"Uh-huh." She wasn't interested. "What time is it?"

Clark looked down at his watch again. "Oh look! It's time to fondle your tie!"

"Clark."

"7:02."

Well, that was better than she thought. But they were still another minute out. Not that it mattered. Her brother wouldn't be there yet. He had a 'close enough is good enough' concept of punctuality. That drove her crazy.

She slid the stick into neutral as she rounded a corner wider and faster than she probably should have. She was shaving time.

"Someday they'll invent a braking system." Clark barked at her as he pulled himself back upright. "When they do, I'll teach you how to use it."

"Sorry!" She said in a very 'sorry, not sorry' tone. Then she popped it back into gear and hit the gas.

Clark didn't care. He knew why she was motoring. This was kick off day. It was the same reason he was wearing a tie. And a jacket. And his church shoes. Ugh, his church shoes. They were still brand new. He wiggled his feet and wondered if wearing them was a such good idea.

"You know where you are?" his wife asked, over her shoulder.

Clark looked up. "Sure. I'm right here. And we're going over there." He pointed straight ahead.

Jericho giggled. It was fun watching him pretend he had a sense of direction.

"What?" He said, knowing full well why she was amused.

She slowed and stopped at a red light. "You could find your way home?" She knew he couldn't.

"With or without crying?"

"Without." The light turned green.

"Nope." He said flatly. "Probably not." But there was no 'probably'. They both knew his only navigation skill was calling a cab.

Jericho revved it into second. Then, realizing she wasn't going to make the next light, dropped it into neutral and let it coast. She looked back at him, through the mirror, as she applied the brake. Tie and jacket? He didn't look half bad.

"Mom was at McKelly's last week." She said, trying to sound nonchalant.

"Okay." Poodle didn't care where his mother-in-law shopped.

"She said they had one of those all-white John Travolta disco suits in the front…"

"Nope!" He already knew where this was going.

"Oh, come on." She pleaded. The light changed and she put it back into first. "You could take me dancing."

"Since when did you want to go dancing with Moby Dick?" He wiggled in his seat, like he was doing the twist. "Maybe a little peg leg polka there, Captain Ahab?"

"You're being silly. Come on. You'd look good."

"No, *you're* being silly." He said back. "John Travolta puts on that suit and jumps around, he looks good. I do the same thing; I look like an avalanche." Then before she could reply, Clark leaned forward.

"That's it up ahead, on the right."

Jericho drove to this parking lot every day. She knew where they were going. But she didn't say anything. He just wanted to change the subject. So, she let him. At least for now.

"If you're going to repeat that last corner," Clark said, "I need a seatbelt."

Jericho slowed down and flipped on her turning signal. "Are there even belts back there?" She had no idea. She was always the driver.

Clark shrugged but didn't check. They wouldn't fit anyway, so why bother?

"I don't believe it." Jericho said, cruising into the lot. Her brother was there ahead of her.

As they rolled over, Milk stood up and put his cards away. Jericho pulled up alongside him.

"Why do you always have to keep us waiting?" She asked.

Milk smiled. "I got lost." He pinched his sister's chin.

"You getting in on this side?" She asked, pulling the emergency brake.

Milk smirked and said, "Be easier on the other side."

"Not for everyone." She mumbled. Then she leaned over her husband's legs and pushed open the passenger side door.

"Thank you." Clark said.

Because there was no front seat on the passenger side, climbing out was a chore. Particularly at Clark's size.

To get out, Clark had to drop to the floor and scootch himself forward. That meant bringing his chest as close to his knees as his belly would allow. It was like doing a set on a rowing machine. He would be purple by the time he was standing upright.

He didn't want to do that. So he sat there, with the door open, hoping some other option might occur to him. But the clock was ticking.

"Clark." Jericho said, reminding him she still had to get to work.

"Yes dear." Clark grumbled under his breath.

"What did you say?" Milk chimed in, hoping to start trouble.

"I said 'I'm fat!'" Clark blurted out under the strain of lowering himself to the floor. He butt-bounced across the carpet until he could grab the side of the door opening.

"Earthquake much?" Milk asked, as the whole car rocked in place.

"Shut up Milk." Poodle felt like an accordion. He wiggled a little farther, then swung his right leg out the door. He could breathe again.

After that, he turned. And put out his other leg. But before he could pull himself upright, he felt Milk's hand pushing down on his head, holding him in place.

Poodle started laughing. "I will kick your ass, little man."

Milk started laughing back at him. "You think so?" He reached down with his free hand and started flicking at Poodle's nose. Poodle laughed harder, shook his head, and started slap fighting.

Jericho watched. *"Give them their moment."* She told herself. Then after 5 or 6 seconds, she said, "Okay! That's enough!"

They ignored her. She reached over and poked her husband in the ribs. "Clark!"

He knew better than to ignore that. He knocked away Milk's grip from his head and stood up.

"Get in the car, trouble maker." Poodle barked. Then, instead of stepping out of the way, he stepped forward, chest butting his friend backwards. Milk rebounded and slapped Poodle's tie up into his face.

"Out of my way, punk." He said, as he scooted around the big man and into the back seat. Poodle watched his buddy get situated. Then climbed back into the car.

As they pulled out of the parking lot, Jericho reviewed their plan of attack one last time. It was fairly simple. She would take them to the top of Vancouver Boulevard. That was the main shopping thoroughfare downtown. From there, they would each visit retailers and introduce the idea of the Centennial parade.

"Don't worry about selling," She said, looking in the mirror for eye contact, "This is preliminary work. Letting the retailers know what we're doing. Sales will come."

No one argued, but both men had their doubts. Three weeks

earlier, they were both working at Sonic Star, Sycamore's largest employer. Making pretty good money, too. Then things changed.

"Just recite the pitch we practiced." Jericho continued. "Then leave a brochure and be on your way."

"Brochure. And be on our way." Poodle recited back to her.

Milk turned his head to Poodle, "How far we riding like this?"

Poodle chuckled. "Do you even know who you're talking to?" He had zero sense of direction and distance.

"I'm going to be crippled when I get out of here." Milk had no leg room. His chin rested on his knees. And his feet were trapped under the driver's seat. He started wiggling and stomping them.

"I can feel that." Jericho said, telling her brother to stop. Which, of course, only inspired him to continue.

"You're crippled already." Clark said, tapping his pal in the temple.

"Babs, stop." Jericho said louder.

Milk stopped stomping and pointed at Poodle's church shoes. "Not as crippled as you'll be."

"What?" Poodle asked, slapping away Milk's finger.

"Why'd you wear brand new shoes? We'll be walking all day."

"They're not brand new," Poodle said, holding up a foot. "They're just polished."

"Yeah, sure. You should have worn sneakers."

"You can't polish sneakers."

Milk rolled his eyes. "Wear unpolished sneakers."

"I don't have any sneakers."

"Mom said sneakers on sale at Sears." Milk said.

"I'm not buying sneakers to wear with a tie." As soon as Poodle said that, he realized Milk was tie-less. His eyes grew wide.

"I'm telling!" He whispered. Then he turned towards his wife, "Ma!" he yelled, like a spoiled child.

Milk slapped his hand over Poodle's mouth. "Shut up, Dick."

Jericho saw the slap in the mirror. "What are you two doing?"

Poodle turned his head and leaned away. As soon as he was loose, he told on his friend.

"Milk's not wearing his tie!" He barely got it out before Milk punched him in the shoulder.

"I said shut up Dick!"

Both men were back to laughing and slapping at one another. Jericho pulled over and came to a stop. She watched in the mirror until they realized what she had done. Then they both stopped and sat up straight.

"Are you through?" She asked.

"Wow, she really is your mom." Milk stage whispered to Poodle.

Jericho ignored her brother, checked the side mirror and pulled back onto the street.

"You're not wearing your tie, Babs?" She asked, shifting into second.

"It's in my pocket." He answered. "They make us look like missionaries. Or bible salesmen." When his sister didn't say anything more, he reached into his jacket and pulled it out.

"Can you tie it?" Jericho asked.

"Better than Mr. tattle tale." Milk said.

"Oh, like that would be hard." Poodle smirked.

"Not as hard as your head." Milk pointed at Poodle's shoes a second time. "You're wearing brand new shoes. You're going to get blisters."

"I'm tough." Poodle said, sitting up taller.

"You're a blockhead." His friend answered.

"Blockheads are tough." Poodle snorted at him. "Their heads are made of… block."

"Okay, okay," Jericho saw this turning into another slap-fest. "How about we meet for lunch? Say right at noon? Clark, I'll bring your other shoes from home. You should be okay till then."

"Where?" Poodle was all about the food.

"What does it matter?" Milk tried to slap his friend on the top of the head. "You won't know how to get there."

Poodle was ready for the attack. And knocked Milk's hand away. "Who cares?" he said. "I'll just follow you."

"Oh yeah? I'll run and lose your fat ass."

"Oh yeah?" Poodle mocked. He made a grab for the back of Milk's neck. "Maybe I'll make you give me a piggy back."

"Where?!" Jericho barked over both of them. "Are we meeting?"

"Sal's Slices!" Milk yelled, as he blocked Poodle's grab. He only had one arm free for fighting. Pinned behind the driver's seat, he couldn't turn effectively. "And tell your little boy to leave me alone. Or

I'm going to have to hurt him."

"Clark!" Jericho called out over her shoulder.

Poodle stopped attacking. But mouthed, 'You're lucky!'. Then slid his thumb across his own throat to let Milk know he was a dead man.

Milk gave him the finger. Poodle tried to slap it. And both men had to look out their respective windows to control themselves.

No one talked for another mile or so. The traffic began to increase. And they stopped more frequently. Then Poodle asked a question.

"What are we supposed to do if we do make a sale?"

"Don't worry about sales honey. They'll come." Jericho was watching lane mergers and answered on auto-pilot.

"That's not what he's saying." Milk said. "Shouldn't they sign something? A contract maybe?"

Contracts weren't finalized. This whole project came out of nowhere two weeks prior. And the legal team had no sense of urgency.

That's why she had 2 unemployed, blue collar, family members doubling as her sales force. She didn't have anyone else. At least not yet.

"Have them cut you a down payment check." She didn't really think anyone would do that without a contract. But kept that morsel to herself. "Have them make it out to the Sycamore Chamber of Commerce."

"How much?"

That was a good question. Contracts weren't done because, among other things, pricing wasn't approved. For three nights she was up working on it until after the National anthem sign off on television. She submitted it a week ago. And still hadn't heard.

"Tell them…" Jericho hesitated for a second, then said, "Tell them 50 bucks holds them a spot.

"50 dollars?" Poodle repeated.

"Yeah. And tell them spots are going fast."

"They are?" Milk asked, sounding doubtful.

"Just tell them!" She couldn't believe she was making it up on the fly. But it kind of felt good. She kept going. "We'll send somebody back later to work out all the details. And the final costs." This was way more fun than she would have thought. "And one more thing. 10 percent off if they secure a spot today. But only today. Understand?"

Both men said they did.

Two blocks later, Jericho pulled over and let them both out.

"Excited?" she asked.

The two men looked at one another. Then Poodle said, "Yeah. Sure."

Jericho sighed. Should she have expected anything else? She hugged them each, one at a time.

"Make me proud fellas."

They both watched her get back in the car. She tapped the horn and held up a satchel of brochures. Poodle reached through the window and took it.

"See you at lunch." He said.

She waved. Then drove away.

They watched until she was out of sight. Then Milk asked, "Want a beer?"

A beer sounded good. But starting now meant napping by lunchtime.

"I'd rather have a meal." Poodle answered.

"You didn't eat this morning?"

Poodle patted his stomach with both hands. "Only once."

"You poor malnourished child." Milk frowned. "Come with me."

They walked off in search of a Diner.

Chapter 2

They headed opposite of the way Jericho had driven off. Milk said he knew of a diner, a few blocks away. Without talking about it, they agreed it was pointless to be out this early. Everything was closed. And would be for at least another hour or two.

Unbeknownst to them, Jericho had already reached the same conclusion. She may have had doubts about their skill sets. Or about their maturity. But one thing she knew, without a doubt, was that the first thing these two would do, would be to go on a food hunt.

If it took them an hour while shops were closed; nothing was lost. But if they did the same thing while stores were open? Well, that's why she dropped them off at 7:00 AM.

After the first block, Poodle looked over at his brother-in-law. "You really bring beer?"

Milk smiled. "Now you want one?"

"I don't want one." Poodle answered. "But you got my mouth all watery thinking about wanting one."

"They're on ice, back in the truck." Milk flipped a thumb behind them.

Poodle didn't punch Milk in the shoulder as much as he pushed him with a fisted hand. That sent Milk sideways, forcing him off the walk.

"Meep-Meep!" he said, pushing an imaginary car horn. He swung wide and avoided a parked car. Making squealing tire sounds, he pantomimed steering himself back onto the curb.

"That was a close one." he said stepping back into the rhythm of their walk. "What if I had wrecked? You wouldn't know where to go."

"I don't know where we're going now." Poodle said.

When they got to the next cross street, Milk pointed and made a left. His brother-in-law followed him.

"Know what street this is?" Milk asked as Poodle caught up.

"If I tell you, we'll both know."

Milk remembered the time Poodle tried that little remark on Mrs. Fahey, the 9th grade math teacher. He wasn't paying attention. So, she asked him a question. That answer won him a quick trip home. The rest of the class howled at his nerve.

Anyone else would have been sent to the principal's office. But Poodle, who was already known as Poodle by then, was a foot taller than Mr. Limbaugh, the principal. What was he going to do? Use a hickory switch?

Milk clapped his hands and said, "Now class!" impersonating Mrs. Fahey's cackle. Poodle was amused that his friend remembered. They walked on. Poodle took in the ambiance of downtown as Milk led the way.

In the mid 1960's, Sycamore's civil leaders passed an ordinance. It decreed that all future development had to preserve the antiquity and integrity of downtown. For the most part, it worked. That is to say, development in downtown stalled out.

Pillars, brickwork, and gargoyles were expensive. And architects were on to other ideas. Nobody was interested in re-inventing nostalgia.

It did, however, work well for development beyond city limits. Suburban malls and industrial parks were popping up in the surrounding townships. Was that their ulterior motive? Poodle had no idea.

But he liked what he saw. He liked simple. And found a certain level of security in growth that had slowed to a crawl. He started life as a farm boy. And still was, at heart.

Life was always changing. You couldn't stop it. The kids were growing. His parents had passed. Jericho was now making him help her hide her wisdom, twice a month, with some shampoo in the sink she called a rinse.

He didn't mind any of that. But if his town was somewhat sleepy, he was in no hurry to wake it up.

It made him think of Sonic Star. And for the first time since his pink sheet, he thought about the situation from a perspective beyond himself.

He frowned. This was going to be tough for a lot of people. He didn't understand, nor care to know, how economics might work. But he couldn't see how people could survive without jobs. Somebody better figure something out.

He was lucky. His wife was still working. He thought about his wife and smiled. He really was lucky.

It was still early enough that the Sun was below the skyline of rooftops. Everything was bathed in a uniform smear of indirect light. 'The delight of twilight' as Poodle and Jericho's wedding photographer had once remarked.

Everything Poodle saw, as they walked, had the feel of an old black and white photograph. He began to appreciate that phrase as they clipped along.

"So, are you going to do it?" Milk asked without looking over.

"Do what?" Poodle answered.

Milk jacked a thumb to the left, and they cut up another intersecting street. He didn't say anything, but by now, he knew his pal was lost. Poodle only had a two-turn deviation limit. Then his sense of direction shut down.

"Are you going to go around introducing yourself as Clark?" The very idea tickled Milk.

Poodle didn't know. And he didn't want to talk about it. He grunted some sort of guttural sound. But that was it. He kept walking. Milk toyed with the idea of asking again. But decided to leave it alone.

Up until the summer before 7th grade, Poodle had always been Clark. He didn't know why he was given the name Clark. No one else in his family wore it. He was the first. And in his mind, probably the last. He never intended to hand it down. It didn't mean anything to him.

There was no great-great-great Grampa Clark that single handedly held back the British at the Battle of Sycamore. For that matter, there wasn't even a Battle of Sycamore.

And there wasn't some long lost, insane Uncle Clark that wore a tinfoil hat and used a homemade crystal set to contact alien planets. Although, Poodle thought that would have been cool. He would have liked that guy. That Uncle Clark would have been fun.

But mad scientist Clark didn't exist. Nor, in his family, did any other Clark. However, he did have an Uncle Bob. And in 1953, Uncle Bob bought some beach front property along the Gulf shore of Alabama.

Two years later, Uncle Bob had built himself a summer home. And Clark and his parents went down to visit. They intended to be gone two weeks. But managed to stay the season.

When Clark left Sycamore, he was a skinny 11-year-old with wavy brown hair and green eyes. His height and weight were nothing unusual. He resembled what you might expect when looking at an active pre-teen. But when he returned to start school, things had changed. His eyes were still green. And his weight was the same. But having gone through what his mother later called the 'Guiness world record of growth spurts', he was suddenly 6 feet tall. He was so lanky, he looked as if he could snap himself in half with a sneeze.

But there was more. For reasons no one could ever explain, his hair went from brown and wavy to bone white and wire-y. His father said the brown would return when he wasn't in the sun all day, every day. But that never happened. From the sideburns up, he looked like an albino Airedale.

And with a new appearance came a new name. By the time lunch arrived on the very first day back at school, he was Poodle. And had been Poodle ever since.

He looked over at Milk. "How you going to introduce yourself?"

"Won't know till it happens."

That seemed fair. Poodle didn't want to think about it either. He changed the subject.

"Where you taking me?"

"Where am I taking you? You're taking me. I'm just showing you how to get there."

"Oh, I'm paying?"

"You are."

"You're too kind."

"Not really." Milk pointed. "Right there. You're going to love it."

Poodle looked over. On the far side of a large parking lot, was a small stand-alone building. It didn't look like a diner. It was larger, and odd shaped. It looked more like a retrofitted auto parts store that was now an eatery. Above the glass double doors was a wooden sign. It read: SPROUTS.

"*SPROUTS?*" Poodle made a face. That sounded hideous.

"Why you bring me to a lawn and garden shop?" he asked. "I thought we were getting something to eat."

"Relax. They only sell tractors at harvest time. Right now, it's granola food. For the groovy people." He tapped Poodle in the chest. "Might want to lose the tie there, hipster."

"I like my tie. It took me 40 minutes to tie it."

"It shows."

"Come on man, you've never been to this place before." Poodle said, hoping this was all a joke.

"Yeah, I have. But it's been a while."

"Been a while because… you OD'd on whole grains?"

"No man, they only use whole grains when they run out of cardboard."

"Oh good." Poodle pretended to clap. "I like it when all the food has the same terrible taste."

Milk reached the door. Then winked at his buddy. "Then you're going to love it here." He stepped inside. And held one of the doors open for Poodle to follow.

The place was clean, brightly lit and the industrial ceiling had been painted black, to go unnoticed. There was also the scent of toasted cinnamon, which lightly floated in the room like incense. Poodle took a deep breath. Who knew tractor sales and service smelled so good?

"Oh man!" He said, licking his lips.

"Told you." Milk said, holding up two fingers to the hostess.

She was high school aged. Tall, thin and pretty. Class president material. Over her skirt she wore an apron that was more for display than function. She stopped at the cash register for menus before walking over.

"Two today?"

Both men nodded. But before they followed her, Poodle said, "Those cinnamon buns smell fantastic."

"Oh? Oh, those are pancakes." She said, "The chef is trying something new."

Chef? Milk had met 'Chef'. He was a kid named Matt, barely older than the hostess. There was nothing Chef-y about him. But he didn't say anything. He just followed her into the dining room.

As they passed the counter full of swivel stools, Milk waved. Chef Matt was on the other side of the server's window, rearranging hash browns on the short order grill. Matt waved back. Then he turned to Timmy, the busboy.

"Dude!" He called over his shoulder. "You just missed the return of the son of Frankenstein!"

Timmy was a 16-year-old high school drop-out. He was perpetually stoned and useless as an employee. But he was the first and favorite nephew of Tiny, the owner. So, he had a job. As long as Timmy showed up every day and did half of what Matt told him to do, he got paid. Otherwise, Tiny would box his ears back. So far, it was a workable arrangement for all involved.

"He did what?" Timmy looked up from a sink full of dishes. He couldn't remember who they were just talking about.

"Oh, he sure did!" Matt snapped back. Timmy was like a puppy. It took nothing more than sounding excited to get him all worked up.

"Mr. Hurley brought him in. Dudes got to be 7 feet tall!" He held the spatula above himself to demonstrate the height.

"Whoa!" Timmy answered back.

Matt waved him over to the window. "Look man, look." He pointed over the counter ledge with the same spatula. "They're in disguise. They all dressed up like some kind a Born Agains."

Timmy peered over the ledge. "Whoa!" he whispered. "Frankenstein got fire and brimstone on his side. Damn!" The two cooks fist bumped each other.

The hostess directed her two newest customers to a booth against the back wall. Poodle was pleased. He'd have room to spread out. When they were seated, she asked about coffee and set down the menus.

"Your waitress will be right with you." She said. Then turned and walked back to her station.

Poodle picked up the menu. But before he looked at it, he glanced around the dining room. It was about half filled. From their ages, he guessed that most of the customers were college students. There were a few, maybe a dozen, slightly older people. He assumed they were professors.

Judging by clientele alone, he expected everything on the menu to be inedible. Fake meat. Fake milk. Fake cheese. Everything 'all-natural' and none of it being what it claimed to be. Except tofu. Goddamn tofu always stood proud. Poodle hated tofu. Just the thought of it made him gag.

But man, that aroma smelled so good! How could all that boiling tree bark and cobwebs create that scent? He sighed. Worst case, he'd just sip coffee and sniff the air.   Assuming the coffee was real.

He noticed that Milk was just sitting still, with his hands folded, watching everyone else enjoy their meals. He slid the other menu over, closer to him.

"You ain't hungry?" He asked.

"Oh yeah," Milk answered. "I just already know what I want."

Poodle tilted his menu up so he could read it. It was a single, laminated sheet, that continued onto the second side. He nodded to himself a few times as he read. When he flipped the page over, he asked, "Those pancakes as good as they smell?"

Milk nodded. "Cakes are good. That's what I'm getting."

"How about the coffee?"

Milk's face scrunched. "Coffee's coffee. Unless you burn it."

"Good. So, it ain't toad stools or nothing, right?"

Milk grinned. "Why would they make coffee out of toad stools?"

"Cause toad stools is all-natural." Poodle bobbled his head, impersonating a helium balloon. His way of mocking the air headed tree huggers.

"What's not natural about coffee beans?"

Poodle pointed at the menu. "What's not natural about ham and eggs? Don't see that anywhere on here."

Milk waved him off. "Have the pancakes. They're good." Then, changing tone, he said, "Oh my God. It lives."

Poodle turned in the direction Milk was looking. An older woman had come out of the kitchen. She was tired and weathered looking. With an insulated coffee urn in one hand, and two empty ceramic cups in the other, she walked over to the hostess.

The hostess shook her head, then pointed at their booth. The woman glared over. She had mean eyes. Even from across the room you could see they were mean. She was staring right at Poodle.

"That our waitress?" Poodle asked.

"Yup. That's Shelly." Milk said.

"She looks like a regular ray of sunshine."

"Oh yeah." Milk answered.

Shelly walked up to the edge of the table and let the coffee pot slam down with a sharp thud. Both men jumped. She let out a cackle of approval, just to let them know she had done it on purpose.

"What do you want?" She said, without looking, as she reached into her apron pocket for her pad.

"Is that coffee, in there, real coffee?' Milk asked, pointing at the urn and sounding doubtful.

"What the hell else would it be?" She glared at Milk. Poodle was certain his pal was about to get the wooden spoon. Then her features softened.

"Where you been Milk?"   she asked.

Milk offered a half smile. "Just laying low."

"I heard about Sonic Star." She said. "Saw it on the news."

"Yeah. Didn't make the cut." He waved a finger between him and Poodle. "Got us both."

She turned her attention to Poodle. That momentary sliver of civility was gone. The beacon of mean was back. Her eyes narrowed and focused on the knot of his tie.

"You're a Witness to the Apocalypse." She sneered. "Cops are looking for you."

What the hell did that mean? Without thinking, he put a hand up to cover his tie. He looked over at Milk.

Milk clapped his hands together. "She said you're a witness. You've been saved. Testify my brother!"

That was no help.

"I don't know what you're talking about." Poodle said back to her. She wasn't listening. The 'order up' bell had rung behind her. She was looking over her shoulder to see what plate was on the window ledge.

When she turned back to them, Milk poked some more, "Shelly, why you want Poodle to testify?"

"Poodle!?!?" She pointed at his hair. "Ha! Let me guess why. Poodle." She said his name like she was spitting poison.

The bell sounded again.

"Goddamn it." Shelly muttered through clenched teeth. She shoved the pad in her apron pocket and, without comment, walked back to the kitchen.

Milk winked. "She's a real sweetheart, isn't she?"

Poodle sneered. "As pleasant as steaming cat piss."

Milk made a sour face and waved a hand in front of his nose. "Cat piss. Pew."

Poodle poured them each a cup of coffee. He sniffed it before he tasted it. Milk watched him, shook his head, but said nothing. Then Shelly was back.

"Okay, where were we?" She focused on Poodle.

"I'll have a stack of those cinnamon pancakes." Then added, "Please."

"Cinnamon vanilla," She clarified, just to be difficult. "Short or tall?"

"Tall. Please."

"You want try some black bean sausage with that?" Milk asked, pretending to be helpful.

"No."

"It's really good."

"I'm sure it is."

"How about a few strips of that soy bacon? Mmmm…" Milk said 'soy' like it was a magic word. Then smacked his lips for emphasis.

Poodle didn't answer. He was watching Shelly's expression.

She wasn't amused. "You can punch him. I don't care."

"Thank you." Poodle answered.

"What about you Milk?"

"I'll have what I always have. And those sausages too, please."

Shelly wrote it all down. Putting her pad back in her apron, she said, "Your girlfriend was in last week."

"My girlfriend? I don't have a girlfriend." Milk said.

"Yes, you do." Shelly said it with as much lilt in her voice as two packs a day would allow.

Milk didn't argue. He didn't answer at all. Shelly waited. Then continued.

"She was in with two other gals I never seen before. They sat on Lona's side, so we didn't talk none. Just waved."

Milk nodded but still sat quiet. Shelly was dirt digging. Milk and Lydia used to be an item. Not all that long ago either. Apparently, inquiring minds still wanted to know.

To Poodle, that went a long way in explaining how Milk came to know this place. SPROUTS was much more Lydia's style than his. He might eat all these hedge clippings without complaining. But they weren't his first choice.

The silence was turning into a standoff. Then, another bell sounded. Shelly smiled and went back to work.

"She's a real sweetheart alright." Poodle muttered as they watched her go.

Milk looked over. "She's fine. She just got a case of the snoops. What woman don't?"

Poodle held up the coffee pot. Milk slid his cup sideways. Poodle poured. Then he topped off his own.

Chef Matt had been watching Shelly talk to the boys. He saw her roar over Poodle's name. It had been him that had rung the bell. He could have waited. But he loved pissing her off. Particularly when she was in the middle of enjoying herself. As he did that, he had turned to Timmy.

"She-devil just ripped Frankenstein a new one." He said.

"Whoa! Maybe monster brimstones should get some holy water too. Toss it in that bitch's…"

"Door!" Matt cut him off.

The hostess came in to refill her silverware tray.

"Hi Terry." Timmy offered her a weak smile.

She ignored him and grabbed a handful of utensils. They were pre-wrapped in cloth napkins. Then she did it a second time, and a third time. When her silverware tray was full, she finally acknowledged the busboy.

"Table 9 is empty." Then she left before he could say anything back to her.

Timmy watched her go. Then turned back to his sink of soapy dishes. "Toss it in her face too." He grumbled.

At that, Matt made a loud sizzling sound and grabbed his own face. "Ah-h-h-h!!!" He withered in place like the wicked witch did when Dorthy soaked her. Both boys laughed.

It was probably best that Terry the hostess didn't hear Timmy wishing that she got her face boiled off with holy water. It would have just fueled her fire. She was already mad.

When Shelly came back to answer the bell, she told Terry there was no silverware on the back booth. And then added that the little bitch needed to get off her ass and do her damn job.

It's not that Shelly was wrong. But she could have worded it nicer. Could have perhaps, if today wasn't her sixth consecutive 10-hour shift. It was only 8:00 AM and her feet were already killing her.

Terry, the Hostess, took the silverware bundles out to the back booth. She glanced around at all the other tables as she passed them. She didn't want to hear about it a second time.

When she reached the booth, she grinned an insincere smile and set two rolled up napkins in the center of the table. As she turned away, Milk spoke up.

"Your sister still got her sheep?" he asked.

Terry turned back around. This time she really looked at him. Not the quick, cordial glance she gave everyone that needed to be seated. But a hard look. A look she could use if she were talking to a police sketch artist.

Nothing. She didn't know this guy. But he wasn't being coy, or clever. He wasn't flirting with her. He was asking a real question.

"No. She sold it at the auction at the end of the season."

Milk turned to Poodle. "Her sister raised a ram lamb for… FFA? Is that right?"

"No. 4H." Terry answered.

"Oh, sorry. She going to sell fruit again?"

That was it. That's how this guy knew her sister. She smiled.

"You're the guy that bought all the cherries."

Milk half shrugged. "Well, a few of us did. I was the guy that showed up and paid." Then he turned to Poodle. "Remember when ma was bombing everybody with pies last year?" He pointed at Terry. "They had some kind of a fund raiser."

Poodle did remember. And he shook his head. "Those pies were good!" He looked at Terry. "Thank you."

"It was my sister and her team. They picked all the fruit. Then Tiny let them use the kitchen to can them." She pointed behind herself as she spoke.

"Tiny?" Poodle didn't know who that was.

"He owns the place." Milk said. Then to Terry. "How's he doing?"

She waffled her hand and grimaced. "You'd do better to ask Shelly. He's lost a lot of weight."

Milk nodded. Then after a moment of silence, he stuck out a hand.

"I'm Babylon Hurley. My friends call me Milk." Terry shook his hand.

"Hello. I'm Terry Smith. Nice to meet you."

"You as well." Milk pointed at Poodle. "And this is my brother-in-law Poodle."

Terry looked at Poodle's haircut. "That's not really your name. Is it?"

Poodle extended a hand. "Yes and no. I'm Clark. Clark Canderankle." They shook hands. "Everyone calls me Poodle. You're welcome to as well."

"Get on your shining armor, bro." Matt said as he turned towards Timmy. "Your damsel's in distress."

Timmy, having been outside, had no idea what was going on in the dining room.

"What did I do?" he asked, checking his shoes to see if he dragged anything inside.

"No man," Matt said as he handed Timmy a 2-ounce ladle. "It must be monster mating season. Frankenstein's running off with his new bride." He started pushing Timmy towards the swinging doors. "He's taking Terry."

"Brimstone Frank snagged Terry? No way, man!"

Matt pushed the door open. "Check it out."

Timmy reluctantly stuck his head through the doorway. He could see their booth at the far end of the dining room. "Whoa!" he gasped, recognizing the back of the hostess.

Matt gave busboy a firm nudge to the shoulder. "Go check to see that she's okay. Go on man. Chicks love heroes."

Then giggling, he ran back to the service window so he could watch.

When Timmy looked back at him, Matt flicked his wrist, egging him forward. Timmy started walking towards the booth. His gate was slow and uncertain. Milk saw him coming, ladle in hand.

"I think someone called out the cavalry." He said. Then he tilted his head towards the kitchen.

Poodle looked up. And Terry turned around. But Matt had already ducked out of the window.

When Timmy saw them looking his way, he waved. Then he began walking towards them with a bit more confidence.

"Oh my God!" Terry whispered to herself. What was he doing? He was coming right towards them. She flickered her wrist, dismissing him back to the kitchen. He ignored her and kept walking forward.

"Hey Timmy." Milk said, when he reached the booth.

Timmy stopped next to Terry. His feet were shoulder width apart. His face was stern and his posture erect. He was now holding the ladle handle in one hand and slowly tapping the dipper repeatedly in the palm of his other. He looked like a stoned out, unwashed version of a POW commandant. He meant business.

He looked at Milk and nodded crisply. "Mr. Hurley."

Then he nodded at Poodle. "Frank." His voice was cold.

Poodle turned to Milk and mouthed, "Frank?"

Milk held out a hand parallel to the tabletop, then raised it to indicate Poodle's height.

"*That little shit!*" Poodle thought, realizing he had just been dissed. Then he smiled politely.

Timmy kept his eyes straight ahead. "Everything all right Terry?"

"Everything's fine Timmy. Go back in the kitchen." Then she muttered, "You moron."

That unglued him. Whatever bravado he had been able to call upon as he crossed the room, trickled out of him. He was suddenly lost.

"Well..." he struggled. "Well, how is everything?"

"I just said everything is fine." Terry repeated. "Go back to the kitchen."

Timmy didn't like being bullied. He tried to regain control of the dialogue.

"Well... how's the food then?" He tried to sound confident.

"They don't have their food yet." Terry said softly through clenched teeth. "You need to..."

"Hey!" It was Shelly, slapping Timmy on the back of the leg with a wooden spoon. "Get your ass back in that kitchen." She ripped the ladle from his hand. "And gimme that!"

Timmy grabbed the back of his leg. He considered saying something, thought better of it. And retreated.

Shelly looked at Terry. "They got their silverware?" Terry nodded. "Good-bye."

As Terry walked off, Shelly turned back to her customers and pointed her spoon at them. "What are you two doing?" She asked suspiciously. She didn't know what was going on, but she knew she didn't like it. "What the hell my busboy doing out here?"

"That lovesick puppy?" Poodle asked.

"He came out to save a damsel in distress." Milk added. "From Frankenstein."

Frankenstein made Shelly smirk. So Poodle stuck his arms straight out and growled like Karloff's version. Shelly lowered her spoon.

"I don't want you two causing trouble." She said.

"Okay by us." Poodle said back to her. After he dropped his arms.

She wasn't completely sold. She lowered her voice so the other tables couldn't hear her.

"I'll throw your apocalyptic asses to the street." She threatened.

Milk noticed Matt discreetly peering out at them. He gently tapped three fingers on the table wondering if Matt would understand.

Two seconds later the bell rang. Milk smiled. And Shelly's eyes narrowed.

"Don't push it with me, Milk." She said.

"Hon, we just came to have something to eat." Then as if on cue, both men slumped their heads down. And stared into their coffee cups.

Shelly walked off to the kitchen, muttering to herself.

After a few seconds of sitting perfectly still, Milk whispered, "We got scolded."

"Yup. Probably going to get detention." Poodle added.

"Or expelled." Milk said.

"Let's not get expelled until after we eat." Poodle suggested.

"Agreed." Said Milk.

Chapter 3

Jericho left the boys and drove all the way back home, to get shoes for Poodle. It was easier for her to run late than it was to leave early for lunch. And doing it this way, it was done.

She didn't expect to find a parking spot when she finally pulled into the lot. But there was, two spaces down from her brother's truck. She pulled in and turned her car off.

Before she got out, she took a moment and stared at the brick wall in front of her. She did this every day. Priming the pump, as it were.

She went through the checklist in her head. Today was the day. It was going to be a good one. She believed in herself. And with good reason. Jericho was a rising star at Abbott Industries.

That wasn't something that was happening to the women around her. Professional life was still pretty skewed and unnecessarily unfair. Even in the modern world of 1978 America. She was still the rarity.

But she was building a solid track record. She had worked hard. It was paying off. She was getting noticed.

Then two weeks ago, out of nowhere, this parade project was dropped in her lap. Raoul had presented it to her as if she had a choice. But he also told her to push everything else to the side. This project already had legs and they needed her to take charge.

Already had legs? She had never heard of it before. Shouldn't there have been some preliminary meetings?

And what good was this so-called centennial parade, anyway? It wasn't selling anything. From what she could figure, trying to project a budget, they were going to take a bath on this. A bad idea, all the way around.

Sometimes, before falling asleep, she wondered if she was getting set up to fail. She didn't really believe that. That wasn't the culture at work. But still, it kept crossing her mind. Mostly, just when she was tired.

"We'll get to the bottom of it today." She told herself. *"That budget isn't approved; I'm using it anyway. I don't have time for this shit."*

She giggled. Swearing, even to herself, made her blush. It wasn't something she normally did. She checked her look in the clip-on mirror behind her visor. She looked good. She winked at her reflection and flipped the visor closed. Regardless of what was going on, she looked composed, focused and ready to win. That was a good place to start. She stepped out of her car.

"The boys will be fine," she told herself, walking across the lot. *"No different than hiring teenagers."* Part of her daily mantra, was reminding herself that at least a portion of this arrangement was keeping them busy. Like teenagers, they were responsible to a limited extent. Once that got old, mischief and goofing off was the rule of order.

But there was a plus side to hiring them. They were low-cost, ice breakers for a new campaign. Their responsibilities were minimal. She told them they were the sales team. She trained them like they were, but she wasn't expecting much in the way of results. And, until she had a real sales staff, they weren't at home all day with nothing to do.

It had been her mother's idea to put them to work. Pearl had visions of her son inviting all his unemployed co-workers over to their house.

She just knew they would sit around all day, beer burping the alphabet. Then lie. Say they were doing repair work. When all they were really doing was cluttering her garage with disassembled lawn mower parts.

She was having none of it. Babylon was her son. He lived with her. He looked after her. But she felt no obligation to endure his hooligan pals. She put the twist on Jericho's arm.

At first, Jericho was against it. She didn't want them working for her. For the very same reasons Pearl didn't want them to stay at home. She lied. She told her mother the men were mature enough to do the right thing. Every morning, they would peruse the want ads, make phone calls, and aggressively chase down any job leads they found.

Pearl thought her daughter was nuts. And told her so.

"They're not going to do any of that." She said with a snit. "They're going to screw off. Shoot pool. Or go bowling." She wagged her finger. "Even when they stay home, they won't do anything. They'll drink beer all day and fall asleep tying fishing flies at the picnic table."

Jericho didn't want to agree. She defended them. Until the next Saturday, over coffee, when Pearl made Jericho look out the kitchen window.

Pearl had sent her son out to rake up the rotten apples, under the tree, before mowing the lawn. When Jericho and Clark came over, Poodle went out back to help him.

Now Pearl was holding back a curtain, emphasizing her position. Jericho looked through the glass. She could see her brother overhand pitching rotten apples to her husband, who was trying to knock them out of the park with a tennis racket. Everything around them, in every direction, was sprayed with mushy apple guts. Including both of them.

"That's what you're leaving to its own accord." Pearl sneered, rapping the window with a knuckle. Then she tapped her cigarette ash into the sink and went back to the table.

There was no ignoring the truth after that. Even Jericho's kids, who were actual teenagers, behaved better. She came up with a plan that night. And the next day, informed them that they were no longer unemployed. To her surprise, neither one of them gave her the fight she expected.

"Hello Jeri." Theresa, the first-floor receptionist waved as Jericho came through the door.

Theresa had just turned 40. When she was younger, she was an athlete. But now, when she stood, you could see that beer was beginning to win the girth war. She still looked good. All 5 foot 3 of her. And you certainly didn't want to rouse her wrath. She had put many a man in his place. But she was no longer an athlete. And for the most part, content with it.

She sat in the entryway, behind a round desk, alongside a modest switchboard. She wore conventional office attire. And to the unsuspecting, she was just another secretary. But to those in the know, she was the undercover, first line of defense for the entire building.

Years earlier, when the owner, Eric Abbott, was first starting out in business, he had been accused of sending scabs to cross a picket line. The union retaliated. They sent protesters to wave signs and carry on, outside his office. Which they did.

But things got out of hand. First there was name calling. Then shoving. Then fists. Before the day was over, both the fire department and the police had to be called. Office windows were smashed and Eric's car, parked across the street, had been set on fire.

Since then, Eric took security very seriously. He had trained officers on every floor. But he liked the idea of a rough and ready Theresa and her misleading appearance at the front entrance. She was pleasant and capable. And gave off a much more relaxed and welcoming vibe than any two crew cuts with SECURITY stamped across their breast pocket.

Eric Abbott would have interviewed Theresa based on her experience as a security officer alone. She had worked 3 years at a Federal Courthouse in a larger metropolitan area. But there was more. Her resume also listed Brightonboro Entertainment as a previous employer.

That was a name he recognized. Brightonboro Entertainment was the parent company of the Allenville Alleycats. They had, at one time, been the fiercest collection of Roller Derby Queens to ever play the sport.

On her interview, Theresa showed him her tattoo. Or rather, all 4 of them. They were grouped together in a bunch, on the triceps, just above her right elbow. Each was a straight line, about an inch long. All of them were close and parallel to one another. They were, in a manner of speaking, the notches on her gun handle. Each 'tat' represented a nose she had broken with a swift back stab of her elbow. Each of those were earned on the Derby track.

The tattoos also represented the primary reason behind her forced retirement from the sport. Still, Eric was quite impressed. He offered her the job on the spot.

"Good morning, Theresa," Jericho said, walking over to the desk. "Any messages?"

Theresa looked at her clipboard, already half filled with the day's phone memos.

"Nope. Nothing yet."

That meant Jericho's interview hadn't cancelled. At least so far.

"No news is good news."   she said, holding up crossed fingers.

Theresa knew Jericho was looking to hire sales staff. She held up her own crossed fingers in solidarity.

"Today's the day." She said with a smile. Then one of her phones rang. Jericho headed to the elevator.

Her office was on the third floor. Somedays she took the stairs. But the elevator was there and she was already running late. She stepped inside.

The elevator doors opened the third floor. She stepped out. Just before reaching her office door, someone spoke behind her.

"He's looking for you."

Jericho turned around. It was Carey, Raoul's secretary, walking towards her.

"Oh. He's looking for me." Jericho said without expression. "How unusual."

Carey ignored the sarcasm. "Love the shoes." She said.

Jericho held up a foot to show off the shoe. "Thanks." Then both women began walking.

"Isn't this your big sales kick off day?"

Jericho chuckled. "Kick off? Yes, it is. Big? We'll see."

"Sorry. But that's what he wants to know about."

Jericho stopped to unlock her office door.

"Tell him I'm pretty sure they've found a place to eat." She opened the door. "And most probably have gotten barked at. At least once."

Carey followed her into the office. She felt bad. She understood this wasn't Jericho's first choice. She didn't go around touting her family as something more than they were. Eric had set a start date. And without any notice, Jericho didn't have much choice.

"Pretty soon you'll have…ah…" Carey paused, she didn't want to word this incorrectly, "a full sales staff."

Jericho held up a hand. "Thank you." It was only the first day. The morning of the first day, and she was already tired of thinking about it. "Please tell him I'll be down in a few minutes."

Carey agreed and left.

The office door was solid oak. Jericho thought about closing it. Possibly locking it. She stood still for a moment and let the thought pass. She sighed and went to the window.

On the one hand she was exhilarated. On the other, she was scared shitless.

"How could a person be both at the same time?" she wondered. And yet, she was. Maybe it was time to open that drawer.   She looked over at the desk.

It was beautiful. Over 100 years old. Dark mahogany with polished brass handles and hinges. It had to weigh as much as Jericho's car. And it was the envy of the entire building.

Even Eric Abbott had asked for it. No one knew it was there until the former storage room, that became her office, was cleaned out.

Before the building was leased by Abbott, for this business, it had been owned and occupied by Emmett Financial Corporation. It was still owned by EFC, but they had outgrown it. Their board decided to relocate to the new Celestial Mall in the suburbs.

When they left for their new home, a great deal of 'stuff' was left behind. It wouldn't project the right image for the brand-new super mall. All of that 'stuff' was piled into a former VPs office and forgotten about.   Until 5 years later, when it was time to clean and create another office.

The desk, when discovered, couldn't be moved. That was because it was wider than the doorway.   It wasn't even close. You could eyeball and see there was no chance. They had to have positioned it in the office before the original walls had gone up. Which explained, in part, why such a gorgeous, hand carved piece of furniture had been abandoned. To move it, you would have to destroy the desk or knock a giant hole in the wall. And now, since both desk and wall belonged to the landlord, neither option was available.

By default, Jericho got the desk.

"Open it." It was Raoul, her boss, and Eric Abbott's right-hand man. He had been told she was in. And deciding not to wait, walked down to her office.

Raoul was in his early fifties. He was slim, with short cropped hair and a thin, Ronald Coleman moustache. Somehow, that almost pencil thin line above his lip managed to exaggerate his perpetually sour expression. He was efficient, but not well liked by most of the staff. They thought he was haughty. And petty. They would impersonate him behind his back, always giving him a French accent that he didn't really have. He was in fact, Canadian. But no one knew him well enough to know that.

Jericho looked up and smiled. And shook her head no.

"What's the point of such a fantastic discovery, if we don't utilize it?" He pretended to be flustered.

"We wait for success. That was the deal." Jericho was still smiling but her tone was firm.

Raoul enjoyed playing hardball. "Let's just peek at it." He said. "I'll close the door. We can make sure it's still there."

"It's still there." Jericho said, knowing she was going to give in and let him have a glance.

Raoul started to close the door. "You can never be too sure." He said in a hushed tone.

She looked at him, trying not to grin. "Should I draw the curtains?"

"And have people talk? Don't be cheeky." He walked over to the desk. "Well?"

Jericho reached down and pulled open the bottom left drawer of the desk. It was the largest drawer and held a metal skeleton for a hanging file system. There were no files in it. It was empty.

"Oh heavens," she said with a deadpan expression, "We've been robbed." She attempted to close the drawer but Raoul stopped her.

"Don't toy with me." He said, waving an impatient finger at the drawer.

When they first discovered the hidden 'drawer within a drawer', Raoul had tasked Carey with calling over to EFC and making discreet inquiries. She found out that one Walter White, retired vice-president, was the last known occupier of the desk in question. That led Raoul and Jericho to assume that it was the beneficent Mr. White who left such a generous gift behind.

Jericho reached into the drawer and felt along the top ledge of the desk frame. Finding the stopper with her finger, she pushed it up. It clicked. Raoul reached down and gently pulled the drawer open another 14 inches.

It revealed an unopened bottle of Macallan scotch and four 'wee dram' glasses. The space had been customized to hold those exact accessories. The stemmed glasses dangled upside down, one in each corner of the hidden cabinet. And the bottle itself rested on a velvet cushion in the center.

There was a note, addressed to no one in particular, threaded around the neck of the bottle. It simply read, "To success"

Having already found pressed numbers on the bottom of the bottle, Raoul was sure the whiskey was at least 30 years old. If it wasn't for Jericho, he would have sampled it already.

"Happy?" Jericho asked.

Raoul held up his hand, holding an imaginary glass. He looked at Jericho. "To success." he said. Jericho held up her own hand.

"To success." she repeated. Then they 'clinked' their knuckles before pretending to drink.

"Maybe we should just…" But she didn't let him get any farther. And pushed the drawer shut with her foot. He raised an eyebrow at her.

"Your self-control is what I both admire, and most despise about you, my dear." He walked back around the desk.

"To success." She said a second time, with a victorious grin. She liked being right. It irritated him.

He frowned. Then he pointed at an overstuffed chair, inviting himself to sit down. "Let's talk about that." He said, having a seat.

"Ugh!" Jericho groaned. Then she pulled out her own chair, at the desk, and sat.

Raoul watched in silence until she was done positioning herself.

"I'll go first." He said, leaning back. "Eric has met with the local press. First article came out yesterday. Did you read it?"

"No."

"Wrong answer." Before she could respond, he kept talking. "Larger, in depth, follow up article in the Sunday regional section." He looked at her sternly. "Read it."

"Yes sir."

"He has 2 radio interviews in the can. No release dates yet. He is going next week to do the same for television."

Jericho noticed he was looking at the ceiling and counting off on his fingers as he recited the tasks accomplished.

"We are in the phone book as the Chamber of Commerce Annex." He looked towards her. "You receive your phone book yet?"

"Yes. Last week."

"Good. Did you look us up?"

"No."

It was his turn to groan. He stared for a moment, then continued,

"Phones will be here, installed and running before the end of the week."

"Stop right there. Why are we in the phone book before we have phones to answer?"

"It's that miracle of modern science we call ineptness." He offered a sour grin. "That wrong will be righted shortly. Practice cultivating your most pleasant voice."

Speaking with the public was glossed over when she agreed to the new job. It didn't change anything. But the more she could avoid it, the happier she would be.

"And you have feet on the street?" He leaned forward in his chair. "Any updates."

"Raoul, it's barely been an hour."

"So, any arrests?"

"No."

"Any fires?"

Jericho crossed her arms. "We have a small one scheduled for 11:30."

Raoul smoothed over his moustache, before saying, "Don't you have an interview then?"

Jericho rolled her eyes. "Yes. In fact, I'm going to kick you out so I can prepare."

"Kick me to the streets?" He put his hands on the arm rests to pull himself up. "I suppose." Then he paused. "Any questions for me?"

"Yes. Two things. First," She waited until they made eye contact. "The budget."

He waved a dismissive hand. "It's been approved."

She had been expecting more excuses. "No alterations?"

"Nope. Fine the way it is." He nodded, hoping to add an air of finality to the matter. "Move ahead. Full speed." He waved his hand like a propellor.

"Oh, you're so full of..." Jericho began to blush.

Raoul's eyes lit up. "Say it."

"Nonsense!"

Raoul wagged a mischievous finger. "That's not what you were thinking." He purred.

"Which brings me to point two." She said, trying to get the conversation back on track.

"Point two." Raoul repeated.

"This parade is a losing proposition." She said, lowering her voice. "That's why I don't believe you showed the budget to Eric."

He cleared his throat slightly. "Well, you may be right." He said, showing signs of becoming impatient. He raised an eyebrow. "And for the record, that's not a question."

"You said question, not me. But I do have one." She waited.

Raoul knew where this was going, so before she asked, he said, "Raise the prices." He tried to sound bored.

"If we raise prices, we will lose customers faster than we cover expenses. And it's a parade. The whole idea is to have people participate."

"So, what are you telling me?" Raoul looked at his nails.

"I'm telling you our boss is too smart to take a bath on this. And yet… We're going to. What. Is. Going. On?"

Raoul smiled. It was an insincere, used car salesman smile. "He loves our city."

"Don't make me swear at you." She said and cocked her head like an impatient parent. Waiting.

And, still more waiting. After Raoul realized she wasn't going to let it go, his smile faded. He shifted in his seat. Then he straightened his cuffs. And spun his cuff links. Finally, he exhaled and looked at her.

"This stays in this room."

"Of course."

"It's not announced yet. And it won't be for some time. But…"

"But…?" She propellered her hand like he did earlier.

"Eric Abbott will be running for the upcoming open State Senate seat, in the next election."

Jericho did not see a connection. "Okay?"

Raoul frowned. "He will be running as the 'get things done' candidate. Creating this parade, resurrecting the local Chamber of Commerce, are all demonstrations of how he gets things done."

It was Jericho's turn to frown. "He's losing money."

Raoul corrected her. "He's not losing. He's investing. It's the cost of success."

She stared at him, taking it in. Raoul continued.

"When Sonic Star announced their lay off, Eric decided that this,"

He sat forward and opened his arms over the parade notes on her desk, "was the perfect counterpoint to demonstrate his capabilities. That's why the sudden, big push, from out of nowhere."

Now things were making sense. Sort of. But it also created more questions. She'd have to think it through.

"Hello!" Raoul said, snapping his fingers.

"Sorry." She said. "Sonic Star got me thinking about the boys." That wasn't true. She deflected to give herself more time to think about what he just told her.

"Yes." Raoul said. "Our feet on the street. You gave them coffee money?"

"I'm sure they headed straight for breakfast as soon as I pulled away." She said.

Recognizing his chance for an upbeat exit, Raoul grinned. "Well, there you see," He lifted himself out of the chair. "They're catching on to this whole salesman routine faster than we expected."

"I hope you're right." She said, still thinking about Eric Abbott's unannounced secret plan.

"Keep me apprised." He said. Then opened the door and walked back down the hall.

*****

The man Jericho was to interview later that day was Bobby Cowl. He had just given himself that name and was rather pleased with it. He felt clever. And wondered if anyone would figure it out.

He was torn about that. It was supposed to be a riddle. A sort of understated irony. But what good was a riddle if no one could solve it? Maybe he should sprinkle a few clues about.

"Tsk, tsk." He said out loud. "Don't be over eager. You'll undo everything."

There was a short knock at the door. Before he could answer, it opened.

"Hey, Lenny…"

Bobby Cowl raised a hand, stopping the man in mid-sentence.

"It's Bobby. Bobby Cowl. I told you that. You need to remember."

"I remember."

"Well, you need to start using it. And using your new name as well."

The man was fidgeting. And not fully listening. He looked over his shoulder and down the hall.

"Did you hear me?" Bobby asked firmly.

Yeah. Yeah, I did." He turned back around. He scratched his head, and looked bewildered, as if he had just woken up.

"How come you changed your name to Bobby Cowl this time?"

Bobby grinned. He had been waiting for this. "Because I rob from the rich and give to the poor."

That did nothing to clarify things.

"I, I think there's already a guy that does that." The other man offered.

"Yes. I'm that guy." Bobby answered.

"But he ain't Bobby Cowl."

"I'm in cognito." Bobby whispered, clearly amused with himself.

The other man stared at him, trying to make sense of what he was just told. He pointed at Bobby.

"No." He said. "You're in your skivvies."

Bobby looked down at himself. He had forgotten that he was still in his underwear.

"They're boxers." He said, feeling like maybe he should cover himself.

"Oh." The man continued to point. "Is that the brand?"

"What are you talking about?"

"In-Con-Gee-Toes. Is that the brand of boxers you're wearing? They don't look no different than your other ones."

"Stop looking at my underwear!" Bobby snapped.

"Sorry." The man stopped pointing.

Bobby huffed. He took a breath and tried to clarify things calmly. "It's pronounced, 'In-Cog-Knee-Toe'. It means in disguise."

"Boxers ain't much of a disguise." The man pointed again. "I can see all of you."

"We're not talking about the boxers…"

"A mask." The man interrupted. "A mask would be a good disguise. Skivvies ain't no disguise. Unless you're going to wear them on your head."

This was pointless.

"Why are you here?" Bobby barked.

"Oh yeah," The man smiled, remembering what had sent him upstairs. "Max locked himself in the safe again."

"Oh, for God's sake!" Bobby groaned. "This is the second time this week."

It was really the third. But pointing that out wasn't going to improve anything.

"And another thing," Bobby said looking around for his trousers. "He's not Max any more. We've all got new names. I'm Bobby Cowl. Your Billy Red. And…"

"Max is Max." The newly named Billy Red interrupted. He said it with such finality that Bobby was taken aback.

"You sitting there like you never talked to him. You think Max is going to answer to anything but Max?" Billy let out a 'Pfft' of indignation. "Guess again."

He was right. Max wasn't going to play. And Bobby wasn't going to start a fight he couldn't win.

"Alright, Max is Max." Bobby conceded. "But what the hell is he doing in the safe?"

"Figuring how to break out of it." What could be more obvious? Billy was confused why Bobby would even ask.

"Well," Bobby grumbled, he resented looking like the foolish one. "Maybe we should let him sit in there and think about it a bit more!"

"It's air tight." Billy said.

"Oh for God's … Is he alright?" Bobby asked. He stood up and grabbed his pants.

"He was." Billy answered. "We were tapping back and forth. Then he stopped. So, I come get you."

Bobby snapped his jeans and zipped his fly. "Come on!" He barked, walking out of his room barefoot. Looking for his shoes would take too long.

Chapter 4

Poodle pushed away his empty plate.

"That was much better than I expected." He said, wiggling the coffee urn to see if there was any left. He had eaten everything. He had even tried a piece of Milk's black bean sausage. His taste buds would have never recognized it as a pork sausage impersonator. But it had a tolerable taste of its own.

Milk spoke without looking up. "You didn't talk at all for 10 minutes. Easy."

"It's an equilibrium thing." Poodle pointed at one ear. "If I talk while I eat, I can fall out of my chair."

Milk looked down at their seats. "It's a bench. In a booth."

"Even worse." Poodle said, trying to catch the hostess's eye. "I could roll under the table, get stuck, and never get up again."

"How's that worse for me?" Milk asked. He stabbed his last bite.

"Ha-ha." Poodle got Terry the Hostess's attention and motioned like he was writing out a ticket. She pointed at the cash register. Poodle slid sideways to get up.

"Be right back." He said. "Leave the tip." Then he walked off to pay.

When he got to the front, Shelly was already there, calculating the bill. She looked up at him.

"Hated it?" she asked.

"No. I thought I was going to." Poodle said, surprised at his own honesty. "But it was good."

"When I first started here, I thought the place would close in a month. But people like it." She looked at the crowd and sarcastically added. "Smart people." Then she handed him the bill.

Poodle pulled out his wallet. "How about you? You like it?"

"Nope."

"O-o-o-kay." He handed her payment.

She took the money. Rang it up. And counted out the change. When she closed the register drawer, Milk was standing next to Poodle.

"Good to see you again Milk." Her tone was flat. She was already on to the customer behind them.

Milk stepped out of the way and let the other person square their bill. When they finished, he reached out and set a fifty-dollar bill on the counter.

"Who's doing what for Tiny?" Milk asked.

"I… I don't know." She answered. "I been thinking about it, but… I don't know."

"Let's start with this." Milk said, sliding the fifty towards her. "You close at all this week?"

"Thursday." She said.

"I'll come by. We can toss a few ideas around. Will Millie be here?"

With her thumb, Shelly wiped at one eye.

"She's been running their place on Townsend since he…" She swallowed. "She's not here much. But I'll tell her to be here Thursday." She took a deep breath and looked at Milk. He was grinning.

"What?" She said. It was more a challenge than a question.

"That one eye looking kind of raccoon there, woman." He said, pointing at her face.

Shelly looked down at her thumb. It was smeared with mascara.

"Goddamn it." She muttered. "Take your change." Then she covered one eye and walked back into the kitchen.

Poodle reached over and picked up his change. "She left your fifty." He said.

"Yeah, I see." Milk picked up the bill and got Terry's attention. She walked over.

"We're starting a little fund raiser for Tiny." Milk handed her the money. "I tried to give this to Shelly but she had an emergency."

Terry could see Shelly through the server's window. She was re-doing her make-up in a compact mirror. "I'll give it to her." Terry said, with a chuckle.

"Thanks. Nice to meet you." Then he and Poodle stepped outside.

"This guy pretty sick?" Poodle asked as the door closed behind them.

"Starting to think so." Milk said, pointing the direction to walk. "He's lost a lot of weight. About 100 pounds, from what I heard."

"They know why?"

Milk shook his head. "All they do is keep testing him."

"Poor bastard." Poodle said as they started back towards Vancouver Boulevard.

They walked in silence for two blocks, Then Poodle spoke up.

"Think we can do this?" He asked.

"Find our way back?" Milk teased. "Pretty sure I can. Need to hold my hand?"

"Need to knock you senseless." Poodle said, motioning like he was going to backhand his pal.

"Might want to wait until we're on a street you recognize." Milk said.

"Good point." Poodle lowered his arm. "But I'm talking about making sales."

"Oh." Milk thought about it for a second. "I suppose eventually."

"What do you suppose for today?"

"Today?" Milk hadn't expected that. "I suppose today is not very likely."

Poodle sighed. "Me too. But I'd love to surprise Jeri. She'd go out of her mind."

"She was out of her mind when she married you."

"Well, that explains that." Poodle said with a smile. "How do you want to do this?"

Milk stopped walking. "Let's start out like she said. We'll each take one side of the road. If you think of something better, we'll try it."

Poodle agreed, but didn't sound convinced.

"It's a straight line. You're not going to get lost."

"Shut up Milk."

They started walking again. In a short while they were back to where Jericho had dropped them off.

"Take this side," Milk said. "I'll cross over."

"Hey. What's that?" Poodle asked, pointing at a bright white glow, across the street. It was a half block up and looked like a lighthouse beacon. They both walked towards it.

When they were almost on top of it, they realized the gleaming beam was reflected sunshine. The still rising Sun had crested the rooftops behind them. It exploded into a blinding floodlight as it bounced across the street, towards them.

"Wow!" Poodle said, squinting. "That's incredible!"

They stood and watched. When cars went by, they would slow down to pass through it. And every driver raised a hand to protect their peripheral vision.

"Kind of dangerous." Poodle thought out loud. Then turning to Milk, "Think anyone's ever wrecked?"

"Can't imagine not."

The sun continued to rise. And eventually, the search light beam faded. The boys crossed over for a closer look.

They found six glass doors. But the glass in each had been removed and replaced with polished aluminum. They reflected like mirrors.

Except that only three of the mirrors were normal. The other three belonged in a fun house.

"Ha-ha! Look at you!" Poodle laughed and pointed to Milk's reflection. His legs were huge. And his head had all but disappeared.

Milk stepped forward. Then stepped back. The size of his reflected head expanded and shrunk.

"That's you trying to think." Poodle said.

"Oh, it hurts. It's hurts!" Milk groaned. He grabbed his head and continued to rock back and forth.

Poodle laughed and stepped in front of a different mirror. He began to clap out measured time and dance around, watching his reflection contort. He looked at Milk and began to sing.

"Na-na, Nah-h-h – na! Na-na, Nah-h-h -na! Hey hey-ey," He wagged a finger at his friend. "No-o tie!"

Then he repeated the chorus. This time Milk joining in.

"Na-na, Nah-h-h – na! Na-na, Nah-h-h -na! Hey hey-ey," They both wagged fingers and shouted. "No-o tie!"

It was fun, and funny to make grotesque caricatures of themselves in the mirrors. They were having a time of it. Jumping. And dancing. And making goofy faces.

But it didn't last. The door farthest away from them opened. Both men stopped abruptly. Poodle straightened his tie and cleared his throat. He looked down to make sure he hadn't spilled any pamphlets from his satchel.

A young woman stepped through the door. She was smiling and held it open for a second, slightly older woman to immerge. Neither woman was thirty yet.

"Don't stop." The first woman said. "We came out to watch." The older woman agreed by smiling.

Milk shrugged. "Better than being chased away."

"With those moves? Not a chance." The first lady was teasing him. She waved her hand, telling him to go on. But she knew he wouldn't.

"Hello." Said Poodle. "I'm Clark. This is Babylon."

"Yeah. We recognized you from Soul Train." The second woman said. Then the two ladies started giggling.

Poodle blushed. "What is it that you do here?" he asked, stalling to regain his composure.

"You don't know?" The first woman asked. Then pointed straight up, to a sign above them.

Warehouse of Mirrors.

"That would explain the bright, shiny doors." Milk said.

"Uh-huh." The first woman agreed. "That's why you're here, right?"

"Actually, we're salesmen." Poodle answered.

The women looked at one another.

"Salesmen?" The older one asked. She sounded doubtful.

"First day." Milk said softly.

"No kidding?" she answered. "What do you sell? Bibles?"

"*I've got to lose the tie.*" Poodle thought. He smiled politely and handed them brochures.

Each woman took one and glanced it over.

"You're not lawyers?" The first woman asked.

"Why would you think we're lawyers?" Poodle asked.

"The people across the street don't like our doors." She answered. "They said they were sending lawyers to talk to us."

"Dancing lawyers?" Milk asked.

"We were wondering." The first woman said.

Poodle looked across the street. The building was empty.

"They're just moving in." The older woman explained. "They want our doors gone before they do."

"We're not going to be able to help with that." Milk said. Then pointing to the pamphlets, "Any interest in the parade?"

The first woman waved her brochure like a handheld fan.

"How about we hang on to these?" she said. "And I call you if we do."

"That works." Milk handed her one of his cards. She took it without looking at it. And handed it to the other woman.

"Well, good luck." She turned to go back inside. When the door opened, she looked back at them. "Feel free to work on your moves." Both women giggled and they were gone.

"No, I don't feel foolish. Why would you even ask me that?" Poodle asked, to no one in particular.

"You'd feel less foolish if you lost that tie." Milk said.

"I like my tie." Poodle said, as much to convince himself as Milk.

"You look like a bible salesman."

"Hey, that reminds me," Poodle said, "What did that waitress mean by the apocalypse thing?"

"She meant you look like a bible salesman."

That didn't sound right. "That's was a weird way to say it."

"She was just squawking to hear herself." Milk said, with a dismissive wave, "Tiny's her cousin. She got a lot on her mind."

They were talking about people Poodle had never met before. So, he dropped it.

"Look," Milk said, "We're just getting started." He motioned for them to start walking. "Those ladies took the pamphlets. We did what we were supposed to do."

Poodle couldn't argue that either. He nodded and started walking. After half a block, he made a resigned sigh.

"Let's get going." He said. And started across the street.

"Race you to Sal's!" Milk called over.

"Which is located… where?" Poodle had a hand over his eyes, like a sailor looking for a shore line.

"Just keep going." Milk waved an arm down the street. "When you get to a sign that says 'Sal's Slices', you've arrived."

"*No kidding.*" Poodle thought, as he turned and headed down his side of the street.

Chapter 5

Three hours later, both men had a much better understanding of how sales really worked. No one was interested.

Overall, people were polite. And generally took the brochures. One woman even looked at it before setting it to the side. But most often, they were told that the owner wasn't there right now. And, of course, no one ever knew when they'd be back.

It didn't take long to figure out it was probably the owner that was telling them that the owner wasn't in. Where do you go from there? Call them a liar? Start a fist fight?

One time, in a place called Tops Plus, Milk was told they didn't accept unsolicited sales visits. He asked if he should have called ahead.

The young clerk said, "Yes, you need to make an appointment first."

Milk thought that was absurd. So, he asked if it would be best if he called ahead first, to notify them that he would soon be calling, so he could set up an appointment? The woman wasn't amused. Nor ruffled.

"Yes, that's almost right." She replied, still folding a shirt, "Generally, how it works is, people come by to arrange a phone call, that will schedule another call, so they can set up an appointment to see one of us in person." She frowned at him. "But not today, we're closed." Which they obviously weren't.

"You my dear," Milk thought, as he tipped an imaginary hat, *"Will be going places."* He set a brochure on the counter and saw himself out.

As morning dragged on, the absurdity of their routine became obvious. The whole walk in. Drop off. Walk out, was pointless. No one was going to remember them. Nobody cared.

Milk stopped between stores, in the shadow of a parked dump truck. No particular reason. There was simply no hurry to visit the next place. And it was starting to get warm.

He took off his jacket and looked at his watch. He thought about something to drink. Then wondered where Poodle was. He looked up and down both sides of the boulevard. Nothing.

"How can you get lost walking a straight line?" He wondered. But if such a thing were possible, his buddy was the guy to do it.

He remembered a small bar around the corner. At least, it used to be around the corner. The Graveyard. It catered to second and third shifters back when Sycamore was firing on all cylinders. He wondered if it was still open. That reminded him of the lay-off. He sighed. And looked at his watch.

He hadn't been by The Graveyard for a few years. But was starting to like the idea of sipping a cold one. He looked up and down the street again. Where the hell could that boy be?

*****

Poodle's first day was fairing far worse than his friend's. By the time Milk was wondering where he was, Poodle was on the run. Literally. And had been for half an hour.

It started when he walked into Floyd's Stationary. The air conditioning was running. It felt good. He was hoping whomever he talked to would be chatty, so he could linger.

Mr. Floyd came out from behind the counter with a finger pointed at Poodle. He was not smiling.

"You've got a lot of goddamn nerve thinking you can show up here." Floyd said. He stopped at the counter's edge. But was visibly shaking. He looked like he was ready to charge.

Poodle stopped just inside the doorway. There was a ceiling fan blowing down on him.

"Excuse me?" Poodle was confused, "Have we met?"

"Everybody in this goddamn town knows who you are. And you're going to pay, you son of a bitch!" Floyd dropped his finger, but continued to shake.

"Pay for what?" Poodle asked.

"You and your goddamn friends think you're so clever. Dressing up like Christians; taking advantage of the meek and the mild."

"It's just a tie, mister." Poodle raised a hand to the knot at his collar. "I can take it off, if you want." He hoped he sounded calmer than he felt. Floyd was foaming at the mouth.

"I don't give a goddamn about your goddamn tie!" Floyd pointed at him again. "You're going to hell. After you go to jail!"

Well, this was going nowhere. He'd get farther arguing with a rabid raccoon. Poodle sighed. He was hot. And getting hungry. He should just turn around and leave. But this guy was such a total jerk, he thought he should give him two cents worth first.

"You know," Poodle said, as calmly as he could, "For someone claiming to be concerned about the meek and the mild, you sure drop an awful lot of 'GODDAMNS' there, mister." Poodle made a point of yelling the curse word.

That was a mistake.

Enraged, Floyd went back behind the counter and pulled out a pistol. Poodle didn't know one hand gun from another, but when he saw it, he was certain it was a cannon.

"Maybe we'll send you to hell first!" Floyd roared as he slammed the pistol onto the glass counter top.

It shattered, spraying glass everywhere. Poodle thought he saw blood. But didn't look twice. Floyd screamed. And grabbed his hand. Poodle was long gone.

Ten blocks later, Poodle's heart was still racing. *"What the hell was that?"* he thought. He had zig-zagged his escape at every intersection or alley he saw. He was certain that crazy son of a bitch had been hot on his tail.

He looked back. No sign of him. Then he leaned up against a building, hoping to catch his breath and clear his head.

He started to think about what Shelly the waitress had said. This guy was saying the same sort of crap. What were they talking about?

Then he realized he had dropped his satchel. Did he leave it in that store? Did he drop it along the way? He had no idea. But it didn't matter. Unless it magically jumped out at him, it was long gone. There was no way he was going back.

"Son of a ..." he muttered to himself. Maybe he should call the police. That guy was nuts. Maybe. But he should figure out where he was, first.

He looked around. He didn't have a clue. Which struck him as funny. Because he never had a clue. Why would this moment be any different?

"Ok, get organized." He said to himself, under his breath. He took off his jacket, loosened his tie and started back the way he came. "Let's see what I can remember."

*****

Milk turned the corner. No Graveyard. He was standing in front of a pet store. A rather shabby one, at that. Kittens, in a display case were scratching the window, trying to get his attention.

Did he have the right street? He was pretty sure but not completely sure. It had been a long time. And he wasn't going inside and ask. He knew himself. He'd come out with 40 kittens. He scratched at his chin, thinking what to do next.

"No!" Some voice from the street behind him began shouting. "Are you stupid? Leave it on!"

Some scruffy guy in a black bomber jacket was standing behind a parked Chevelle. Milk thought it was a '70 or maybe a '71. Still looked sharp. There was a young woman in the driver seat. Guessing from the one-sided conversation, she had never popped a clutch before. Milk walked over.

He didn't bother to introduce himself. "You drive. I'll push." He said.

The younger man turned and sized him up. It was clear he didn't like being told what to do. He was tall and scrawny, with block letters spelling PAIN carved into his knuckles. In a previous life, he would have done well as a junk yard dog.

Milk didn't say anything more. He just waited. Although 40 was coaxing him forward from the horizon, Milk hadn't slowed down much. He played softball, rode a bike, and played pickup basketball with the other CYO coaches in the league. Poodle still had a bench and loose weights in the basement. They worked them in the winter, when there wasn't much going on outside.

"Yeah. Okay." The kid finally muttered. Having credible assistance didn't improve his demeanor any. He walked to the driver side door. "Get out."

When the woman exited the car, the young man nodded slightly to Milk. Then turned to push. Milk leaned into the trunk and did the same. They went about ten feet when someone else on the street leaned into the trunk, next to Milk. The car picked up speed.

Milk saw the kid jump into the driver's seat. He tapped the third man's shoulder. They both stopped pushing. The car rolled another 8 feet, jerked, and the engine turned over.

Milk held out a hand to the third man. "Thanks." They shook hands. Then he looked down the street at the Chevelle. The young woman was running to catch up with the car.

"You're making a big mistake honey." Milk muttered to himself. He glanced over to see if the third man had heard him. But he was back to being alone.

*****

At the Sonic factory, back when he was employed there, Poodle was almost never on his feet all day. He was on and off a tow motor. Plus, they all got breaks. And he had access to water. And a restroom.

So, as much as Poodle wanted to deny it, Milk had been right. He was wearing the wrong shoes. His feet were killing him.

He snarled and told himself not to think about it. He wasn't going to stop. He would grumble through the pain, from one rejection to the next. Eventually, he would meet up with Jericho and Milk for lunch. Then he could change his shoes.

Sal's Slices meant pizza. He had been there before. And he liked it. He told himself he was getting a large one. All to himself. And a pitcher of beer. And he wasn't sharing either. They could get their own.

But first things first. He had to figure out where he was. Stopping at the corner to read the signs didn't help. Spruce and Juice? Where the hell was that? And nothing looked familiar.

He realized he was in a residential area. Lots of one, and an occasional two-family home. He must have strayed farther than he thought. And had no idea how to get back. Then he heard something.

It was faint. At first, he thought he might be imagining it. But he stood still and listened. People were singing. But where?

Poodle walked around in a small circle. He had one ear cocked higher in the air than the other. And a finger, blocking out sound, in the lower one. Would that even help? He thought about what someone looking out their window might think.

"Well, if they send the cops, I'll find out." He thought. And he kept listening.

It sounded like opera. He hated opera. But right now, he didn't care. People singing opera meant people who could tell him how to get to Sal's. Where was it coming from?

The breeze faded and the sound died. Hmmm. He waited. When the breeze returned, so did the faint sound of song.

Poodle knew which way to go. At least, he hoped he did. His feet were not letting him forget about them. Over the next block, the sound got louder. Could it be someone's record player or radio, escaping through a window? That wouldn't do him any good.

But as he continued, he realized the singing was some group's rehearsal. They were stopping and repeating the same section, over and over. As he drew closer, he understood why. They weren't particularly good.

He kept trudging on until he found himself standing in front of the slowly twirling, red and white stripped pole of Pagano's Barber Shop. This was it. This was the source of the singing.

He squinted to see into the big picture window. The shop used to be a single-family house. He could make out two barber chairs. Someone was sitting in the one farthest to his left. The other was empty. No one else was in the room.

Poodle took a step forward. He could see past the window glare. The man in the chair was asleep. His feet were up. His head was back and his mouth was open, fly hunting style. There was an open newspaper resting across his chest, like a blanket. It appeared he had been that way for a while.

"Well, at least I know it wasn't him." Poodle thought. He considered slapping the window with the palm of his hand. Just to watch the guy jump. It was funny to think about, but he knew he wouldn't really do it.

Then the music stopped. Poodle stopped as well, ear to the air. The sleeping man couldn't be bothered to notice.

When the singing started up again, it was coming from behind the building. There was a small walkway between the hedges next to the barbershop and the chain link fence of the house next door. Poodle looked around. Nothing said KEEP OUT, or more importantly, BEWARE OF DOG. He followed the stone path.

The singing grew louder. And somebody was playing an instrument. Something low. And not very loud.

As he walked, the side of the house became the side of an add-on garage. A drive way was in front of him. Assuming the overhead door was open, he would peek inside.

When he did, he saw 3 rows of folding chairs, in an arc, around a small band riser. On the riser, with a music stand and a baton, was a slim, college aged conductor. He had a short, neatly trimmed beard. His hair style was scruffy, but combed. It made Poodle think of a well-dressed beatnik. He was facing the other way. And couldn't see Poodle leaning in.

But everyone else could. And all of them were between 60 and 80 years old.

"Holy mackerel!" Poodle thought. *"I've stumbled onto the crypt-keeper chorus!"*

He looked behind himself, half expecting something mummified to grab at him. When he looked back, several of the chorus members were looking in his direction. He smiled and waved passively.

They whispered amongst themselves and kept looking at him. Others started doing the same. When the conductor noticed, he looked over his shoulder. Poodle figured it was time to go. But the young man smiled, waved him in.

"Big finish now!" The conductor raised his voice over the singers.

That's when Poodle noticed the tuba player. At the conductor's command, the tuba got noticeably louder. But only for a second. With a stern index finger from their leader, the tuba quickly quieted down.

The tuba was being played by a pudgy, middle school aged Tomboy. She was easily half a century younger than almost everyone in the room. Besides the conductor, she was the only other person to have a music stand. But her stack of sheet music was loose. And most of it was laying ignored on the ground in front of him.

The singers squeaked and squawked and got louder, doing their best to achieve that big finish. But the quality of song didn't improve any.

The baton sliced the air and suddenly they were silent. The conductor signaled for a 5-minute break. Then he pointed at the kid in the back.

"Teddy tuba, you know what to do."

"It's a sousaphone!" The gal yelled back. But she was already up. And with the instrument still around her neck, she pushed a walker over to one of the older ladies. The woman was already standing and waiting for her. She took the walker. And then they began traveling together.

Poodle watched as they slowly crossed the room. The conductor walked over to him.

"Didn't mean to interrupt," Poodle started.

"You're fine." The young man said, extending a hand. "I'm James."

They shook hands. "Clark Canderankle. Nice to meet you."

"You're the new neighbor?"

"No. No I was just walking past and heard. Was that opera?"

"Well, from an operetta. Not necessarily our strongest piece though."

"You'd be in a bad way if it was." Poodle thought. Then asked, "What else do you guys do? Besides opera."

"Mostly the Mitch Miller sing along kind of stuff."

Poodle scratched an ear. "Much demand for that?"

James smiled and waffled his hand in front of himself. "We do the nursing home circuit. Pretty well received there."

"I didn't know that was a thing." Poodle said.

"It's not." One of the old men said. He was up and walking towards them. James waited until he arrived, then made introductions.

"This is Al Burdick. One of our tenors. And he's right. It's not really a thing. We're volunteers. But they like us. And these guys..." James waves a hand to the rest of the room. "They just want to sing."

"It's nice you have a place to do it." Poodle said, glancing around the make shift rehearsal room.

"My uncle owns the barbershop." James said. "He's an old opera guy."

"That him around front?" Poodle asked.

Both Al and James chuckled but didn't explain why. "No, that's Gus. A different uncle." James said. He turned slightly and looked out at the group. He pointed at a slim man with a full head of silver hair.

"That's uncle Frank, right there." Then he pointed at the middle school kid helping the elderly lady. "And that's my niece, Teddy tuba."

"It's a sousaphone!" Teddy yells over her shoulder. She has one hand on the walker and the other, very gently, on the elbow of the woman walking with her.

James ignored the outburst. "We practice once, maybe twice, a week. Play out when we can."

Poodle nodded but his attention was on Teddy. "Shouldn't she be in school?"

James agreed with a slight shake of his head. "They know she's here. The school owns the tuba."

"It's a sousaphone!"

"Kid's got good ears." Poodle said.

James chuckled. "The sousaphone is lighter and designed for marching bands. Teddy switched over because she's getting to a certain age."

"Oh." Poodle answered to be polite. But didn't understand.

James turned his back to Teddy then drew an imaginary circle around his mouth.

"Shut up Uncle James!" Teddy yelled from across the room. "I can see you!"

"She has a chap ring from playing so much." James said softly. "She thought if she switched instruments, it would help."

"I said shut up!"

Poodle looked over at Teddy, then squinted trying to get the features of the young girl's face into focus. In defiance, Teddy puts a hand over her mouth and chin.

Poodle turned back to James. "Didn't help, did it?"

"Nope." James had also turned back around. He's entertained that his young niece is upset.

"I'll kill you, Uncle James!"

"Put a cork in it, Teddy!" Uncle Frank barked without bothering to look at his great-niece. He is up and steadying himself on the back of a chair.

"I'll break your hip, old man!" But there was no malice in Teddy's voice. It was just the posturing of youth.

The woman she was walking with has stopped. They are now in line for the restroom. She reaches over and gently slaps Teddy's arm. Her way of telling the girl to behave.

Uncle Frank has walked over to the three men. James makes introductions.

When Frank and Poodle stop shaking hands, Al said, "He looks familiar, don't he, Frank?"

"I've looked like me my entire life." Poodle said.

As Frank took a second, more measured look at their guest, Teddy walked up. Everyone but Frank saw her cross the room.

"Right there, old man." Teddy said, poking her uncle in the hip with an index finger. Then she made a loud popping noise and grabbed her own side, pretending to be in pain.

"That's enough Teddy." James warned.

Without taking his eyes off Poodle, Frank reached over and pulls Teddy towards him. Teddy puts her head on her uncle's side and wraps both arms around him. Frank ruffles the young girl's hair.

"You going to break my hip with a hug? That your big plan?" Frank rubbed his knuckles on top of her head.

"Shut up old man." Teddy mumbled and squeezed her uncle's waist.

James opened his mouth to reprimand his niece. But uncle Frank raised an eyebrow, dismissing it. Then he turned back to Poodle and shook his head.

"I've never cut this man's hair." He said. "Looks like a Bob job."

"Bob job?" Poodle didn't understand.

"Roberts Brothers." Al offered.

Poodle lit up. "Yeah! I been going there my whole life. My old man took me as a kid."

"We all used to bowl together." Al said. "Back when we still bowled."

James looked at his watch. "We got to get back to it, if we're going to have enough time."

That caused uncle Frank to look at his. "Skip the adagio," he said. "We should work the songs people know."

Poodle remembered he was an intruder. "I should get going." Then added, "But I do have a question. How do I get to Sal's Slices from here?"

"It's about 10, maybe 12 blocks." Al said. "You know the neighborhood?"

"No."

Al offered a slight smile. It was as if he could tell Poodle was geographically impaired. "I'll draw you a map." He said, walking off.

"Thank you." Poodle answered, pleased with his good fortune. He could handle a map. Then, surprising himself as much as anyone else, he asked, "Anyone ever consider being in a parade?"

James and Frank stared at him for a few seconds. Even Teddy turned a confused eye on their guest. Then Frank spoke.

"I can't even get everyone to walk across the room without falling. A parade would be impossible."

"I was thinking more like riding on a float. You could have your chairs. Everyone could sing." Poodle tried to sound optimistic.

Frank shook his head no. "Every time the float started or stopped; we'd all capsize. We fall out of chairs now. We ain't even moving."

"Uncle Frank." James' tone was curt.

"Aunt Phyllis did." Teddy's head was up and off her uncle's side. "She was just sittin' there. Then BAM! Ass over tea kettle."

"Teddy!" James barked. "Language!"

Teddy kept talking. "Gravity did a snap the whip." She flicked her arm as if she were snapping a wet towel. "Now she got that big eggplant chinstrap on her face." She rubbed her hand across her own jawline to show the size of the bruise.

James knew where the chinstrap remark originated and glared at his uncle. Frank looked away. James took a step towards Teddy.

"Mrs. Merideth needs you. Now."

"But Aunt Beth isn't…"

"Now!" James pointed to the back of the room.

Defeated, Teddy slumped away. But after two steps, she whipped around with a poisonous sneer, pointed at James, and said, "Maybe I'll break your hip too!" Then she double timed it to the back of the room.

The men all watched her run away. Then James sighed. "She's really is a good kid."

"Seems like she is." Poodle said.

"Kid's alright." Frank said, looking over his shoulder at Teddy. "She herds the whole gang like a sheep dog. Always knows where everybody is."

Al and James both nodded in agreement.

Poodle waited a second, then asked, "Is everyone here related to one another?"

"Not to you." Frank said with a smirk.

"Touché." Said Poodle.

James used a finger to draw a ring in the air, meant to include everyone in the room. "They all grew up together. Been in this same neighborhood forever. Teddy and I have never not known all these people. So, in that regard…"

"I get it." Then out of nowhere, Poodle snapped his fingers and said, "The Razor's Edge."

"What you say?" Frank asked.

"Your bowling team. The Razor's Edge. Took me a minute to remember. I could picture your jackets but I couldn't think of the name."

"How you know that?" Al asked. He had just walked back with a half sheet of paper.

"My dad used to tend bar at the Phelp's." Poodle struck a pose like a body builder. "Short, stocky, fireplug of a farmer looking guy. Ben Canderankle."

Both the older men smiled. Al wagged a finger at Poodle.

"I remember you! You were always late!"

Poodle blushed and smiled back. "Yeah, yeah, yeah. Even when I was on time, I was always late." He looked over at James, who had been left behind in the conversation. "My old man was a farmer. But… things changed. We had to move to town." Poodle ran his hand through his hair. "For a while, he tended bar at the Phelp's. A couple nights a week."

"They sponsored our team." Uncle Frank added.

"Sometimes he went right from the machine shop to the bar. When he did, my mother sent me over with dinner." He looked back at Al and Frank. "You know why I was always late?"

Both men shook their heads. "Girlfriend?" Al asked.

"Naw," Poodle answered. "I wanted a beer. I wanted to sit at the bar with everybody else. Of course, he said no." He looked back at James. "I was only 13." He clarified. "But one day, he started crabbing at me about how long he had to wait. I said gimme a beer, I'll get there on time. He said no, get there on time and I'll give you a beer."

James was mildly shocked. "You ever get one?"

"Hell no. I used to run, I mean run, from our house all the way to the bar. Sometimes I rode my bike as fast as I could. Didn't matter. He was already hungry. So, I was late."

The two older men started chuckling. "He had your number." Al said.

Poodle agreed. "Yeah, I was too dumb. And he knew it."

"Van's here!" Teddy shouted from the back of the room. Everyone looked over at the garage door opening. A big, white airport limo styled van was backing into the driveway.

James looked at his watch and let out a sigh of disappointment. "Why's he so early?"

No one said anything.

"Okay everybody!" James shouted. "That's it for today. Thank you everyone." He looked at Poodle. "Excuse me for just a minute." And started walking towards the van.

Frank stuck out his hand. "We got jobs too. Otherwise, sheep dog gets after us." He cocked his head towards Teddy. "Nice to meet you…again."

Poodle shook hands with both older men. Al handed him the map. Poodle thanked him. Then walked back over to James, who was adjusting a portable step, in front of the van door.

"You guys need a hand?" Poodle asked.

"We do this all the time. We're good. But thank you."

They shook hands. Poodle walked back along the side of the building. He stopped at the road and looked at the map. It seemed simple enough. But then, how'd that work out for him every other time?

"We'll see." He put the note in his pocket and started walking.

Chapter 6

Two blocks down from watching the Chevelle drive off, Milk found a watering hole. It was a weathered and worn, two-story store front called the SLIP. He had never heard of it.

It looked like apartments on top. There was no doorway for the stairwell, so Milk assumed it must be in back. Not that he cared. The neon OPEN sign in the window was his priority.

"*Nice.*" He thought. And walked up onto the patio in front of the entryway steps. There was a screen door leading inside. He knocked sharply and went in.

"Didn't I tell you…" An older man, kneeling behind a pulled-out refrigeration unit, stopped yelling in mid-sentence. He sized up Milk. "Sorry, thought you were my youngest."

"No, just me." Milk said, moving forward, "Got a challenge, huh?"

The old man groaned, and got to his feet. "I been on my back, inside this thing, for half an hour." He pointed the piece of pipe he was holding, at the unit. When he did, something black dripped out onto the floor.

"About ready to beat the hell out of it." His hands were filthy. "Sent my boy to the hardware store. Thought that was him clowning around when I heard the knock."

"No, that was me. Sorry." Milk said. He was standing at the bar now. The other man pulled out two bar rags, set the pipe on one and started wiping his hands with the other.

"We're opening a little late today." He tilted his head towards his refrigeration project. Then, getting a better look at his patron, "What you selling?"

"Actually, I came in to get away from selling."

"Keep that attitude and I'll buy you a beer." He smiled and nodded for Milk to have a seat. "I hate salesman. Nothing personal." The man finished cleaning his hands. Then tossed the rag on top of the gooey drip he had left on the floor.

"I'm not a fan either." Milk said. The man cocked his head at him, then laughed.

"I know, I know." Milk said, "Today's my first day. I thought it might change my attitude. Bu-u-u-t..." He sighed.

"First day, huh?" The man pulled back the tap on a draft. "What you do before?"

"Worked the dock and sometimes one of the lines at Sonic Star."

It was the other man's turn to sigh. "That's going to fuck this town." He poured Milk a draft. Then handed it to him.

"Thank you." Milk took the glass. He didn't want to start on the 'what's going to happen now?' conversation. So, he changed the subject. "I'm drinking alone?"

"Ah, my kid sees me having a beer, he'll think it's a day off. I can't get that knucklehead to..." The old man stopped himself. "You know what? I've got to get some tools." He pointed to an open door next to the bar. "I'll be right back." Then he walked away.

Milk sipped his beer. It tasted good. Good enough that he could have talked himself into making a day of it.

"Enjoy your beer. Get back to your job. At least you have one." He told himself.

Because he mentioned Sonic Star, he started thinking about the whole lay off thing again. Quite a few of the guys he knew were going to be hurting.

Compared to guys with kids and house payments, Milk was sitting pretty. He had sold his own house when he moved back in with his mother. All that money was parked in the bank.

And his mother's house was paid off. Had been for years. She was even collecting on the old man's pension, to boot. Neither of them had any expenses. They were covered. At least in the short run.

Milk took another sip of his beer and heard the screen door open. He turned. Some kid in torn jeans and a KISS tee shirt was walking in. He had a Medusa styled haircut and looked as stoned as Timmy back at SPROUTS. Milk raised a hand in greeting.

"Hey, how you doing?"

The kid said 'Hey' but didn't make eye contact.

Milk had time to kill. "Want to buy a parade?" He asked.

"What? Uh… No." The kid answered and looked around like he was searching for something he dropped. Then he stood in the middle of the room, scratching his elbow.

"It comes with your own marching band." Milk blatted out a fog horn sound while pantomiming a trombone.

This time the kid looked at him. "Yeah, sure."

"You'll be the most noticed person, wherever you go. Grocery store. Ball Park." He repeated his trombone impersonation.

"Hey dad!" The kid walked past the bar and into the back.

Milk took another pull of his beer. A minute later, both men came back into the bar area. The older man looked over at him.

"Kenny says you sell marching bands?"

"Well," Milk grinned, "I work for the Chamber of Commerce. We're selling spots in an upcoming parade." The older man looked at his son. Milk continued. "A parade that will, most likely, have marching bands. I was teasing your boy. Said he should buy one to follow him around."

"Probably should," the older man said, still looking at his son. "Least then I could figure out where you are half the time."

The kid flopped his hands against his outer thighs in exasperation. "Man! I told you; traffic was messed up!"

"Traffic." His father clarified. "It was the traffic that was messed up?"

"Well, yeah! What else would it be?"

The older man turned and looked blankly at Milk. Milk held up his hands as if out of ideas. The man turned back to his son.

"You get the pipe dope?" he asked.

"Well, yeah." His kid answered.

"Good. Where is it?"

His son had to think about that. Then said, "In the car."

"I sent you to get pipe dope because I wanted you to leave it in the car?" The old man had raised his voice. He pointed towards the parking lot, silently telling his boy to get it. The kid stomped off.

Milk waited for the old man to say something. When he didn't,

Milk said, "Never knew your place was here."

The man seemed perplexed at that. "Started out as my old man's place." He said. "We been here almost thirty years. You don't get over this side of town much?"

"Live in the subs." Milk said. "I've been to the Graveyard a few times. But it's been a while."

"They moved." The man said, walking behind the bar. He picked up a six-ounce juice glass and held it under the tap. He looked at Milk's glass. But Milk gave him the sign that he was fine. The man took a sip of his own beer. And continued.

"It's just THE YARD now. They bought the old police impound. That's on… Salisbury Park?" The man wiggled a finger in the general direction of where you would find it. "They built a building. And use the lot for volleyball, mini-golf, stuff like that." Then he remembered his boy was still gone. "Where the hell did he go?" He set down his beer and walked to the screen door.

Milk took the opportunity to finish half his beer in a single swallow. Then said, "You guys have work to do. Thanks for the beer." With a second swallow, he finished it. Then he set a business card on the bar top.

The man turned his head. "He'll be back in a minute. Stick around for the fireworks."

Milk stuck out his hand to shake. "I'd rather watch from a safe distance. Thanks again." They shook hands and Milk left.

Outside, the kid was bent over, rummaging through his trunk, trying to find the pipe dope. Milk thought about sneaking up behind him and doing another trombone blat. Or maybe pushing him in and closing the lid. But when he walked past, he just said, "Probably rolled under the front seat." And kept going.

He knew which direction to wander, to get to Sal's. But it would be a lot shorter walk if he could find some way of cutting across diagonally.

That part left him uncertain. He had always been in a car before. And never did this on foot. He walked a block. And then another. Then recognized the area.

He was on the edge of the original residential section of the city. Home of Sycamore's industrial forefathers. A 6 block by 6 block square of former one family mansions that were now cut up into 3 and 4 family apartments. They were old and worn down. It made them look sad. But at the same time, it was somewhat nostalgic to look at them.

Two kids whipped past him on a Huffy single speed. One riding the seat. The other standing and pedaling. They could have taken him out. But Milk had heard their laughter and jumped out of the way.

"You're pulling my pants down!" the driver shouted over his shoulder. The kid behind him was clutching belt loops for dear life. Both were red faced and laughing as they roared by.

Milk waved a fist, in mock anger, as they sped on their way down the street.

More nostalgia. He smiled. And kept walking.

In another two blocks, he saw a small park. It was in the center of a quad of houses. Maybe he could cut through there. Save some time. He moved off the sidewalk.

Getting closer, he saw what he thought was a wooden shack. Who would build a shack in a park? He stopped and squinted.

His eyes weren't what they used to be. But he could still see okay. Just not as well far away. Or close up. But overall, his vision was fine. He didn't need glasses. No matter what his mother said. But he did wonder about that shack. He kept moving towards it.

When he got within a weak outfielder's throw to second, he could make out two children. And the shack wasn't a shack at all. It looked more like a lemon-aide stand. They had a sign but he was still too far away.

At 40 yards, the children realized he was a sales prospect. The taller of the two lifted a pitcher off the counter wiped underneath it. He looked at the shorter one and said something. Milk couldn't hear them. But right after that, the smaller one pulled out a stack of paper cups and set them near the pitcher. It was a little girl. She waved.

Milk waved back. The sign came into focus. It read, '5 cents a glass!'.

"For what?" Milk wondered. More beer would be nice.

The pitcher was white ceramic, with bright yellow sunflowers painted all the way around it. It was very pretty. But you couldn't tell what was inside.

At last, Milk stopped in front of them. He looked them both over. The taller one was a young fellow, around 10, and needed a haircut. The shorter one looked enough like the taller one, that Milk figured they were brother and sister.

He smiled. They smiled back.

Milk fished around in his pocket. Although he had plenty of coins, he was feeling around for nickels in particular. The two kids waited in silence.

"What you selling today?" he asked, as he pulled out four nickels.

Neither one said anything. He waited. They just stood there.

"Hello?" Milk asked.

The little girl waved at him again. Milk smiled and waved back. Then he waved at the young boy a second time. The boy smiled and waved back at him. Then they all started laughing.

Milk took a few steps backwards. Then, pretending to walk towards them for the very first time, he acted overly surprised and excited to see them. He waved both hands this time. The kids looked at one another, giggled, and each waved both hands back.

Milk paused for the silliness to dissipate, then put a nickel on the counter. The little girl, looked at her brother. He nodded 'yes' and the little girl pulled a cup from the stack and set it on the counter. But she didn't let go of it.

At first Milk was confused. But then he saw the boy needed both hands to pour. The little girl was making sure the cup didn't spill.

"Nice system you got there." He said. But again, neither child responded.

After the older one finished pouring, the younger one moved the cup towards Milk.

"Thank you." He said, bowing his head slightly. The kids looked at each other, giggled some more, and each bowed back.

"It's like seeing double in a mirror." Milk thought. Then he remembered the mirrored doors from earlier in the morning. He wondered if mirrors might mean good luck. Breaking them was bad luck. At least that's what he'd always heard. He wondered if the opposite could be true. He had no idea. If he remembered, he'd ask Jeri. Would she know? Probably not. But it would be fun to annoy her with this kind of stuff.

Milk picked up the cup and sniffed. It was, in fact, lemon-aide. He tasted it. Kind of weak, very cold, and plenty sweet. But overall, not bad. Something a kid would like.

When Milk finished, he set his cup down, and put another nickel on the counter. He tapped the ceramic pitcher.

"Your mother knows that you're using this?" He was teasing. "I don't want to get in any trouble."

Both kids stopped and listened but neither responded. Milk pointed at the pitcher again. "This your mama's?"

At the word 'mama' both children looked down at their feet. Then the little girl turned in to her brother for a hug.

"*Aw Geez!*" Milk thought. Not sure of what he had just done.

"Look, I'm sorry." He said. "I didn't mean nothing. It's a nice pitcher, that's all."

The little boy patted his sister's back. Milk just stood there and waited. After a short time, the little girl looked up. When she did, the boy directed her attention to the used cup.

She let go of her brother and held the cup. But her smile was gone. The boy poured a second cup. When he set the pitcher down, he looked at Milk. With effort he said, "No Mama."

It took Milk a few seconds. "Your mama's gone?"

The little boy nodded.

"I'm sorry. I didn't know."

The little boy nodded. Then he reached out and patted Milk's hand, telling him it was okay. Honest mistake.

Milk stepped back, looked out towards the horizon and blinked a few times. Then he cleared his throat and stepped back up to the counter.

"Here, here, here…" he said, waving an arm like he was erasing a blackboard. "You can't stand there looking down. You'll get stuck that way." He reached into his pocket. "Look."

He set a nickel on the counter. Then holding out his right hand, palm up, he pointed to the little girl, then to the nickel, then he tapped his finger on his palm.

"Put it in my hand, honey." But she wasn't looking at him. He waited. Then looked at the boy. "You want to try?" He repeated the motion of instructions, saying, "It's a cornball trick. But if you've never seen it before, it's kind of fun."

The boy looked at him. Then he said something Milk didn't understand, to the girl. She nodded. And the boy put the nickel in Milk's palm

"Now watch this." Milk closed his hand over the nickel. Then he showed them his empty left hand. And closed that one as well.

"Are you ready?" And with a very loud fake sneeze, he made both children jump.

"AH-CHEW!"

The children laughed at being startled. Milk nodded at his right hand. Both kids looked at his balled-up fist. He opened it to reveal and empty palm. The little girl opened her mouth in disbelief.

The boy pointed at Milk's still closed left fist. Milk smiled and opened it to display the very same nickel.

The kids were amazed. They had never seen a magic trick before. At least, they'd never seen that one.

But Milk wasn't done. He nodded for them to look at his hands again. When they did, he clapped them together, without warning. The kids jumped and giggled.

Milk separated his hands. The nickel was gone again.

He slowly turned his hands over, so they could see the other side. The little boy bent down and peered at the counter beneath his hands. Still no nickel.

Milk reached over slowly and gave the little girl's ear the slightest of tugs. Then he handed her the nickel as if he had just found it there.

She smiled and put it in their little pay tin. Milk looked over at the little boy. He was already feeling around his own ears.

Milk smiled. "You got to give me a minute, buddy."

Then the little girl pointed behind Milk. "Padre."

Milk turned around and saw a man crossing the park towards them.

Chapter 7

Even with a map, Poodle managed to make a mess of the directions. He didn't know where he was. And his feet were back to throbbing again. He needed to get off them. Even for just a few minutes.

He looked around for a bench or a bus stop. There was nothing. He kept walking, grumbling to himself. Maybe he should untie his shoes.

Wouldn't that be a sight? With any luck, loose laces would make him trip. He could skin his knee or tear his pants. Besides how was he going to retie them? There was no place to sit.

He kept walking until a car racing through a red light caused him to jump back to the curb. He swore and stepped into the street, hoping the driver could see his finger in the rear view.

Then, he saw it. On the other side of the intersection. A big steaming cup of coffee painted on a store front window. That would work. That's what he wanted. Having a cup, or two, and maybe a donut, would get him off his feet for five minutes. That's all he needed. He crossed over.

But at 5 feet from the door, he realized the steaming cup wasn't coffee at all. It was tea. And printed on the little paper label, dangling from the tea string, it said, "Readings and Fortunes".

"Oh crap." Poodle thought. He didn't need his fortune read. He already knew his fortune. His feet were killing him. And they weren't going to stop killing him unless he got off them. Besides, he didn't even like tea. Why would he? No one ever served doughnuts with tea. No wonder we threw the damn stuff in the harbor.

He looked around for somewhere else to go. There were other stores. But nothing that made him think he could go in and have a seat. Then he smelled a faint whiff of jasmine. He didn't know it was jasmine. He just liked the smell. It was nice. Very light. And made him think it might be good, even without a doughnut. He cupped his hand over his eyes and leaned closer to the glass.

Inside, he could see a white doily on an otherwise empty wooden table. It was a nice table. Oak. And looked hand crafted. It sat in the center of a small room. Two wooden chairs were pushed in around it. They both looked hand crafted as well. Looking off to the side, he could see another, smaller table, by the wall. An unlit antique lamp sat on it.

It was too dim to see much of anything else. The only light in the room was coming through the front window, which Poodle was obstructing. He chuckled at the absurdity of blocking his own view. Then leaned away from the glass.

"They're not even open." He thought. Then he smelled the jasmine again. Was that tea? Or perfume? Maybe it was incense. He couldn't tell. But it made him think that maybe somebody was in there.

He tried a second time to look deeper into the room. But it was too dark. He leaned back and sighed. It would have been nice to sit down. Even if they didn't have coffee. Or donuts. He looked at the door. Painted in cursive, on the bottom of the door window, it read "Come in. We've been expecting you."

"Nice touch." He thought. Then he tried the doorknob. It turned. And a little bell jingled when he pushed it open.

"Hello?" he called out. And rapped his knuckles on the door for good measure.

It took a few seconds before a woman yelled back. Poodle couldn't understand what she said. He stepped inside and repeated himself. Closing the door, and the bell jingled a second time.

Now that he was inside, it was easier to see. The room was simple and sparse. There were odd sized, antique picture frames hung on two of the walls. One contained a landscape painting. The others held black and white photographs.

There was a braided rug covering most of the floor. At the far end of the room was a draped doorway leading deeper into the building. Poodle waited, assuming the woman would come out or say something else.

After a short time, the drape in the doorway billowed. Then someone's arm reached out and pushed it to one side. An older woman, with her grey hair pulled up into a disheveled bun, came through the door. She was pushing a rolling tea cart in front of her. She walked with a slight limp, as if she had a tender hip or knee. As she came closer, Poodle could see a single plastic hair curler bouncing off her shoulder in time with her steps. She wore a faded, floral housecoat and untied, high-top sneakers. She also had a cane hooked over one wrist.

"Been expecting me?" Poodle thought the message on the door should be updated.

He said hello. She didn't answer. She was focused on steering the cart onto and over the braided rug. Poodle watched her and thought of a slow-motion space buggy bouncing over the surface of the moon. On top of the cart, a ceramic tea set rattled and jiggled as she crept along. He stepped forward to help, but the woman waved him off. Besides the tea pot and the cups and the saucers, Poodle noticed a plate of cookies rattling towards him.

"Cookies!" He suppressed a grin. Not quite donuts but who was he to complain? He'd even suffer a cup of tea for a few of those. She stopped her lunar rover in front of the doily covered table. Nothing had tumbled or overturned. She let out a slight sigh, then motioned for him to sit down.

"I'm not here for a ..." he started.

She held up a hand. "Tea first."

Poodle considered repeating himself, then looked at the plate of cookies again. *"Oh, what the hell."* He thought, pulling out a chair. He'd explain himself in a few minutes.

The woman waited for him to sit. As she did, she discovered the lone curler. She pulled it out of her hair, with one hand, and put it in her housecoats oversized pocket. Then, she let go of the cart and maneuvered the cane into her hand. She leaned on it for balance. With her free hand, she emptied the cart top onto the table. Again, Poodle offered to help. She ignored him.

"You thought this was a coffee shop." she said as she pulled out her own chair.

"I did." Poodle confessed.

She nodded but didn't say anything more. She poured the tea and slid one cup towards him. Poodle took it and thanked her. She passed the plate of cookies saying, "Not quite doughnuts." She said in sing song voice, "But who are we to complain?"

"Well, that was a little weird." Poodle thought. Then pulled the plate towards him.

"Thank you." he said softly.

She waved a hand in front of herself, addressing her attire. "I forgot you were coming." She said, with a shrug. "Sorry." She didn't seem all that concerned.

"Forgot?" Poodle pondered that. Then, trying to be polite, said, "Well, at least I didn't keep you waiting."

She smiled, letting him know she appreciated his humor. She tapped her temple. "Age is catching up with me."

Poodle acknowledged her remark with a grin.

"An absent-minded psychic? This ought to be interesting." He thought.

She looked at him as if he had said that out loud. And for a second, Poodle wondered if he did. But she didn't say anything more.

They ate in silence. The tea had more aroma than flavor. And the cookies had less flavor than the tea. But still, Poodle had a second cookie. And then a third, just to make sure his assessment was correct.

"You like them." She finally said. It was more a statement than a question.

"Very light." Poodle answered, eyeing how many were left. "Did you make them?"

"I don't bake." She said, bringing the teacup to her lips. "I used to. But not anymore." She sipped her tea.

"I don't bake either." Poodle said, again trying to make polite conversation.

"But your mother-in-law does." The woman said.

Poodle thought about that for a second. Lucky guess? Either that or this lady was pretty good. He agreed with her, and said, "Yes. Yes, she does. She's very good."

She smiled and pointed her cane towards his belly. "I can see that."

Poodle felt his cheeks flush. She didn't have to say that. But, then again, here he was, showing up unannounced. And helping himself to her cookies. That wasn't exactly polite. So, he let it go. And took another cookie.

"Guilty." He said, patting his belly.

The woman offered a dismissive wave, "I was just teasing." she said, "There are far worse sins than 3-layer chocolate cake."

Now that was getting pretty precise for lucky guesses. Poodle stopped chewing and looked at her. She smiled. But it was the tell-you-nothing smile of an accomplished poker player.

"*She's reading me.*" Poodle told himself. "*I must have some kind of tells.*" He wondered where this conversation was headed. And reminded himself that he could always get up and walk out at any time. He smiled back.

"Worse sins perhaps," he said, picking up his tea cup, "But I'm not sure there's a better one." He patted his belly again.

They both chuckled at that, then Poodle continued. "This is all very nice, thank you. But I didn't come for any kind of a reading."

"You came to rest your feet. And so, you are."

Poodle nodded. "You're pretty good."

"Moselle Sayer. Knows all, tells all." She said, with a slight roll of her eyes.

"Nice to meet you Ms. Sayer. I'm Clark. Clark Canderankle."

"But you prefer Poodle. Nice to meet you too, Mr. Poodle."

"Just. Poodle. No mister." He said. Then added, "You're freaking me out a little bit."

She brought a napkin to her lips, then leaned towards the cart.

"So soon? Come now." She said, pulling up a small wooden box from a lower shelf on the tea cart. She set it on the table in front of her. It made Poodle think of some aristocrat's snuff box from revolutionary war days.

"Tea leaves." She said.

It opened with a dull pop and she took out a few dried pieces. After examining each of them, she selected one and she rubbed it between her fingers. It crumpled into small pieces that fell in front of her onto the table.

"I thought you guys read them from the bottom of a teacup." Poodle said.

"Don't believe everything you see on TV." She said with the slightest of sneers. Then, looking over at him, she continued, "Besides it's all just part of the show."

Part of the show? Yeah, that made sense. He felt himself relax. "You mean this is all just a trick? It's not really real?"

He was sure that's what she was telling him. But why she would admit that. And how, if it was all just a trick, did she know about Pearl's 3-layer chocolate cake?

"Oh no, it's real." She said pushing the tea crumbs around in a small circle. "But it wouldn't be entertaining without a show." She was hunched over now, and peeked up at him. Lowering her voice, she said, "And that's all people want. Truth is somewhat… secondary."

Poodle wasn't following. He lifted a cookie from the plate and watched as she divided up the tea crumbs into three separate lines. She continued.

"You see, people don't come to me because they want an answer. They might think they do. But they don't. Not really. That would spoil their fun."

"You kind of lost me." Poodle said. And started to think about how many steps it would take to reach the door.

"Think of it this way," she offered, "People love their own imaginations. It's like having a toy thought balloon. They fill it with hope. Or fear. Or anything in between. They love watching it get bigger. And bigger. You still with me?"

Poodle said he was.

She went on. "They come to me for validation. To re-enforce how important their great big balloon must be. It is, after all, theirs." She giggled. "An honest answer would pop that little balloon." She snapped her fingers as she said 'popped'. "That wouldn't be any fun, would it?"

Poodle understood that a popped ballon was no fun. "So, you put on a show for them?"

"Yes." She now had the tea crumbs in 3 reasonably equal piles. "I make sure that there is nothing more important than the fleeting whim their imagination has captured. I 'ooo' and I 'awww'. And then I send them off with a riddle. Or a conundrum. Something they can ponder and fondle until they decide to come see me again." She brushed a loose lock of hair out of her eyes. "Much more fun than a deflated balloon."

Poodle leaned forward. "Why are you telling me this?"

"Because you didn't come for a reading. You came to rest your feet." She looked over at the empty plate. "And eat a dozen cookies."

"A dozen? Really? Ah, sorry." He changed the subject. "But don't some people come for the truth?"

"They all think they do. But no one ever does."

"I would want the truth." Poodle said.

"Oh really? Moselle Sayer smiled. "Let's see." She closed her eyes and began to hum. Then she reached out and pinched the center pile of leaves. And as she lifted her arm upward, she sprinkled the dust back down onto the table.

Poodle watched in silence. He couldn't figure out what her angle was. She seemed to know things. But it still didn't make any sense. And unless she held him hostage with another dozen cookies, he was out of there.

"Well, there's no way around it now." She said as the last of the dust settled.

"No way around what?"

"You're going to jail."

He didn't expect that. But surprise only lasted for a second.

"Okay. This is where she tries to hit me up." He frowned at her.

"No. It's the truth." She said. "It will happen today." Then she tilted her head as if she were looking over a pair of glasses. "And it gets worse."

"I'll miss the jail house evening meal?" Poodle pushed his chair back. It was time to go.

"Ha-ha." She said flatly. "No. Your wife will find out."

"Oh man, come on. That's not even funny."

"This is why people prefer riddles and conundrums." She sat back, looking slightly smug.

"I'm really getting arrested?" He started to stand up. Then sat back down so he could brush cookie crumbs off his shirt into his empty palm.

"Thank you." She said, watching him empty his crumb filled hand over an empty plate. "You're getting arrested. You're going to jail. It's also a case of mistaken identity. So, you won't really be charged with anything."

"And my wife has to find out?"

"Afraid so."

Poodle shook his head. "Afraid it's time to go." He stood up and pulled a pair of singles from his front pocket. "For the cookies." And he set the bills on the table.

Seeing the money made Moselle Sayer mad. She pushed back her own chair back and stood up.

"You're a nice man," she said, wobbling on her cane as she took a step, "for a future convict."

Choosing to ignore her, he said, "Nice to meet you Ms. Sayer." Then turned to go.

"Yeah, nice to meet me." She scooped up the two dollars. "Like it was nice for you to meet that miserable bitch waitress this morning! You didn't listen to anything she said either!"

"*Miserable bitch waitress...*" Poodle stopped in mid-step. How did she know that? He had no idea. But it didn't matter. She just proved that she did. What had Shelly told him? He rolodex-ed through his head, trying to recall everything Miss Congeniality had barked about. Then he remembered.

"That Apocalypse thing!" he turned around. "What is that?"

Moselle Sayer stared at him with an outstretched arm and a sour expression. Poodle realized he had insulted her by leaving the money.

"I was trying to be nice." He said as he took back the two dollars.

It took Moselle Sayer a few huffs and a snort before she regained her composure. Then, in a deliberately reserved tone, she said, "They're a gang of thieves. Run by a man that has delusions of grandeur." She sneered. Then added, "Among other things."

"I don't know what that means." Poodle replied.

"He believes he's a larger-than-life type of hero. Like the guys in the movies."

"He thinks he's Flash Gordon?" Poodle asked. It was the first movie hero that came to him.

"Not him so much." Moselle said, shifting her weight and looking at her chair. "But that's the idea. He fixes..." That wasn't the word she wanted. She paused.

"He fixes things?" Poodle asked.

"No," she said, still trying to remember the word. "He fix, fixtures...?"

"Appliances."

"No."

"Shoes."

"No! He doesn't fix anything." A curl of hair fell in front of her face. She blew it out of the way, with a snort. "He fix, fixtu? Fixtulates..." she snapped her fingers. "He fixates! That what he does."

"Is that some kind of a dance?" Poodle said, as he thought about sitting back down. He was hoping she would offer him more tea.

"Ha. Ha." Moselle wasn't amused. "He thinks about things so much he turns into them. Now he thinks he's that folk hero guy. What's his name?"

"Bob Dylan?"

"No."

"Peter, Paul and Mary?"

"What the hell is wrong with you?"

Poodle grinned. He couldn't remember a time he didn't enjoy being a wise ass.

"He's that old legend." She shook her head, not remembering his name. "The one that lived in the woods."

"Tarzan?"

"No." She frowned. "Tarzan lives in the jungle. This guy lives in the woods. With a bunch of other guys. Looks like Errol Flynn."

"Captain Blood?"

Captain Blood didn't live in the woods. This guy was a numb skull. But she didn't correct him on the woods. He wouldn't care. She just continued because she was getting tired of his antics.

"Not Blood. But you get the idea."

She raised an excited finger. And opened her mouth. But after a few seconds, she dropped her hand to her side. "Damn it," She sighed, "It was on the tip of my tongue. Anyway, now he's this guy. And he got himself an idea. So, he puts on a disguise..."

"Wait a minute," Poodle interrupted. "Are you're saying he put on a disguise because he became this new guy? Or he became this new guy and put on a disguise to become another new guy?"

Moselle raised an eyebrow. She didn't think he was paying attention. She winked at him. "Crazy shit, huh?"

"It's making my head spin."

"Anyway, his disguise idea worked. So now he's going to keep being that guy."

"Which guy?"

"The second guy was just a disguise." She explained.

"I though the third guy was the disguise."

She put her cane free hand on her hip. "I ain't Abbott. You ain't Costello. Understand?"

Poodle was hoping to get a little more milage out of that. But she didn't want to play. Just as well, he should be leaving.

"This guy sounds crackers." He said, hoping to wrap up the conversation and be on his way.

"Don't think he's not smart. Because that would be a mistake." She warned.

None of what she just told him sounded particularly smart to Poodle. But he didn't say that. He just wanted to leave. Politely, if possible.

"But he is crackers, you're right about that." She spun her index finger in a circle near her temple. "His success got him thinking God is on his side."

"What?" Poodle thought that was ridiculous. "No way."

"That's what he's thinking." She shook her head in dismay. "In his mind, he's got a divine directive."

Well, divine directive certainly didn't sound very good. Poodle thought about that for a second.

"No. That couldn't be right." He said, Then, a wave of doubt floated through him. "Could it?" he asked.

She frowned. "Do you think the universe would a provide divine directive, to a lunatic? Tell him it was okay to steal?"

Poodle had no idea. As far as he knew, the universe didn't tell anybody anything. "Probably not." He said softly.

Moselle's frown turned into a sneer. "You know!" she pointed at him. "When you sit in church with your wife and your mother-in-law, you *could* pay attention."

"Hey! I do." Poodle snapped at her.

"You do not!" She snapped back. "You spend the whole time thinking about this week's game!" Her tone had become mocking. "And next week's parley picks! O-o-o! A-h-h!"

She caught him dead to rights. That was true. Poodle had no idea what went on in church. Nor did he care, beyond the snacks in the basement, after Mass. He was just there as chauffer. Then something occurred to him.

"Hey, do you…" he wiggled his fingers around his head, "follow sports?"

"No!" She barked loud enough to make him jump. "Enjoy your almost break even gambling for what it is. Dumb luck and random chance." She turned and took a step away from him.

Parleys didn't sound near as much fun when she described them that way. But he didn't argue. He was already back to thinking about getting arrested. If she knew all that other stuff, why would she bullshit him about that? She didn't want money. She got mad over two dollars. Maybe she was right. But how?

Poodle swallowed hard. Then spoke soft. "Shelly said I should lose the tie. Think that would help?"

"Keep you out of the paddy wagon? Nope."

Poodle sighed. "What if I call my wife first?"

"And tell her what?"

"I don't know." Poodle realized how desperate he sounded and looked at the floor.

"Call her if you want." Moselle said, pointing off in the distance. "There's a phone booth at the top of the hill."

Reaching into his front pocket to check for change, Poodle bobbed his head. It probably wasn't a good idea to call Jericho. He'd mess it up and make it worse. Worse than what? He didn't know. But he didn't know what else to do. Maybe something would occur to him as he walked to the phone.

Moselle Sayer turned back around and watched him fumble for change. For a big guy he was looking pretty sorry. Her demeanor softened.

"How are your feet?" she asked.

"Better." He said, trying to sound optimistic. And they were. Getting off them, even for a few minutes helped.

"Keds are on sale at Sears. But only till Tuesday. Tell your wife."

"Thank you." Then, feeling awkward, he added, "I'll see myself out."

Moselle waited until the door shut behind him. She walked to the window. And could see him heading up the hill.

Standing still, not thinking about anything in particular, that elusive fragment of thought finally bubbled into her mind.

"Robin Hood." She said softly.

By the time Poodle topped the hill, a healthy level of skepticism had returned. The fact that his feet were hurt again only encouraged his doubt.

He couldn't explain how Moselle Sayer knew what she knew. It had to be a trick. And with each aching step, it was getting harder and harder to believe that a random encounter with a human dust rag guaranteed his impending arrest. It wasn't right. It had to be a con. He just couldn't unravel it.

Maybe she was setting him up so he would come back. She as much as told him that's what she did. Gave people riddles, those were her exact words, make them want to come back. Maybe she was doing that to him.

The pay phone was on the far corner. He stopped for traffic and thought about what he would say.

"Hi honey. My feet hurt. I lost my satchel. And all of the brochures. I've been turned away at every business I've entered. But none of that matters because some crack pot gypsy lady sprinkled tea dust and now I'm going to jail!"

No. He wasn't doing that.

Traffic cleared but he didn't move. He wasn't going to admit defeat. Not on the very first day. So, he decided he'd call and not say any of that. Tell her it was going slow. Ask about her day. Then he could listen to her voice. He liked that idea. Besides, the pay phone would only give him 2 or 3 minutes. He could say he didn't have any more change. Ma Bell would keep it short and cut him off.

Poodle crossed the street. With his feet hurting again, he found it easy to be angry. And when he discovered the pay phone coin slot was jammed with month old bubble gum, he was ready to scream.

"Who the hell would do that? Little bastards." He stared down at the rock hard, overflowing pink glob.

He took a business card from his wallet and tried using the corner to dig out the gum. But that didn't work. He creased it in half, creating a card stock hoe, and tried again. The gum held firm.

"Aw-w-w!" He groaned as his paper tool crumbled. "Damn it!"

He reached into his pocket for a penknife or screwdriver or some other object he already knew wasn't there. He felt a quarter. That might work. He pulled it out and scraped at the gum. Nothing.

"You've got to be kidding me." He thought, then struck the quarter against the top of the pink mound, like a miniature pickax. Nothing.

He tried again. Nothing. With more force. Nothing. Then again. Nothing. His face turned pink. As pink as the all-day triple bubble he was trying to dislodge. Nothing.

"Come on!" he spit out between clenched teeth. Then, with one final show of force, he jammed the quarter as hard as he could. And scrapped his knuckles all the way down the front of the phone.

It tore back his skin. He screamed and swore. And, on instinct, jammed his fist into his mouth. He could taste blood. He hated blood. He hated tasting his own blood. He gagged and spit it out. But the air burned his wounds and he shoved his knuckles back in his mouth again.

"Oh my God!" He yelled at himself as he tried to dance away the pain. "You moron! What did you do!"

He bounced around the booth for a few more seconds and told himself he had to see how bad it was. What if he needed stitches? What if a bone was sticking out? He knew he needed to look. But he didn't want to see. He stopped dancing. He opened his eyes. Then he saw it. Laying on the ground.

He had knocked the phone receiver from its cradle. But the cord had already been cut. And it fell all the way to the floor.

"I couldn't have called anyway." He pushed it with his foot. "Son of a bitch." If his knuckles still hurt, he was too angry to care.

He stepped out of the booth. He had just passed a small drugstore, a half a block back. He looked down at his knuckles. At least two of them were bleeding. He pressed his wounded fingers against his chest, to apply pressure. And started back down the hill.

His knuckles bled the whole walk back. He checked them several times. But they wouldn't stop. He figured he might need more than band-aids. Maybe gauze and tape.

At the entrance to the pharmacy, he sized up his own reflection in the door glass. He looked like he someone had emptied a revolver in his chest. There were 6, maybe 8 bloody spots on his shirt, from trying to stop the bleeding. But he was still angry. It made him sneer. And he walked in.

A short, high school girl wearing a blue 'Nathan's Drugs' smock was restocking a shelf. She was down on one knee, with her back to the door. Poodle walked up to her.

"Bandages." He commanded.

He took her by surprise and she looked up. Poodle, who was already a foot taller than her, appeared twice that size, from one knee.

He was angry. And he was bleeding. It was right out of a movie. She stood up quickly and took a step back. Then pointed down the walkway.

"Aisle four." She said. But didn't look at him.

Poodle turned towards aisle four. Then stopped. And turned back.

"Thank you." He said, trying to sound sincere. But she was already gone.

At a sunglass's kiosk, he stopped to look at himself in the 3 x 5 mirror. He put on a pair of shades and held up his bloody hand, next to his face, so he could see the reflection.

"May I help you?" The voice came from a dark-haired man wearing a tie and a lab coat. He was standing in the middle of the walkway, ten feet ahead.

Poodle put the glasses back and held out his hand. "Scrapped up my knuckles."

The man was indifferent to the blood. "Let's get you cleaned up." He waved for Poodle to follow him. "Come on." Then he started walking.

Poodle followed. In three steps he had caught up. "Sorry for the trouble." His anger was beginning to subside.

The man stopped at aisle four, grabbed a box of gauze, a roll of tape, and a can of antiseptic spray. Then said, "Restroom's over here. There's a counter and a sink."

Poodle followed and said, "I'll pay for everything." But the man didn't answer and kept walking.

In the men's room, the man set the spray on the counter. He motioned for Poodle to wash his hands.

Poodle began cleaning up. The man pulled a small pair of scissors from his lab coat pocket. He cut 4 short strips of both the tape and gauze. He left them on the counter.

Poodle began feeling foolish.

"Sorry for the trouble." He repeated. The man still didn't respond.

Poodle dried his hands and wrapped the gauze around his fingers. Then, as he was taping it in place, he realized that lab coat man had gone.

When he finished bandaging his wounds, he opened the door, to exit.

Two uniformed police officers were in the hallway, waiting.

"You need to come with us." One of them said.

Chapter 8

On the one hand, Jeri was ready to ring her husband's neck. How could he get himself arrested? This job wasn't that hard. She had watered it down to little more than an errand. Just deliver the goods and move on.

On the other, she understood it was all a mistake. The police were looking for someone else. But still… She had to go to Raoul and tell him she was leaving. And she needed him to cover an interview for her. Which of course prompted Raoul to ask what was so important.

She could have lied. Or told him to mind his own business. And for a second, she considered both. But it was related to work. He had a right to know. The company's interest was his job.

So, she told him. He listened. He seemed more curious that upset. Possibly intrigued. She finished and waited for his assessment.

"They always manage to add a bit of color, don't they?" He said with a wry smile.

She was glad he liked them. She felt fortunate. It didn't have to be that way. He wasn't that way with others. The rest of the staff found him cold and distant. Sometimes he could be difficult due to his general indifference to things outside of work.

But he liked her family. And she was glad of that. She remembered when they first met. At the time, she was certain it was going to be a disaster.

A year earlier, when Eric had first committed to resurrecting the Chamber of Commerce, he had Raoul organize a charity golf tournament.

It went unspoken, but the charity was a secondary consideration. The opportunity for the retailers to gather and mingle was the primary objective.

Eric was quite impressed with what Raoul, with a little bit of help from Jericho, had created. But his enthusiasm fizzled when he realized that Abbott Industries would not be participating in the actual golf tournament. Raoul hadn't found any takers.

Raoul explained that he didn't golf. Eric didn't care. He said, it's captain and crew. You just need to be a member of a team on the links. Find people.

Everyone worked hard for Raoul because they had no choice. He was stern and had high standards. But no one was willingly going to recreate with him. Jericho offered herself and the two boys. Raoul begrudgingly excepted.

They golfed respectably. The boys, having been promised beer and buffet, were enthusiastic. And played to win. They didn't care that neither Raoul nor Jericho could play. Those two just rode along, hit balls into the woods, kept the score card somewhat accurate.

Until the 6th hole. For reasons unexplained, on the 6th hole, Raoul drove his ball 145 yards off the tee and onto the green.

The boys went ballistic and began howling his name like a wolf call.

"Rah-Rah, Raoo-oo-oo-ll!!" They tossed their heads back, arched their spines and carried on with abandon.

And they didn't let up. It continued at every hole. Everyone they caught up to, and every group that passed them, saw and heard the ritual. It was fun. And inviting.

If anyone from any other group joined in, Milk and Poodle would howl all the harder. Sometimes they put their heads together like they were doing bluegrass harmonies.

At first Raoul was embarrassed. Then mildly entertained. Entertainment slowly gave way to annoyance. But, by the time they returned to the clubhouse, a curious thing had happened.

Howling at Raoul had become a spontaneous, drunken cult ritual. Everyone that saw him howled. Across the parking lot. In the restroom. Everywhere.

People he had never met came up to shake his hand. Jericho, knowing Raoul was a closet germaphobe, found that part of the day most entertaining.

He had become an instant celebrity of sorts. Even among the few sober people in attendance, he was a hit.

While everyone was enjoying the buffet, Eric got up to say a few words. He thanked everyone for coming. He thanked the golf course. He announced the money they had raised. He announced the winner of the tourney.

And finally, when he called out Raoul by name to thank him for organizing the event, the room erupted. Everyone howled. Even some of the clubhouse staff stood up and clapped.

Eric was stunned. He, better than anyone else, knew Raoul could be a cold fish. When his first in command stood up to acknowledge the crowd, Eric called him up. The applause continued. Eric whispered something in Raoul's ear.

Raoul never revealed what his boss said that day. But he beamed brighter than a spot light. And always kept a soft spot for his two new golfing companions.

That had a lot to do why he was tolerant and unchallenging when Jericho first proposed hiring them as sales staff. They had no skills. From Raoul's perspective, they also had no couth.

But they did have his blessings. And they came on board.

Now one of them had been arrested.

But Raoul wasn't shocked or scandalized. He was completely calm, if not modestly amused.

He knew it was nonsense. Because he was already aware of the Witness to the Apocalypse gang. And their brief robbery spree. He knew Poodle had nothing to do with any of that. And he was sure the police did as well.

"It was over in Mumsford." He said. "Didn't get much news coverage around here. Lots of local retailer word of mouth though."

Jericho had never heard anything about the robberies or the gang.

Raoul had found out through Eric. Eric owned property and had business connections in Mumsford. His contacts told him as much as they knew. Which wasn't very much. Some band of thieves had posed as founders of a new church. One of them went around, looking for a back room or storage area to lease so they could hold their spiritual gatherings, once a week.

They found some well-intentioned, if not overly naïve, business owners willing to let them do that.

But what this insincere Christian was really doing was casing various establishments to rob. Which his gang did. Three places, all in one night. Two of them were break ins. The third was robbing the gracious host that had invited them in under false pretenses.

The local police didn't have much to go on. A few people gave a rather vague description of an older man with a handlebar moustache that originally came around. What almost everybody could describe in detail was the 7-foot-tall thief that held a gun on them, while they were being robbed. He wore a mask and didn't talk. But everyone remembered his height.

Everyone, including Pete Floyd, from the stationary store. Somewhere between smashing the glass counter top and getting eleven stiches in the ER, Floyd had called the police and reported Poodle. He was sure he had come face to face with the thieving giant.

The cops were given the same relative description when they took the call from Nathan's Pharmacy. They thought they had a gang member.

But the description given by the victims was of a much thinner 7-foot thief. And probably younger. Lastly, although the man had worn a mask, he hadn't covered his head. He had a dark crew cut. Poodle's hair was something all the witnesses said they would have remembered. As well as his girth.

So, the cops took down Poodle's vitals, snapped his picture, inked his prints and let him go. That's when he called his wife for a ride.

"Take him to lunch." Raoul said, after he finished sharing everything he knew.

Jericho said she would. She didn't mention that the three of them were already planning on meeting up. Raoul didn't need to know that. Besides, if he was telling her to do it, then he was paying for it.

"Maybe the cops told him something we don't know." He added. "Could be fun. Find out." Then he rubbed his hands together.

"You just love the gossip mill, don't you?" Jericho teased.

"It's not gossip if you can dress it up as news." He answered, waving the back of his hand like a broom, to send her away. Then he added, "Wait. What's on your afternoon calendar?"

"I have that second sales interview."

"Have her send them to me." He looked at his watch.

"I should be back in time."

"If you are, fine. No harm in both of us talking to… him or her?"

"Him." She said. Raoul nodded. And Jericho left.

When she pulled up, Poodle was standing outside. She saw his blood caked shirt.

"What did they do to you?" she asked.

He got in the car. "I did that myself." He said. Then he told her about the phone booth.

He expected to hear about it, ruining a new white shirt and all. But she just said, "Change your shoes." and pulled out onto the street.

She remembered his sneakers. He grinned.

"I love you baby." He said, taking off his shoes. For a minute he considered finishing the day barefoot. But he liked his toes. And the way this day was going, he should protect them.

"Honest to God, I didn't do anything." Poodle finally said, when the silence became too much for him.

Jeri looked in the mirror and said, "I know." Then proceeded to tell him everything that Raoul had told her.

He listened. Then offered her the parts about Shelly, and Mr. Floyd, and needing to go to the pharmacy. Initially, he left out the part about the fortune teller. He wasn't sure why. In part because he couldn't remember her whole name. Moselle was such an odd name that he completely overlooked her last. Also, it was so weird that he thought Jeri might ask a hundred questions that he wouldn't be able to answer. And he felt dumb enough already. But eventually he told her. She listened.

"I've heard of that Moselle lady." She said, when he had finished. "Some of the gals in my book club have gone to see her."

Poodle decided to skip over what she had told him about those seeking her services. Those women would get in a snit and it would eventually get back to Mrs. Voodoo herself. Poodle didn't want that hanging over his head.

But it did make him wonder if this Moselle woman could cast spells. If she could, he was going back with a whole wheel barrow full of cookies. And talk to her about that Floyd dude. Poodle was sure that's where his trouble started.

That little turd had sliced himself pretty good. Poodle was sure of it. Could Mrs. Knows All - Tells All conjure up an infection? Not gangrene or anything. Just something painful. Keep him crying for a week or two.

"What?" Jeri was looking at her husband. He was smiling.

"Plotting my revenge." He said between huffs and puffs. Tying his sneakers in a moving car was more work than he expected.

He sat up and looked out the window. He figured someone at the Pharmacy called the cops too. He couldn't really blame them. He was pretty frightening looking. Now he'd have to take his shirt off to go into Sal's. Or maybe not. He could go in, as is, and invite another encounter with Sycamore's finest.

They drove for a while in silence. Each reviewing their understanding of the situation. Finally, Jeri asked, "You hungry?"

"No, they fed me in the lock up."

"They did not."

"You're right my dear," he said, straightening his posture, "They did not. And I am starved."

Jeri smiled. She understood that 'starved' meant he hadn't eaten in 40 minutes or more. But it also meant that he was feeling better soon. She wondered if her brother was doing any better than her husband? Honestly, how could he do any worse? Arson? She didn't want to think about it. They needed to focus on the positive.

When she hit 3 green lights in a row, she made a point of telling him.

"See that? Things are getting better already." She said.

"Oh my God!" He yelled, pretending to be in a panic. "Skip lunch! We're going to the race track."

Skip lunch. Like that would ever happen.

"Look for a parking spot." She said, pointing to the passenger side of the street.

It took them another block but they found one. Poodle eventually grunted himself out of the car. He took off his shirt and put his jacket back on over his tee shirt. If someone looked, they would see the soaked through stains. But it was a far cry better than the assassination attempt he had just taken off.

They walked up the street to Sal's Slices.

Inside, the lunch rush was over. People still occupied most of the booths that lined both walls. But those people were full. And their dishes were dirty. Most of the square tables in the center of the room were empty. One or two of them had been pulled together earlier for larger groups. They were empty as well.

A busboy was cleaning up after all the exited customers. He was moving slow. It was hot. Hotter than outside. Poodle wished he hadn't worn his jacket.

The counter to order was all the way in the rear of the building. Poodle tried to march straight back there, but Jericho grabbed his arm.

"I don't see him. Do you?" she asked.

"He's not here." Poodle said. Then tried to read the specials board from where he was. But it was too far away. He started to step towards it but his wife grabbed his arm again.

"Someone wants you." She said. And turned her head towards a young child, standing on a booth cushion, pointing at her husband. A nun, in habit, was sitting at the same booth. She was trying to make sure the child didn't fall. But put no effort into trying to dissuade her from seeking Poodle's attention.

Poodle looked over. Then wiggled his fingers at her in a childish wave. "Hi honey." He said, knowing she couldn't hear him.

When the little girl saw him wave, she rubbed the top of her head and pointed at him a second time.

"Yes honey," he said, wanting to get back to the menu. "Just like a poodle."

The little girl stopped pointing. And motioned for the nun to come with her. Then she hopped off the booth cushion and walked over. The nun followed.

They all stood in the middle of the room, looking at one another. No one was quite sure what to say. Jericho spoke up.

"Hello. I'm Jericho." She offered.

The little girl tapped at the nun's sleeve.

"The Poodle?" The nun asked. She had an accent.

"Ah, yeah." Poodle said, putting his hand on his chest. "That's me."

The nun and the little girl looked at one another. They each shook their heads, in agreement. Then the nun handed Poodle a folded note.

He opened it.

"What does it say?" Jericho asked, moving to his side so she could read it, too. Poodle read it aloud.

"Emergency! Stop. Come right away! Stop. No time for questions.

Stop. Follow these two immediately. Stop."

"Why did he keep writing stop?" Jericho asked.

Poodle pointed to the letterhead. Milk had drawn a line through the original, CHRISTIAN CHARITY CHILDREN'S HOME, and had written WESTERN UNION below it.

"It's what they do in telegrams. He thinks he's being funny." He said. The he looked at the nun.

"You get this from a guy named Milk?" He asked her. She looked confused and didn't answer.

"Maybe Babylon? Or Babs?" Jericho offered.

The little girl tugged at the nun's sleeve. The nun looked at her then handed Poodle a second folded note.

Poodle opened the note and read aloud. "I said no time for questions. Stop. Follow these two immediately. Stop." Poodle started to laugh.

"What is he doing?" Jericho said. Poodle held up a hand and waved her to stop.

"You think she's not armed with another dozen notes?" he pointed to the door. The nun and young girl led the way out. Poodle looked at his wife. "Let's go find him."

The nun and the young girl had arrived by tandem bicycle. They walked it over to where Jericho had parked. Then they got on, with the little girl in front, and both began pedaling.

It was obvious from the beginning, that bicycling was not a required skill set at the convent. As the nun pedaled, she white knuckled the hand grips. And occasionally panic shuttered for no reason. But all their progress, as slow as it was, came from the 7-year-old in the front seat. She was at ease. And knew where she was going.

Jericho followed behind her at a speed so slow the needle laid on zero the whole time. Twice people coming up behind her honked before she waved them on. And once, on a modest incline, her little bug stalled.

Poodle suggested Jericho push them, bumper to fender. Jericho ignored him.

"How fast do you think you'd have to push them before she screamed and dove off?" he asked. Jericho told him to be quiet.

"The little one would love it. She's not afraid." But with a glare from his wife, he dropped it.

After several more blocks, Poodle thought he should get out and push the bike himself. They'd go faster. He'd trot along and keep them rolling.

Trot along. Who was he fooling? That would work for two blocks. Then his heart would give out. He scratched at his ear and looked to the side.

But in the end, what seemed like an eternity, was little more than 10 minutes. They arrived at the Children's home. It was big and brick and looked like a cross between a hotel and a cathedral.

"I heard Babe Ruth came here once," Poodle said, looking at the building. "Came to visit the kids."

The nun tapped the little girl's shoulder and they came to a stop on the sidewalk. Jericho turned into a large gravel lot, on the side of the building. She parked the car, turned it off. And set the brake.

Everyone was still intact. No spills. No heart failures.

She opened her door. And heard laughter. She looked off to the backyard.

"Are you kidding me?" She said. Poodle turned when he heard her.

A small army of children was running around on a sandlot ball field. In the center of the mob, standing on the pitcher's mound, waving, was her brother. Holding a kickball.

Chapter 9

Jericho had been impressed with her own composure when she heard her husband had been picked up by the cops. Needless to say, she had been surprised. And concerned. And even somewhat annoyed.

However, she understood that none if it was anything he had done deliberately. It could all be fixed. And then they would move forward.

But now? Now she was mad. What was her brother doing, blowing off his job to play kickball with a gang of children? He didn't even know any of them.

But she was stone cold professional. She wasn't going to make a scene. She'd deal with him in her own good time.

Milk called a time out and told all the kids to get some water. Most of the kids continued to run around like they hadn't heard a word he said. He walked off the mound and headed to the bug.

"This is your idea of an emergency?" Jericho said, when her brother reached her. She wasn't smiling.

But Poodle was. He was psyched. He even had sneakers on. He came around the car. Milk looked at his blood-stained tee shirt.

"What happened to you?" He asked.

"I got arrested. How about you?"

"I got a 5-cent lemonade and a free beer." Milk said, spinning the kickball in his hands.

"Cool. Want to trade?" Poodle asked.

Before Milk could answer, Jericho snatched the ball from him.

"So, we're done for the day, is that it?" Jericho's voice was low but her tone was furious. She turned her head between them. "You both look like you're done for the day. Am I mistaken?"

For a few seconds, neither man said anything. Poodle looked at his feet. They both liked the idea of being done. But neither was going to say that. They were barely half way through their very first day.

Then Milk looked up, "This is Father Phillip. He runs the place."

Jericho turned around. A young man had walked up behind her. He was slender, with a hawkish nose and short, dark hair. And except for his collar, he looked like any other thirty something. Poodle stuck out his hand.

"Hello Father." He said, "I'm Clark. Clark Canderankle. And this is my wife, Jericho."

Father Phillip shook his hand. "Very nice to meet you." He said slowly, taking in poodle's shirt. Then he looked down. And saw Poodle's sneakers. "Have you come to play? Exciting game. Very close score."

"We're keeping score?" Milk asked. But no one answered.

Poodle wanted to tell the priest that 'Yes.' he had come to play. Kicking the snot out of a rubber ball and running the base pads would feel pretty good after the morning he had. But that wasn't the deal with his wife. He just smiled. And stood as if he was mute.

Jericho was astute enough to read the situation for what it was. On a certain level, this was a PR moment. There would be no gain in being a hard liner. All anyone would understand from that position, was that she was being a bitch. And she ruined the party. She might not be able to salvage the rest of the day, but she could save face. It was one afternoon. And her husband needed a serious make over before he could go out again, anyway.

A few of the children had circled around the adults. Some were watching and waiting. A couple kept asking when they were going to play again?

Jericho gently tossed the ball to the priest.

"So, it's You, Clark, and Babylon against everyone else?" She asked.

All the kids started yelling with excitement. The priest smiled and shook his head.

"Oh, we want to be fair." he said. And handed the ball to one of the older boys. "You poor kids wouldn't stand a chance against us supermen."

The kids started booing and yelling that they would win. Father Phillip laughed and held up his arms for everyone to quiet down.

"No, no." Father Phillip said, "We're already in the middle of a game. We can't stop now. Come on!" He waved an arm towards the field and all the kids began running.

The adults followed at a much slower pace. Poodle, who had already crossed his fingers, side glanced at his wife. Her eyes were straight ahead. And she was as tight lipped and stern looking as he expected. This was going to be tough to navigate. He looked at his brother-in-law.

"How you working this game?" he asked.

"It's not really teams, as much as turns." Milk answered. "I'm all-time pitcher. Father Phil has been catcher." He looked over at the priest. "But I think he might be ready for a break."

"That would be great." The priest said. He looked at Jericho. "I'll ask sister to get us some lemonade. The kids made it this morning. For their stand."

"The kids made it." Jericho repeated in her head. She wasn't sure if she was supposed to be impressed, or forewarned.

The priest turned back around, looking in the shade of the side lines for some assistance. The nun that biked them over, was coming towards them, walking down from the building. She was carrying the same floral pitcher Milk had questioned. Behind her was an older gentleman, carrying a pair of lawn chairs under each arm.

Poodle was focused on getting his assignment right. "Okay. I can cover that." He said to his brother-in-law, agreeing to step in as catcher.

"Kids old enough to catch the ball guard the bases." Milk continued. "Everyone else is in the outfield. We rotate turns so everyone gets a chance to kick. When they score or get out, they go back to defense."

"Simple enough." Poodle said, hoping he wouldn't have to keep track of who's turn it was to kick."

Jericho physically distanced herself from her husband and brother. She had no issue with the priest, the charity, the staff, or any of the kids. She would be pleasant and personable with all of them.

But her family was only too eager to misinterpret her professional poise as forgiveness. She was pissed at her brother. And it was spilling over onto her husband. And she wanted to make sure they both kept that in mind. The cold shoulder was a good place to start.

"How many kids are here?" Jericho asked the priest.

"From the sound, you would think a lot more. But right now, we have 19." Father Phillip answered. "The facility can hold up to 40."

"It's just you and Sister bicycle?" Poodle asked, from behind them. He was pointing at the nun. The older gentleman had already opened all the chairs and was headed back to the building.

"That's sister Maria." The priest said over his shoulder.

The nun looked over and smiled when she heard her name. But she made no effort to join the conversation.

"She's on-loan to us, for lack of a better term." The priest continued. "A few of the kids only speak Spanish. She's here to assist with that."

Poodle made a confused face. "Does she speak any English?" he asked.

"That, I'm afraid," The priest chuckled, "Is a work in progress." Then he stepped on home plate and held out his hands for the ball.

"We have a few nuns that teach." He continued. "And one that's a nurse. We also have a few volunteers from the congregation that do landscaping, maintenance, janitorial, that sort of thing." He pointed at the old man, who was just reaching the building. "Like Chester there."

The kid holding the ball tossed it to Father Phillip. The priest thanked him and handed it to Milk.

Milk turned to the sea of children meandering the outfield. "Who's turn is it?"

Shouts rang out. And every hand on the field went up. Milk rolled his eyes. And modified his question.

"Okay. Who went last?"

That generated a bit more hesitation. But finally, with some coaxing, one of the smaller kids raised a hand and folded an arm over his head. Milk pointed to 4 or 5 children in the same age group and told them to go over by the priest. Then he turned to Poodle.

"Remember doing the cub scout thing with Harry?" He asked. Harry was Jericho's oldest child and only son. Poodle nodded. "Same idea for this group. Give them a little direction, when needed. Get them to kick it. Older ones..."

Poodle finished his sentence. "Want to do it themselves." Milk turned and headed to the mound.

"Everybody ready!" He shouted to the outfield. The kids yelled back. Milk turned to face home plate. "Play ball!"

The kids Milk had picked were lined up outside the base path. Father Phillip sent up the first kicker. Then he sat down in a lawn chair next to Jericho.

"We are very fortunate. We don't get a lot of guests. Thank you." He handed Jericho a lemonade. "Most people that come here are on business. And don't seem to have much time for the kids."

"*Business.*" Jericho grumbled to herself. But she wasn't focused on the conversation. The 5-year-old girl, the priest had sent to the plate, had stopped short. She froze when she saw Poodle towering ahead of her. Jericho watched. She was all set to tell Poodle what to do. But she wasn't talking to him.

It took but a glance before Poodle understood the situation with both his wife and the kid. Each had happened before. He focused on the little girl and got down on his knees. When that didn't help, he sat back on his heels. He was now half his own height.

"*Hurry honey.*" He thought behind a pained smile. "*I can't sit like this very long.*" He waved her towards him. But she wasn't buying it.

"You want to kick the ball?" He asked her, trying to sound cheerful. And ignoring his knees.

The girl nodded that she did. But didn't move any closer. Poodle sighed. Some children didn't care that he was 3 times taller than they were. Others froze, exactly like this one was doing.

He looked at his wife for help. But Jericho was cringing at what her husband was doing to one of his better pair of trousers. When she saw him look over, she turned her head.

Milk, watching from the mound, knew what that head swivel meant. And, as was always the case with his sister, her annoyance was his opportunity. He turned towards the outfield, waved both arms over his head, and shouted.

"Spider attack! Spiders!"

Then he dropped to a sitting position. And lifted his torso off the ground, so he could spider walk on top of the mound. He zipped back and forth, going nowhere, while a dozen children did the same. Then he waved an arm towards Poodle.

"Get him!" He shouted. And the spider children all marched, in unison, on their prey.

If it had just been Milk on the assault, Poodle would have joined in and spider raced towards him, with the intention of spider punting him through the uprights. But that wasn't the case. There was a whole army of pint-sized arthropod imposters screaming and bearing down on him. They were all too small to play that rough.

He lifted his butt off the ground and did a spider retreat. The whole-time shouting "Can't catch me! Too slow! Can't catch me!" as he backed up.

But he was wrong. They did catch him. And kicked at him. And stepped on his fingers. And tried to trampoline off his belly.

They weren't hurting him any. Even the bigger ones were too small. But he understood someone would eventually get hurt. So, as soon as he could, he flopped over onto his side and rolled away from them.

After 10 feet, He stopped rolling and sat up. He felt like he had taken a ride in a clothes dryer. His head was spinning. He saw one relentless 7-year-old that had jumped to his feet, race towards him.

"Oh crap!" He thought and braced for a head on.

But Father Phillip was there, and scooped up the boy before collision.

"Whoa! Easy now Jimmy. We called time out. Time out now." The priest spun in a circle. The boy's legs flew behind him in a giant arc. When the priest set him down, Jimmy wasn't quite done. He wiggled and squirmed. And wanted to pounce. Father Phillip had to keep a loose grip on him.

Milk had never left the pitcher's mound. He watched the attack from the rear. And was enjoying his sister's angst as much as Poodle's tribulations.

He stood up and brushed himself off. He intended to help his best friend back on his feet. Then he saw a young man, around twelve, leaning on a crutch, behind the backstop. He was scowling. And deliberately keeping his distance.

"What's up with that?" Milk wondered. And waved to get the kids attention. Which he did. But the kid immediately looked away.

Milk walked over. The kid, realizing he was being approached, started to hobble away. But Milk stopped him.

"Hey, I'm going to need your help." He said, cocking his head towards Poodle.

"What?" It was more a challenge than a question.

"Big man doesn't just jump back up. Come on. Bring your stick." Milk waited. The youngster didn't want to help. He tried to look angry. Milk just waited him out.

Some kid in the outfield screamed, "Come on!"

The kid with the crutch spit, said "Fine!" and shuffled to Poodle.

"I thought you were a goner." Milk said, when they reached the newly appointed catcher. He was still on one knee.

"No thanks to you." Poodle said, and took a half-hearted swipe at his pal's leg.

Milk ignored him and looked at the boy.

"Take a step closer, so he can push up on your crutch. You can lean on me if you need to."

The boy let out and 'as if' Pfft, and didn't move. But Poodle didn't wait. He was close enough that he grabbed the crutch. Milk did as well so Poodle didn't pull the kid down on himself.

Grunting, the big man stood up, towering over the other two. He dusted his knees and looked towards the kid, intending to thank him. But the young man was already on the move. He repositioned himself behind the backstop, where he had started.

"So much for social interaction." Milk muttered, as they both watched him. Then Milk cuffed the taller man.

"Let this experience be a lesson to you, for scaring that little girl." he tried to sound threatening.

"How about I give you a lesson in dribbling your head like a basketball?" Poodle answered.

"Wrong sport." Milk said, quickly moving out of reach. He trotted back to the mound. "Let's try this again."

When all the kids were back in position, Sister Maria escorted the first little girl to the plate. Milk rolled the ball. The girl kicked and it dribble back towards the pitcher's mound.

Milk walked off the mound to meet it. Then booted the ball into center field. All the kids in the outfield began running around chasing after it. The little kicker trotted off towards first.

Milk looked at the 13-year-old playing third base. He made a kicking motion. The girl shook her head yes.

"Okay. Next one's yours. Get ready." He said with a wink.

The next batter came to the plate and did the exact same thing as the first. But this time, the girl playing third took the opportunity to launch the ball deep into left field. The two base runners both clapped and advanced.

When the last kicker from the first grouping came to the plate, Milk picked several new outfielders to 'get on deck'. They were 2 or 3 years older than the first group and more comfortable interacting with Poodle.

Father Phillip, who had finally settled down Jimmy, had a brief huddle with Sister Maria and backstop boy.

Jericho watched them. From what she observed, the kid appeared to be bi-lingual. That made her curious. After the huddle broke up, Father Phillip walked back over and had a seat.

"That young man doesn't care for kickball?" She asked.

"Oh, you mean Rodney? I believe he does." The priest answered. "But he's reluctant to play. Very self-conscious, for obvious reasons."

"Was he injured?"

The priest frowned. Jericho thought she may have tread where she wasn't welcome. But after a pause, he continued.

"Like he is with so much of his young life, he's very evasive about his foot. He says he had an accident when he was younger. How much younger? He doesn't say. Claims he doesn't remember any of it."

Jericho looked over at Rodney. He was back to watching the game intently.

"That's really sad." Jericho said, almost to herself. Then, "Where is he from?"

"Says Texas." The priest answered. "But all we have on record is a variety of charities he keeps running away from."

A communal "Ah-h-h-h!" suddenly roared in from the playing field. They both turned to look.

A 10-year-old had gone for two on what should have been a single. He dove under the throw to tag him out at second. As he slid into the base, the ball flew over him, and into the no-man's land between infield and out. Everyone was screaming and the boy made it safely to third before the defense regained control of the game.

"They'll sleep good tonight." The priest said, smiling. "Thank you for that."

Jericho felt embarrassed. The priest was being sincere. And until that moment, she had been indifferent. She had been caught up in wanting her knuckleheaded team out of there, as quickly and politely as possible.

"We haven't done anything." She answered.

The priest politely disagreed. "You did all of this." He waved his hand over the field of laughing children. "We are grateful to have company. Particularly…, is Babylon your brother?"

"Yes. Yes, he is." The priest's gentle soft sell was having an impact. She looked out at her brother, not nearly as mad as she was a minute earlier.

"He said he was selling parades. Then laughed. I wasn't sure what to make of that." Then the priest cupped his hands to his mouth and yelled words of encouragement to the newest kicker.

When he finished, Jericho clarified what her brother had told him.

"He's selling spots in a parade." She said. "The Sycamore Chamber of Commerce has been re-activated. and we are sponsoring a parade in celebration of Sycamore's 100th anniversary."

"Yes, I heard the chamber was active again. I think that will be a good thing." They both unintentionally nodded in unison. Then the priest added, "We were part of the last centennial celebration. Had our own float."

Well, that didn't make any sense. She looked over at him with furrowed brow. "I don't think I remember that." She was trying to be polite.

"Oh, I'm sure you do," The priest said, now somewhat confused himself. "It was America's birthday. It was only, what? 18, maybe 20 months ago."

It was as if his words ignited fireworks behind her eyes. She was suddenly blind. Not by light. But by realization. All her questions and concerns were already answered. Somebody had already done this.

How could they have missed this? Why hadn't they had meetings?

When she started to talk, she realized she was already on her feet. She had no idea she had stood up.

"I… I need to use the phone. Do you have a phone I can use? Just for a minute." She looked around as if a phone might be lying on the ground, on the sidelines of a softball field.

Father Phillip was momentarily startled. But he called to Rodney, "Are you alright?" he asked her, as they waited for Rodney to make his way over.

"Suddenly, I'm euphoric!" She grinned. "I'll explain after the phone. Thank you."

Rodney stopped next to them. The priest explained. And Jericho and the boy headed towards the house.

Both Poodle and Milk watched her walk away. She wasn't headed to the car. So, they probably weren't being left behind. That would be a good thing. Even in sneakers, Poodle didn't want to walk home.

Chapter 10

Rodney led Jericho into the house. He took her up the back steps, through the screened in porch, past the pantry, into the kitchen, and eventually stopped, in a very large parlor.

The room had a 16-foot ceiling. There was a chandelier of cut glass and candles in the center. It was 10 feet wide. And hung down 6 feet. Without the thick coating of dust that had accumulated on it, it would have been magnificent.

The far wall was an entire bookshelf. It went 12 feet in the air. But it was barely a third full. And most of those were magazines and paperbacks. Across the top, Jericho saw the framework remnants of what was once a rolling ladder.

She sighed. This house must have been beautiful at one time. It was still nice. But it was tired. And worn. And it was clear that upkeep was sparse.

Rodney pointed at a small table, next to a sofa that had its back to a wall. On it, a desk phone sat atop a phone book.

"Thank you." Jericho said, as she took a seat and pulled the phone book out from under the phone. It was one of the new ones. She almost said something to the boy about the new Chamber Annex being listed. But she felt foolish and let it go.

She handed the book to Rodney. "I have to make a call. But I need you to look something up for me, in the yellow pages. Have you ever used them?"

Rodney nodded that he had.

"Do you know the address here?"

Again, Rodney said that he did.

"Good," she said. "While I'm on the phone, here's what I want you to do." She explained what she needed from him. He smiled. She made a motion for him to start looking. He opened the book. Then turning a quarter turn away from him, she dialed the phone.

Jericho knew all the direct lines at Abbott Industries. She bypassed the switchboard. And called straight to Raoul's office.

Carey answered on the second ring. They chatted briefly, then got down to business. Jericho explained her call.

Carey wasn't pleased that someone would have to call city hall. She had done that before and didn't like it. They were an impossible bunch, over there. Lots of lip service and phone forwarding, but very little of anything else.

Until you were willing to show up in person and spend half your day in line, you didn't get anywhere. And she was sure that person in line would end up being her. It certainly wouldn't be Raoul. Not that she wouldn't have enjoyed him being out of the building for a few hours. She could use the break. He expected others to work as hard as he perceived himself to be working. And just like his perception, his expectation was delusional.

At least, that's how Carrie saw it. She wasn't like Jericho. She wouldn't give it right back to him. Lord no. She didn't like to admit it, but she needed this job.

The first time she saw Jericho stand her ground, she was sure the girl had announced her own last day. Raoul was so mad at her.

But Jericho had been right. And he knew it. Probably why he was so angry. And then… nothing happened. Except that he started to talk to her more like an equal. It was as if they needed to lock horns before he would respect her.

Jericho finished with her list of instructions. "You got all that?" She asked.

Carey said she did. Jericho thanked her. Then added one last thing. Carey was amused.

"Really? She asked. Then after jotting everything down, she said, "He's not going to like that." She tried to sound serious but was smiling too wide, while she said it.

Jericho giggled. She could tell Carey was grinning.

"Well, if he starts to get all Raoul like," Jericho offered, "Tell him that we're not losing money, it's an investment."

Carey had no idea what that might mean. But she was guessing, from Jericho's tone, that it would burn his butt.

"Might just be worth it." She thought. Then hung up.

As the receiver hit the phone, the door to Raoul's office opened. He and the sales candidate walked past, chatting. Neither noticed her.

That was fine with Carey. Raoul noticed her when he needed something. If he was preoccupied, all the better. The two men strolled through her office, still talking, and walked out into the hallway.

Carey could hear them. But couldn't make out what they were saying. Judging by Raoul's tone, the interview must have gone well.

The voices faded, which told Carey that Raoul was walking him to the elevator. Another good sign. Raoul was quick to dismiss what didn't hold his attention.

Being the secretary she was, Carey got up and retrieved the candidate's application folder from Raoul's office. She was just sitting down when he came in.

For a second, she thought about telling him she already had the folder. But after Raoul stiffly walked past her, without so much as a glance, she decided she would rather have him fail to find it first. She waited.

Sure enough, within a minute of him marching past her, Raoul was grumbling and shuffling stacks of papers. Thinking he would be walking right back out with the file; he had left the door between offices open. She could hear everything.

And when frustration got the best of him and he muttered, "Oh for God's sake!" she turned around.

"You call me, boss?" her voice was innocent. And she batted her eyes, naively.

Raoul was not amused. "Mr. Cowl's application and file. Have you seen it?"

"Is that what you put on my desk, as you walked past?" She pretended to glance around. Then held it up. "This one?"

Letting out a frustrated sigh, Raoul stomped over and took it from her. Then awkwardly handed it back. He only wanted to find it, so he could give it to her.

Carey smiled and took it from him. "You're so efficient, even you can't keep up with you."

Raoul offered a sour smile. He had a pretty good idea of what had just happened. But before he could say anything, Carey spoke.

"Jericho called." She said, deliberately louder than necessary. Then she read the first item. "City Hall has a ready-made list of repeat customers from the last parade."

"Excuse me?" Raoul, was still annoyed about the folder and had been only half listening.

"The Bi-Centennial parade?" She asked. "From two years ago? City Hall has a record of all participants."

Raoul heard that. And understood instantly. He smiled.

"Well done. When is she... retrieving it?" He asked, tapping his fingertips together.

Carey ignored his question. "Item two, tell him Clark is fine. No worse for wear. Then thank him for asking."

"I was getting to that." Raoul said with a frown. He wanted to ask more about the City Hall's records. But Carey kept pushing forward. She was enjoying herself.

"And finally, Jericho said she will be in after lunch. And that will be for 25." Carey looked up from her notes and batted her eyes a second time.

"Twenty-five? Dollars?" Raoul tugged at the cuffs of his shirt. "Could be worse."

"Oh no," Carey corrected, "Twenty-five people."

"What!?!?"

"I asked. Just to make sure." It was hard for Carey not to smile.

Raoul's eyes flashed around the room as if looking for something to throw.

"Get her on the phone." He barked.

"How?" Carey answered softly. She was setting herself up for the line Jericho had told her to use. But the opportunity didn't arrive. Raoul turned purple. Stormed into his office. And slammed the door.

*****

Outside, on the sidewalk, Bobby Cowl was searching for a pay phone. His interview had gone well. He was certain he had the job. That guy Raoul, was easily flattered.

In his mind, the next step was to validate everything he had alleged, on his resume. That wouldn't be too hard. And there was no immediate rush. But he was excited. And wanted to talk to someone. Maybe brag a little about how easy it went.

He decided he should call the Watch Tower. Which was an easy conclusion to reach. He had no one else to call.

The Watch Tower is what he had christened the abandoned bank they were using as a hide out. It went 4 stories into the air. And was easily the tallest building in the soon to be ghost town of Lockland.

As soon as he found a booth, he would call and talk to Billy Red. Billy would be interested in hearing about his success. Max would be hard pressed to care less. Bobby was sure of that.

Max was an odd bird. Bobby was certain that of the three of them, Billy's cousin was the one that was most out there. Hands down.

"But," Bobby reminded himself, *"He was there when we needed him. Loyalty matters."*

After that big warehouse fire in Louisiana, the two would be gangsters needed to hold up somewhere far, far away. Billy's cousin became the answer. They drove north. And the duo became a trio.

"All part of building my band of merry men." Bobby mumbled. Then glanced around to make sure no one heard him.

In truth, if you could get past all his idiosyncrasies, Max was valuable. For one, he was pretty inventive. He created the painter disguise. Neither of the other two would have ever figured that out. And it worked perfectly. Fooled everyone.

And he cracked the combination on the giant vault in the basement. Who knows how the hell he did?

"Or why he keeps locking himself inside it." Bobby thought. That little stunt didn't make any sense to him.

"It's part of being a spy!" Max would always say, whenever he was asked.

Being 'a spy' was a handshake agreement between Billy and his cousin. Something left over from their youth together. Bobby had nothing to do with it. And he was fine with that.

He found a phone. And fished through his pocket for a dime. Then he placed the call, and waited. On the third ring, Max picked up.

"Hello?"

Bobby Cowl rolled his eyes. They weren't supposed to speak when they answered the phone. Just pick it up and listen. He had made them practice that.

After a few seconds, Max repeated himself. His voice was cheerful. And carefree.

"Hello?"

"Don't sing your greeting!" Bobby snapped into the phone. "Don't say anything. Pick up the receiver and wait. In silence."

"Seems a tad rude, doesn't it?"

"Yes. On purpose. There is a reason. We went over this."

"I remember." Max agreed. Being reprimanded did nothing to diminish his demeanor. "Still seems rude."

"Go tell your cousin I'm on the phone."

"Okay."

The line went dead. Max had hung up so he could go relay the message. Bobby pulled the phone away from his head and looked at it.

"Of all the stupid…" But he didn't finish. Was Max that dumb? Or just that antagonistic? It didn't matter. The dial tone had returned.

Bobby swore under his breath and flicked the receiver up and down. It was times like this that made him wish 'henchman' was a real job title. That way, he could put an ad in the paper and interview qualified candidates, rather than be limited to word of mouth.

He found another dime and redialed. On the second ring, Max answered again.

"Hello." He sounded even more cheerful than before.

"Without hanging up, go get your cousin. Have him come to the phone. I would like to speak with him." Bobby made a point of enunciating each word.

Nothing. Not a sound.

Bobby waited. Then he realized what was happening.

"Max, there is no point in not talking now. You already said hello. You're only not speaking because you know it's me. Right?"

"Maybe."

"Well, then, maybe it is."

Bobby would have been hard pressed to explain what he meant by saying that. But it didn't matter. He was focused on his tone. Not his words.

That was because, sometimes, working with these two was like trying to train young dogs. They tuned into your inflection. The sound of your voice. When they did that, actual words were secondary. There was no point in explaining yourself. They were only listening to see if you were upset with them or not.

He paused. Then gently continued.

"Please set down the phone. Go get your cousin. Tell him I would like to speak to him."

"Okay."

"Thank you."

Before running off to relay the message, Max set down the receiver. In the phone cradle. And killed the connection.

Chapter 11

Jericho hung up the phone and sat still, thinking. This was the break she needed. Things were going to be alright. She looked at Rodney. He tapped a spot in the yellow pages, telling her he had found the right place.

She handed him the phone. "You make the call." She said. "I'll tell you what to say."

He agreed and began dialing. She waited. And let her mind drift.

Uncovering participants from the previous parade was going to be a pain. But that event had been executed through government. So, if nothing else, there would be a mountainous paper trail. She just had to find it.

Maybe she'd send over Theresa. And her power packed elbow. Jericho chuckled. Wouldn't that just send shock waves through the collective inertia of city hall? It was fun to imagine.

But she also knew, that if it came down to it, she could get it done herself. And that would put a competent sales team weeks ahead of schedule. She felt bad thinking 'competent' sales team. As lack luster as they were, her men were sincere. They knew they were in over their heads, and they went for it anyway. She was proud of them for that. Plus, without their bungled, convoluted way of doing things, she may have never discovered this lead.

"Hello," Rodney said when someone came on the line. "I'd like to place an order. For delivery."

Back outside, the game was continuing. All the young outfielders had had their turns at the plate. The older, physically larger kids, were now finishing up launching the ball into the stratosphere. Almost every kick was a home run.

Since there was no score, it didn't matter. The blasts into the outfield kept the younger kids running around. Milk only had to make one pitch, per kid, for this age group. So, they went through the line up quickly.

As the next to last older kid, came to the plate, Milk looked to sister Maria. At first, she didn't understand. But as soon as she did, she waved him off and passed. Milk looked at Poodle and Father Phillip.

Poodle leaned towards the priest, "Be warned. He's an excellent bowler."

"Excuse me?" Father Phillip didn't understand.

"I've been watching him. You'll need a plan." Poodle said. "He thinks he can put a spin on it. Pitch you a breaking ball. You'll kick at nothing. Land on your ass. I mean butt. Sorry, Father."

The priest chuckled. "Oh, I've landed on my ass a plenty." He said, patting Poodle's arm. "But go ahead, tell me your plan."

They whispered back and forth for a minute. Then Father Phillip looked around and pointed. "There's Rodney."

Poodle looked over. Rodney was hobbling his way back from the house.

"He speaks Spanish." The priest continued. "He'll help." And after he said that, Father Phillip stood up and pointed to himself, so Milk would know he wanted a turn.

All of the kids squealed and clapped. And the older kids began cat calling.

Father Phillip made a big production of preparing for his big kick. He took off his jacket and folded it several times before handing it off. He did a few deep knee bends. Then started laughing when he realized that squatting that far was a terrible and dangerous idea. He took a few practice kicks, from both sides, as if deciding which leg to use.

Milk watched and grinned. But he wasn't about to be outdone. He turned around and waved his arms at the kids, encouraging them to make even more noise. The yelling and clapping grew louder.

Rodney stopped against the backstop. He was confused by the noise.

"What's going on?" he asked Poodle.

"Just a little good-natured showmanship." Poodle answered.

"Father said you speak Spanish."

Rodney looked at him. But didn't answer.

"Help us pull a little joke on everybody else."

Rodney smiled. "I'm listening."

Father Phillip walked up to the plate. He wasn't done clowning around. He needed to hold everybody's attention as Rodney talked to the nun.

He puffed out his chest and lifted his arms like a body builder, striking poses. The children were screaming and imitating him. They had never seen him act like this before.

As Milk watched, he was casually swinging his pitching arm, at his side. With each swing, he was twisting his wrist looking for just the right feel. He saw Rodney talking to the nun after talking to Poodle. He figured something was up. But that just made it all the more entertaining.

Finally, the priest walked to the plate. But instead of getting ready to kick, he began yelling.

"Who thinks I can kick a home run?" He shouted to the field.

A mixture of cheers and boos and laughter came back at him.

"You don't think I can get around all the bases in one kick?"

With encouragement from Milk all the kids began booing and yelling 'No!' back at the priest.

Father Phillip pretended to be offended. He stomped around home plate. Then, with hands on hips, he yelled, "Can I get around the bases in TWO kicks?" He pointed at himself. And then to everyone's surprise, he pointed at Sister Maria., She would be the second kicker.

This time the kids erupted in clapping and cheers. They wanted to see Sister Maria play.

Father Phillip was satisfied. He got ready to kick. Poodle took his position as catcher. Milk pitched the ball. Father Phillip ran up, ready to launch one.

The ball was spinning sideways as it rolled forward. Poodle had been right. Milk was trying to toss a curve.

But Father Phillip stopped dead, five feet before the ball reached him. And as it started to break sideways, the priest reached out and ever so gently touched it with his toe.

It was softest kick of the day. The ball rolled nine inches away and parked itself in the grass.

"Bunt!" Poodle shouted. But made no effort to get it. The priest ran down the base path to first. All the kids started screaming at Poodle because he was just standing there.

He hollered "Bunt!" again. And when the kids starting yelling for him to pick up the ball, he put a hand to his ear as if he couldn't hear them.

The priest rounded first and looked back. Seeing Poodle clowning around with the ball, back at home, he headed for second. The kids continued to scream and point.

Poodle finally reached down and grabbed the ball. With ferocious showmanship, he whipped his arm towards second base with all his might. But the ball rolled off his fingers, at the top of his toss, and flopped to the ground behind him.

The eight-year-old covering first ran up and grabbed the ball. Poodle, with a hand above his eyes, was looking out towards second base. Then he gazed down at the young first baseman.

"You didn't see where that… Oh, there it is." His eyes were wide as he pretended surprise.

The boy from first was not amused. He made a fist, to punched Poodle in the thigh. But instead, stomped his way to the mound, ball in hand.

By then, Jericho was back at the playing field. She took the same seat and glanced at her watch. It would still be a few minutes. But everyone appeared to be enjoying themselves.

"*I should try that.*" She thought, meaning enjoying herself. Or maybe punching Poodle in the thigh. Both options made her smile.

When Milk got the ball again, Poodle made eye contact with him. Then he tilted his head at Sister Maria. Milk had a pretty good idea what was about to happen.

"Sister!" Milk hollered to the sidelines. "You've got to help Father Phil."

Sister Maria looked up, then over at Poodle. Poodle did the subtlest of "No" nods of his head. Sister waved off Milk.

But Milk knew not to take 'No' for an answer. It was part of the show. He turned to the playing field and started chanting "Sister! Sister!" All of the children joined in.

Sister looked at Poodle. He waved her forward. She walked up. The kids cheered. He positioned her in front of the plate and stood back.

Milk waved all the players in. They weren't going to be fooled with another bunt. He laughed at himself doing that. Then turned and pitched.

As it rolled towards her, Sister Maria stepped out of the way. In two steps, Poodle was at the plate and kicked the ball farther than anyone had done all day.

It felt good. Poodle wanted his friend to pitch another. And maybe a third. But that, of course, didn't happen.

He watched sister trot the base pads. The kids were all the way out, past the uncut grass, still chasing the ball. By the time they had retrieved it, both priest and nun had made it home safely.

During that down time of the ball returning to the pitcher, Poodle peeked over at his wife. He was as discrete as his less than graceful self could be. He didn't want her sending back razor eyes. Or worse. Best if she just didn't know he was sneaking a glance.

But she was waiting for him. She knew what was going through his head. And she wasn't going to miss the opportunity.

When he peeked over, their eyes met. For a second, he panicked. It was too late to turn away. But then she smiled. And gave him a very small wave.

He almost put a finger to his chest, asking if she was waving at him. But he didn't want to accidentally 'dumb' his way into making her angry again. That could happen anytime, anywhere, without any effort on his part. So, he just smiled. And was glad he hadn't been struck dead by ocular laser beams.

When he turned, Milk was walking up with the ball. "My turn." he said.

Poodle smirked. "Oh, you going to show me how it's done? Big guy."

Milk smirked back. And spun the ball on one finger, like a basketball.

"Maybe not so big," he said. Then, without warning, he smacked the ball with the back of his other hand. It bounced off Poodle's chest. And flew straight back. Milk caught it before his big friend even reacted.

"But plenty fast." He winked. He taunted him with the ball.

Poodle lunged. But the smaller man was too quick. Milk jumped backwards. And as his friend was leaning, he bounced the ball off his pal's forehead. It made a loud empty thud.

Then Milk took off running. He wouldn't stand a chance if he was within arm's reach of the big man.

Poodle took off after him. All of the children began squealing and screaming. But it was no contest. Poodle left sprints behind in high school. He was good for about ten yards.

Milk knew that would be the case. And slowed down just enough to get an extra effort out of his friend. Which Poodle did. And Milk dashed out of reach.

He could have stayed well beyond Poodle's grasp the rest of the afternoon. But that wasn't Milk's style. They were keeping the kids spellbound. So, when Poodle put his hands to his knees, to catch his breath, Milk looped around. He was hell bent on kicking his friend in the trousers. Old school slapstick. The kids would go crazy.

But it was Poodle's turn to be quick. As soon as Milk's kicking foot left the ground, Poodle dropped to one knee and turned.

He caught Milk by the ankle and pulled up. Milk's other foot came out from under him. And he toppled. Fortunately, Poodle had sense enough to let go. And no bones were broken.

Milk laid on his back laughing. "Where the hell did you learn that?" He finally said. Poodle was too out of breath to answer. He just looked down at his friend, grinning.

All the kids ran up.

As they did, Father Phillip looked to Jericho. "This is how they are, every day?" He asked.

"Oh no," Jericho answered, with a straight face. "Some day's they're full of energy."

The priest waited to see if she would smile. But her gaze was glued to her boys.

Poodle extended an arm to his pal. Milk grabbed his wrist and Poodle pulled him to his feet.

While they were dusting themselves off, one of the kids yelled. "Do it again!"

Everyone laughed. And Milk said, "We wouldn't have done it at all, except he wouldn't give me a home run turn!" He kicked up his leg like he was punting a football. Both feet leaving the ground for a moment. Then he raised his arms in the air and he looked at all the children. "Is that fair?" he yelled to the group.

A resounding "No!" filled the air.

"He's quite good with the kids," Father Phillip commented, "Keeps them involved. And on their toes."

Jericho nodded in agreement. "He coached Pop Warner for a few years. Both of them did."

Poodle looked across the sea of young faces. The crowd was against him. He puffed up his chest and stepped towards his friend.

"You want a turn? I'll give you a turn." He tried to sound menacing. But he could hardly be heard over all the cheering.

Milk pumped his arms in the air. And did a victory dance, which was little more than skipping, to home plate. The children continued to cheer. Some started to skip as well.

Poodle picked up the ball. Skipping was well outside his wheelhouse. Instead, he sauntered to the mound, rolling the ball between both hands.

If he had been calm, or not caught up in the noise of the crowd, Poodle would have realized he was being set up. As a target. Because what could possibly be more fun, for kids, than watching one adult pummel another with an oversized rubber ball?

Milk loved clowning around. And making the kids laugh. And, to be fair, if Poodle had thought of it first, he would be doing the exact same thing.

But he hadn't thought of it. Until he released the pitch. Then it was crystal clear. The look on Milk's face told him everything.

"*Oh Shit!*" he thought. And instinctively covered his crotch with both hands.

It was too late to run. Or dive for cover. Poodle turned his head and braced for impact.

Milk ran up and kicked for all he was worth.

Watching the ball bounce off the big man's belly, then ricochet straight back and sniper Milk in the forehead, reminded some of the older children of pinball.

Both men toppled over, groaning and laughing.

"Twice in five minutes." Milk mumbled. "Ugh!" He hadn't hit the ground that often since football.

The priest stood up. "Are they alright?"

"If not, they deserve it." Jericho said. She had witnessed far too much of their moronic humor to be concerned. She looked at her watch again. And then at the road.

A small pizza truck was slowing down and turning into the driveway.

Jericho stood up and let out a long, loud whistle. The kind of piercing shrill a southern boy would use to herd the dogs.

Everyone looked over at her.

"Anybody hungry?" she asked.

Chapter 12

Is there a greater unifier, in this world, than food? Possibly. But none comes to mind.

Food does that job very well. We all need it.

When others share it, we're grateful. And if they can't, or don't, life's not quite as good. Because food makes us happy.

And as the Melvin's Pizzeria truck turned into the lot, the crowd that raced towards it, would have been quick to agree. Everyone was excited for food. Everyone wanted some.

Father Phillip took charge of the off-loading. He had the older boys carry boxes, two at a time, up to the house.

With a little help from Milk and a few of the younger kids, Sister Maria created a buffet styled serving line. It ran, paper plates and napkins at one end, through the kitchen and then back outside, for casual dining.

Chester, the Maintenance man, led Poodle to a shelf in the garage. They pulled down five folded paint cloths, which became heavy duty, multi-colored, picnic blankets.

Just before they began the meal, the priest gave a short thanks. Everyone sat still, with bowed head. But as soon as he said 'Amen', the race was on. Everyone chewed, slurped, and said very little, for the next half an hour.

As happy as everyone was, Poodle was happier than most. He got food; free food, at that. And his wife was smiling again. He didn't know why his wife was glad again. And in between bites, he didn't really care. If she was happy, he was back in good graces. At least for the moment.

Before the blessing, Poodle had brought a folding chair over and sat next to her. She was sitting on the ground, at the edge of a drop cloth, next to her brother. On the other side of Milk were the two children he had originally met at the lemonade stand.

Rodney and Sister Maria were also sitting with them. This gave everyone a chance to introduce themselves. And ask a few questions.

The little girl was Anna. She was 5. And her brother was Roberto. He was 7. Milk had been right; they were siblings.

Roberto wanted to know the secret of the coin trick. He asked Milk to show him, so he could practice. Milk said he would. And handed the boy a nickel.

Jericho interjected, "Keep it short. We need to be leaving soon".

No one would argue that it hadn't already been a long, adventurous day. Very soon, it would be time to go. And whether Clark and Babylon agreed or not, there was still work to be done. Jericho had to get back to the office.

Chester had left a lidless metal trash can a few yards away from the picnic area. Kids were beginning to get up and toss out their paper plates and napkins. Sister Maria was quick to get after anyone that didn't self-initiate their clean up.

"We can't let you pay for this entire meal." Father Phillip said, "It's too much."

"Our boss has already paid." Jericho replied. Then added a small lie. "He insisted on it."

Milk and Poodle looked at one another.

"What boss might that be?" Milk asked.

Jericho knew where this was headed. "Don't."   She said.

"Don't what?" Milk asked.

"Don't start." She said to her brother. "Everyone is calmed down now. Let's leave on a quiet note."

"I just asked what boss you were talking about?" Milk answered. He cocked his head. And fluttered his eyelashes. "He sounds like a very generous, very wonderful man. What's his name?"

"You know his name." Jericho wouldn't look at him.

Father Phillip didn't know everyone well enough to realize this was common place. "I didn't mean to start anything." He said.

Jericho turned to the priest. "It's fine. Babs wants me to say his name, so they can howl like a wolf. It's a long story."

Milk cupped his hands around his mouth, lifted his head, and ever so softly, whispered, "Rah, rah, Rah-o-o-o-o-l-l-l."

But it was short lived. Jericho reached over and muzzled her brother. He had already worked up the children a few times. Now they were quiet. As far as she was concerned, his antics were over.

Her brother didn't really care. He just didn't want to be done screwing around. But he knew enough to let it go. He picked up his plate, as well as Anna's and Roberto's and took them to the trash.

Slowly, all the kids began doing the same. It was their routine, and oft repeated, clean-up program. It started and flowed with no instruction from the adults.

After Poodle stood up, Milk commandeered his chair as a table top for the nickel trick. Roberto watched closely. And caught on immediately.

Anna didn't want to be left out. And kept pestering her brother to let her watch over his shoulder.

But Roberto was having none of that. This was his trick. She could go get her own. Milk didn't have to speak Spanish to understand. He had a sister of his own. He led Anna over to another chair, where his jacket was draped across the back.

He reached into the pocket. First to feel for his medals. They were still there. He told himself he should have ignored his mother. And not brought them. She meant well, but it was a dumb idea.

He had mixed feelings about the medals. And about his time in the military. But even on the sourest of days, they still meant something to him. Once he got them back home, they weren't leaving again.

Next to those, he felt his deck of playing cards. He pulled out the pack and handed them to his new little friend.

She took it. And in opening the box, she dumped all the cards on the ground.

"Can you say go fish?" He asked.

Before bending down to help her pick them up, he glanced over at Roberto. The boy hadn't even noticed Milk was up and gone. He was focused on mastering the trick.

Milk remembered himself, as a young boy, up half the night, under the blankets with a flashlight. He could imagine Roberto doing the same thing.

Poodle looked around, trying to find a way to be helpful. He saw Rodney and another young fellow, about the same age, getting ready to square off. He walked over.

Squaring off was something Poodle understood. He had done a lot of it when his parents first moved from the farm into town.

They had him later in life. And he was an only child. Which was fine, when he had a bottomless bucket of farm chores to complete. And an endless countryside as a playground.

But after his parents lost the farm. And his father got a job in the town, Poodle realized how socially awkward he was. So did all the other kids in school. Getting in fights was fairly routine for the first year or two.

He walked up to the two boys. They trying to stare each other down. Poodle cleared his throat. He was almost two feet taller than either of them. And 150 pounds heavier than both of them combined.

When they saw him glaring down at them, with one eyebrow raised, they put their 'stinks like Viking' build-up on hold. They both relaxed their posture. And expected to get an earful.

Poodle pointed at the kid who's name he didn't know.

"Those were a nice couple of kicks. Good job."

The kid didn't say anything.

"What's your name?"

"Jessie." The boy told him reluctantly.

"Well, Jessie. Nice to meet you. You speak Spanish?"

"No." Jessie made a face like he had been offered a turd sandwich.

Poodle ignored the expression and turned to Rodney.

"Then you're my guy, Hot Rod. Would you please tell Sister Maria I need to speak with her?"

Rodney pointed. "She's right there."

"Yeah, I know." Poodle said without bothering to look. "Please go tell her." He waited. Eyes glued on the boy.

"Fine." Rodney spit, as he left to get the nun.

Jessie watched Rodney hobble. He started to snicker, then checked himself and looked up at Poodle.

"You like sports?" Poodle asked.

"They're okay." Jessie sounded too cool for school.

"You ever box?"

Jessie instinctively stood straighter and clenched his fists. "I can fight."

"I imagine you can." Poodle said calmly. "You ever fight in a ring, with gloves?"

The boy hadn't. But didn't want to admit it.

Poodle kept right on talking. "We'll talk to Father. Putting up a ring is easy enough. Might do a few of you some good. How much you weigh?"

"I don't know." Which was true. Jessie was 11. Why would he care what he weighed?

Rodney came back with the nun. Poodle deliberately turned away from Jessie, to address Sister Maria. When he did, he saw Rodney's expression change. Jessie had seen the opportunity to ditch. And took it.

Before Rodney could rat out his nemesis, Poodle held up a hand. "It's okay. He ain't going far. Right now, I need you to translate. Ready?"

Rodney was annoyed. But agreed. Poodle took his time expressing his thanks. Somewhere in the second minute of talking, Milk walked over.

"What are you? A one-man stage show?" He asked.

Poodle didn't understand. "What?"

"Shut the hell up. We've got to go." Milk yanked a thumb behind himself.

Rodney laughed. And adjusted his crutch. He was going to pull a Jessie, first chance he saw.

Poodle looked to see where his pal was pointing. And saw his wife, with her hands on her hips. Tapping her foot.

*****

Even before the good-byes began, Milk had decided he wasn't riding back to his truck, crumpled into the back of his sister's bug. He'd never be able to walk again. Instead, he was going to call a cab. Which he did.

His sister didn't understand why he would waste good money on a cab when they were all headed to the same place. He told her it would become obvious if she let him drive. She rolled her eyes and dropped the subject.

On the trek back, Jericho was her old self, joking and chatting nonstop. Poodle was glad. It was way better than the 'what-for' he had been expecting. He tossed in an occasional, "Oh yeah?" and a couple of "Oh really?" so she knew he was listening. But overall, he let her go to town. She told him about the previous parade. How it changed their situation.

As soon as she told him, Poodle remembered that parade. They had both been there. With the kids, waving ten-cent American flags at all the floats.

But he had no intention of sharing that fact. She'd just ask him why he hadn't brought it up two weeks earlier. Back when, it could have saved her hours, if not days, of planning. He just smiled and listened. And sat pleased with himself that he'd actually learned a thing or two about being married.

But it didn't take very much fading in and out before his mind drifted back to the Witnesses of the Apocalypse. That whole thing burned his butt. And tore up his knuckles. And ruined a pair of trousers. And whatever else he could blame on them. He was still pissed.

When they pulled into the lot, at Abbott, Milk was already there. He was sitting on the bumper, sipping on a beer.

Jericho didn't care that her brother was having a beer. But she didn't want the two of them hanging out in the company parking lot. They both looked like hell. And were supposed to be out, tracking down sales; without torn trousers. And bloodied tee-shirts.

She told her husband they couldn't stay there sucking brews.

He said, "Of course not!" as if offended by the thought. And as soon as she was around the corner, he strolled over to Milk's cooler.

He grabbed a beer and half a handful of crushed ice. He rubbed the ice on his face and the back of his neck. Then he tossed what was left, in his hand, out the door. He closed the cooler lid. Then stared at it.

"You need one?" he yelled.

"Not yet." Came the reply.

Poodle popped the top to his beer. Milk had an empty soup can screwed to the wall, for pop tops. Poodle dropped his in. Then he reached down and opened the cooler again.

"What is that?" He asked, looking at the bread bag.

"Don't you ever get full?" Milk didn't have to be told what Poodle was looking at. "You just had pizza."

"Well thank you. Don't mind if I do." Poodle reached in the bag. It was jerky. He took out a small piece and popped it in his mouth.

When he came back around, Milk slid sideways and made room for him on the bumper. For a short while, they drank in silence. Sometimes, beers just taste better that way.

At the end of his first, Milk crushed the can. Then went and got two more. He handed one to Poodle.

"So, how did you come to get arrested?" He asked.

Poodle gave him a rundown of the adventures he had while on his own. Milked sipped and listened. He occasionally interrupted to explain what he was doing at approximately that same point in time.

Finally, Poodle finished. They went back to drinking in silence.

Someone driving by blew their horn. Both men waved. But neither recognized who it was.

"Well," Milk said, "Seeing how it's been bugging you so bad."

"I didn't say it was bugging me so bad."

"It's not bugging you so bad?"

"It's bugging me powerful bad. I mean, real bad." Poodle said. Then he leaned back to chug the last third of his beer.

"It kind of occurred to me," Milk continued. "That wife of yours..."

"You mean that sister of yours?"

"That's the one." Milk agreed. "She's going to be awful busy tomorrow. Her hands will be full over at town hall."

"Oh, she won't be the one going over there." Poodle corrected, crushing his now empty first can. But when they looked at each other, they both laughed.

"Anyway," Milk said. "While she's not having her hands full at town hall, you and I could go up to Mumsford. Try to make ourselves a few sales there. And maybe have a little look around."

Poodle was intrigued. "What do you think we'll find?" He asked.

"No idea. But we can go snooping. Ask a few questions. Maybe let everyone know it wasn't you."

"Good way to get ourselves shot." Poodle mumbled. He thought about the stationary store owner. He wanted to pay that guy a visit as well. But he kept it to himself.

"And, if a few of my fishing poles just happen to be… well, you know…" Milk winked.

No further discussion was needed. The boys high fived one another. It was time to go home.

*****

Knowing how slowly wheels turned at city hall, Jericho had Theresa call over, in advance, and inquire about the Bicentennial records. Then she decided she would have Carey do it as well.

"If we can't get any information out of them, the least we can do is tick them off." She thought, feeling somewhat amused at her own obnoxiousness.

Is this how Raoul felt when he was all caught up in being Raoul? She had to imagined so. And that led her to thinking about her boss's boss.

Eric was impulsive. A 'snap-to', 'right now' kind of guy. He didn't wait around. He expected results to be delivered as he asked. And he was quite comfortable letting you know how unhappy he was, when he had to wait.

She wondered how well that management style would fit in with state government. From what limited interaction she had with them, they didn't seem any slicker, or more efficient, than their local counterpart. Would it drive him crazy? Would he try to fire everyone?

Somewhere in the back of her mind, she could faintly hear the bell of opportunity ringing. But she didn't have time for that now. In fact, if she wanted time for that later, she had to get some success generated with this project, now.

She walked down the hall. After telling Carey what she needed done, she looked up at Raoul's closed door. Then she picked up Carey's phone and buzzed Raoul.

"Yes?" He answered on the second ring.

"Your 4 o'clock is here." Jericho said.

"I don't have a 4 o'clock." His tone was curt. But uncertain. Jericho imagined he was groping around for his calendar, just to check.

"Well, it's 4 o'clock out here." She said, making Carey giggle. "It's got to be 4 o'clock in there. Did your watch stop?"

"I beg your…" Raoul started, then paused. Realizing who he was talking to, he hung up. A second later he was at his office door.

"Very funny." He said when he saw the two ladies smirking. He stared at Carey until she turned away and began adjusting the paper in her typewriter. Then he motioned for Jericho to come in.

When they were both seated, he raised an eyebrow and said, "Lunch for twenty-five?"

"It was pizza. For children." Jericho brushed away a stray piece of lint from her skirt. "That revelation saved us 2 weeks of cold calls."

He knew she was right. But she could tell, he was searching for something to be dismayed about. So, she changed the subject.

"How did the interview go? And thank you again for covering."

Raoul acknowledged her gratitude and said, "That man is our guy."

"You hired him?" She hadn't expected that.

"No. Not yet. But we will."

"You don't want me to talk to him first?"

Raoul frowned. And made a dismissive wave. "Talk to him when he gets here. Besides, you've got your hands full. At City Hall." It was his turn to smirk.

This was his precursor to 'Carey is far too busy to…'. If Jericho was going to move forward with acquiring the last parade's participation list, she was on her own.

But just to burn his butt, she wasn't going to show any annoyance. He'd have to sit there disappointed. She smiled.

"Sounds good."

They talked for a few more minutes. Raoul let her know that Eric was pleased with the latest updates.

Jericho wished she had been there for that conversation. When there was an advantage, being deliberately incomplete, was within Raoul's wheelhouse. He wouldn't outright lie. But he wouldn't think twice to frame things to his advantage, either. Had he mentioned her in that update? He didn't say.

"I have a convict at home I have to feed, hose down, and send to bed." She said standing.

"You've been gone all afternoon. And now you're leaving early?" Raoul didn't actually care, but he couldn't let it pass.

"Think of it as pre-utilizing my comp time." She said. "I'm going to be rummaging through archives in the city hall basement all this week-end."

"You're waiting until the week-end?" Raoul should have known better than to believe that.

"Oh, I can burn a day tomorrow," she said, headed to the door. "But I'm going to have to go home and rest first."

Raoul smoothed over his moustache. After pondering for a moment, to get the last word, he told her to close the door behind her.

*****

Milk sat in his mother's kitchen, playing solitaire. There was a meat loaf in the oven that still needed a few minutes. And just like any other night, he used dinner as an excuse to avoid the chatter of the television. He found it annoying. Particularly, the news.

His mother, on the other hand, loved television. Especially, the news. Once you turned it on, and sat down, you were free to drift off to anywhere you wanted. Or nowhere at all. Paying attention was merely an option.

And the news, in particular, was all but guaranteed to be rehashed, repackaged, and re-presented the very next night. No matter what. So where was the loss, if you chose to check out for thirty minutes?

When her husband was still alive, Pearl and Damascus would have a drink, and watch the news together. Every night. It was the ritual that officially kicked off each evening.

"Time your cooking around commercial breaks." She used to tell her daughter. "It's a skill worth developing."

Like the majority of other domestic advice that her mother offered through the years, Jericho took that one with a grain of salt. She was glad it worked for her parents. But she'd figure it out her own dinner process.

"What time are they coming?" Pearl called out, over the sound of the TV.

"They ain't coming, ma." Milk counted out three cards and flipped them over.

"None of them?"

"No ma. Poodle's taking Jeri to dinner. Harry's at his frat house, painting." He paused to review over his columns of cards. "I forget what Lizzie's doing."

Pearl sized up her last swallow of Manhattan.

"Hmmm, where they going?"

"I forget. Someplace nice."

"We weren't invited?"

"No, ma." Milk set down his cards and got up to check the oven.

"How come?" Pearl tilted her head and let a cube of ice slide into her mouth. She chewed it.

"Cause it's a nice place, ma."

"Don't talk to your mother like that." She crushed the cube with her molars and rattled her glass, letting him know it was empty.

Milk set the hot pan on top of the stove. Then closed the oven door.

"I mean you'd have to get dressed." He called back to her. "Do your hair. Put on stockings. And make-up."

Pearl sneered at the very notion. "I'm not doing all that!" She yelled.

Her son chuckled. "No kidding." He said it soft enough to be sure he wasn't heard. He walked to the doorway between rooms.

"You want your drink out here? Or at the table?"

"It's time to eat?"

He walked into the living room. And picked up her glass.

"It just come out. You got a few minutes."

"You're not hungry?"

"No. I hate food." He went back into the kitchen to mix her another drink.

"Then come watch the news with me."

"Ah-h-h, I don't hate food that much." He finished making her drink and brought it back to her. Without looking at him, she pointed at the napkin on her TV stand. He set the drink on top of it.

"Thank you." She said.

"Oh yeah." He walked back into the kitchen.

"Did your medals work like we thought they would?"

"Like you thought they would." He thought. Then he yelled back, "They worked fine ma."

"You didn't have them on when you came home. I was worried you lost them."

Milk smiled. *"Well God bless her for noticing."* He thought and walked back to the doorway.

"I got kind of scared about that too." He said. "I put them in my pocket. I'm not taking them anymore."

But the series of commercials had ended. And her gaze was fixed on the talking head on the screen.

Milk was pretty sure she didn't really pay attention to what they were saying. But he also knew there was no talking to her until the next round of ads. He shuffled back to the kitchen.

"Just as well." He thought. He still needed a few minutes.

He hadn't thought about Lydia in weeks. He had gotten rather good at not thinking about her. But now it was test time. Because Shelly brought her up.

His brain wanted to play 'Let's remember'. It kept drifting back, flickering and flashing frozen moments of them together. It was nice. But all for naught. It would be better if he stayed busy until his brain got bored, and left him alone.

He sighed and opened a jar of gravy. Ma hated gravy from a jar. But he wasn't making gravy from scratch for just the two of them. She'd have to get over it.

"Get over it." He repeated to himself. That seemed like sound advice for everyone in the house.

Chapter 13

Sometime after 10 PM, that same evening, a low and steady tapping woke Bobby Cowl. It was the second time that night. And as far as he was concerned, the final one. He sat up on his mattress. It lay on the floor, without a bedframe. Next to him, on the floor, was a small lamp. He clicked it on and stared into space. This was not going to work.

Yes, morse code was a skill. And yes, if they practiced, they would both get better at it. But of all the skills to practice in the middle of the night, pounding the water pipes back and forth, over four floors, was a poor choice. What the hell did they think they were going to do with morse code anyway? Talk to boy scouts? Not at midnight, in an otherwise empty building.

Bobby sighed. He knew this was his own fault. He also knew he had to fix it. Now. Or he might never get another full night sleep.

When Bobby Cowl had hired Max, he had been less than truthful. Like everyone else that Bobby had worked with, Max had a rap sheet. And a long history of run ins with the law.

But unlike everyone else, Max was a God-fearing good son. And when his mother, on her deathbed, made him promise to walk the straight and narrow, he swore he would.

There was no point in asking a man, with such an oath, to be a thief. Even an honorable one. One that would only rob from the rich. And give to the poor. Okay, eventually, give to the poor. Either way, Max would have turned him down. However, the overlap between an espionage agent and a common criminal was extensive. And not overlooked by Bobby Cowl.

From listening to Billy, hours on end, during lock up, Bobby knew of Max's spy obsession. He thought it nonsense, but it provided an opportunity to exploit. Bobby fibbed and told Max that he and Billy Red ran a spy ring. Max was quickly on board.

But he didn't come baggage free. He had his own ideas about the world of cloak and dagger. He would spend whatever money he found, or swiped, on code rings and x-ray glasses. It didn't matter that none of them ever worked. They were spy tools. And he was now a spy.

He practiced secret handshakes and often wore a trench coat. Even indoors. When he took phone messages, he left them in a quasi-cryptic pig Latin that no one could decipher. Including himself.

And sometimes, things like deciding he had to be fluent at morse code, in the middle of the night, became intolerable.

Bobby Cowl walked down the hall to the restroom. There was one on every floor in this building. The door was partially open. Bobby peered inside.

Sitting, cross legged, on the floor, next to the toilet, was Billy Red. He was down to boxer shorts and a tee shirt. He had a stethoscope dangling from his ears. And a pipe wrench in his hand.

"Mmmm-mmm." Bobby cleared his throat. "Where did you get a stethoscope?" He asked.

"Max." Billy answered.

"And Max has a stethoscope too?"

Billy nodded that he did.

"Do I want to know how Max acquired two stethoscopes?"

Billy shook his head no.

"You're banging on metal pipes with wrenches. You don't need stethoscopes." Bobby had the uncomfortable feeling that this discussion would go on for half an hour. Only to start over again when Max finally came up from the basement.

"But we're spies." Billy said it like he was astounded that Bobby didn't remember.

"We're not spies." Bobby answered. His voice starting to rise. "We just told Max we were spies."

"Yeah, I know. But I like being a spy better."

"Oh, you do?" Bobby flashed an insincere smile. "What do you like about being a spy?"

"You get to do cool stuff. Like this." Billy tapped the wrench on the open pipe under the sink. "And you get to have cool stuff too." He put his hand to the stethoscope.

"Well, you got me there. You do get cool stuff." Bobby pointed at the stethoscope. "Have you tried it yet?"

"No. Not yet."

"Well, you're in for a treat." Bobby held out his hand.

"Let me hold that for you." He took the wrench. "That round part, at the end of the elephant truck? Hold that against the pipe. Ready?"

With a nod, Billy said he was. And Bobby gave the wrench a sharp rap against the drain catch.

"Yee-ooww!!" Billy tore the stethoscope from his head. "You did that on purpose!"

"No kidding?" Bobby pointed the wrench head at the discarded stethoscope. "They work pretty good, don't they? Do it again?"

"You tried to kill me!" With the toilet on one side and Bobby on the other, Billy didn't have enough room to stand up. He just sat on the floor and barked.

Bobby looked down at him. "Go find your cousin. And go to bed. Spy school is over. Good night." Then he dropped the wrench, which startled Billy. And he walked back to his own room.

Lying in bed, Bobby thought things over, one more time. Maybe people related to one another wasn't such a good idea.

Normally, Billy was a good soldier. But truth was, he lacked focus. If he liked you, he could be swayed. Even by stupidity.

"I like being spies better." Bobby muttered, mocking his accomplice. He turned off his lamp and kept thinking.

There were lots of reasons to cut Max loose. This was just the latest. And if he ever decided to be difficult, Bobby could find himself in a 2 on 1 stand-off with the knucklehead brothers. He didn't need that to erupt in the middle of the next job.

But on the other hand, despite all his oddities, Billy's cousin had some impressive skills. He could pick locks. And jumpstart cars.

After Billy found this abandoned bank, the one they were now using as a hide out, Max got them in the door, without breaking anything. The next day he showed up with a portable generator. Didn't offer any explanations on how that came about. He was too busy arguing with himself as he dragged it to the basement.

An hour later, they had lights. A week after that, he gave Bobby a fake ID that they used to get the phones turned on. When Bobby asked him how he managed both of those, Max just grinned wildly and say, "I'm a spy!"

Bobby was no fool. He dropped it. At least for the time being. There were more pressing matters to address. Besides, he liked this hide out. A four-story stone building. It reminded him of a castle. And he liked this little ghost town, Lockley. He liked the name. And he liked that no one was around.

At some point it would all change. Somebody, somewhere, still owned this foreclosed bank. Or at least the building. And eventually, they would come around. But Max wasn't the only one that could get things done.

That trunk of cash money Bobby wasn't supposed to know anything about, disappeared the same time that he and Billy did. Right after that big fire. And just before that anonymous tip. Imagine that.

If any sort of real estate person came snooping around, he'd use the money, the fake ID, and sign a lease. Problem solved. Bobby smiled a toothy, devilish grin, as he closed his eyes. He liked being on top.

"Thank you J.T." he thought. *"Thank you for failing to kill us. And thank you for covering our time in the big house. You're just a real swell fella."*

Then he fluffed the rolled towel he was using as a pillow. Tomorrow, he had plenty more to think about. But right now, he had to get some sleep.

*****

If Bobby Cowl had known, that at the exact same time he was thanking J.T. Morris, that Mr. Morris was thinking about him, he would have been surprised. And considered it an ironic coincidence.

But J.T. Morris would have disagreed. What was so ironically coincidental about that? Even though he knew him by a different name, Morris thought about Bobby Cowl around the clock. All the time. Twenty-four seven.

He thought about Bobby Cowl so much, that he had given himself an ulcer, doing so. A serious ulcer. One the doctors now believed required surgery. At a real hospital, with a real surgical center.

J.T Morris was sitting in an Arkansas prison. They had a medical wing. But not a hospital. And certainly not a surgical center.

If there was any irony to be found, it was that Bobby Cowl had both caused Morris's incarceration and provided the ulcer that would soon be setting him free. But abstract association was not a strong point with the convicted felon. So, it was destined to pass unrealized.

Morris grimaced. He put a hand to the center of his sternum and held his breath. He hoped the moment would pass. Burping always hurt. His ulcer wasn't as bad as the doctors believed. But it was real. And it was painful.

At some point, unless he achieved the vengeance he so desperately wanted, his health would deteriorate to a point that surgery would be unavoidable. But, by convincing the doctors that his ulcer was worse than it actually was, they all agreed that he needed to go to the hospital now.

And that was the plan. Escaping from jail was impossible. But escaping, just before they arrived at the hospital, was a real possibility. He had a team on the outside. And they were ready and waiting.

He picked up the last letter that Timothy Reilly would ever send him. Or anyone else.

"You did good kid." He thought, looking it over one last time. Then he crumpled the letter with one hand. And dropped it into the toilet.

Before his mysterious disappearance, Timothy Reilly had been an unemployed college graduate. And a want-to-be investigative reporter. Months earlier, he had written an initial letter to Morris, asking for an interview.

Morris had no interest in talking to anyone. He ignored the request and threw the letter away. But Reilly was more confident than competent. He was sure this story had legs. And wasn't ready to quit so quickly. Besides, he was desperate to pretend he had a job.

He wrote again. And then a third time, finally outlining what he was hoping to achieve. That outline, from Morris's perspective, was an unexpected blessing.

It was clear, from reading the third letter, that Reilly, or someone he knew, was already talking to someone else. And that made Morris smile.

There were no more than five people on the outside that had incriminating information on Morris. But only one of them was dumb enough to open his mouth about it. And that was just the fellow Morris wanted to find.

So, he wrote back and said he had reconsidered. He would be willing to talk with Reilly. They met several times. And exchanged a half dozen additional letters.

In his own mind, Morris gave the young writer every opportunity to reveal the location of his other contact. But Reilly didn't understand the implication of avoiding the question. He was amused that Morris wanted something from him. He thought by being coy, their conversations could go on indefinitely.

But time ran out. And Morris, who was less than pleased, arranged for an associate to drop in on Reilly. See how he was doing. And provide a more persuasive mode of inquiry.

Now the wheels were turning. And soon, the circle would be complete.

Chapter 14

The next morning, Poodle came downstairs, with pillow combed hair, in search of coffee. He had slept later than he intended and was out of sorts. There was talking in the kitchen as he entered. Milk was at the table, chatting with Elizabeth.

Poodle held up a hand of acknowledgement as he walked past their conversation. He grabbed an empty mug from the dish rack.

Milk was wearing his old M3 baseball cap. Back in High School, when the Mythical Milk Machine was their go-to, week-end adventure mobile, the whole gang had those caps. Pearl made one for each of them. Poodle couldn't remember exactly when. Or why.

"Haven't seen that in a while." He said pouring a cup.

"Feeling adventurous." Milk said. Then added, "You still have yours?"

"I do. Somewhere." Then to Elizabeth, "When did your mom leave?"

"She was up and gone when I came down."

"What about Harry?"

Elizabeth, a junior in high school, looked like her mother did at that same age. She was tall enough that she refrained from heels around most of the high school boys. Which sometimes frustrated her, she liked shoe shopping.

She was athletic and carried herself that way. She had a bushel of auburn hair that couldn't be contained, even when she pulled it back. And just like her mother, she could scowl. Which she was doing, right then.

"He's at the frat house. Remember they're painting?" She rolled her eyes.

Poodle sipped his java and ignored her attitude. He already knew that. And as soon as the coffee kicked in, he'd be more than happy to remember that fact for himself. But in the meantime, he intended to utilize the youthful vitality of his daughter's brain power. That was one of the few benefits of keeping children around.

Milk waited for Poodle to look at him, then tapped the face of his watch. Poodle nodded, took a big chug of coffee and headed back upstairs. Ten minutes later, they were on the road.

As they got on the state highway, Poodle looked around the truck.

"Weren't you just in your very own kitchen?" Milk said, keeping his eyes on the road.

"I was. And so were you. And you could have been making me eggs or something."

Milk smiled. "My time was being put to good use."

"A point for that, but..." Poodle patted his belly. "I'm on the verge of missing a meal, here."

Without warning, Milk jerked the steering wheel sharply to the right. Then snapped it back. Poodle flailed sideways towards him.

"Whoa! Did you feel that?" Milk yelled, pushing his passenger back upright. "The whole Earth shook! Don't ever say that again!"

Poodle thumped his buddy's arm with the bottom of his fist. It was a good shot. Square in the shoulder. Milk flinched and leaned away. The truck edged towards the oncoming lane. A passing station wagon sounded a cautionary horn.

"What are you doing?" Milk laughed as he corrected them back into the center of their lane. "You're going to get us killed."

"No! You're going to get us killed!" Poodle barked back. Then, looking down at the hollow legged folding chair he was sitting on, he said, "And you need some seat belts."

Milk offered a doubtful frown. "They don't just come with the chair?"

Poodle pantomimed tugging at a seat belt that was too short. "Nope. Thinking not. No seat belt here."

"Well... maybe somebody left them in the cooler. In a waxed paper bag." Milk said without looking over.

Poodle's eyes lit up. Then they narrowed.

"Not a trick." Milk said.

A minute later, both men were munching from a bag of glazed doughnuts. Milk also brought a thermos of coffee, which they shared.

They chomped and sipped and didn't say much. Farm fields and soon to be housing developments passed on either side. A few of the proto-type homes were open for viewing. By appointment only. Each house was bigger than the next.

Some had pillars on the front porch. And at least one came with a built-in pool, in the back. All the rest of the development area around them was empty, except for the winding streets.

"Think they're on city sewers, way out here?" Poodle asked, between bites.

"City water maybe." Milk answered. "I doubt sewers right now. Eventually, maybe."

Poodle took a swig and looked to see how many doughnuts were left in the bag. He opened it with one hand. The bag sat on top of a plastic milk crate, next to the driver's seat. It was filled with audio cassettes.

"What are you listening to these days?" He asked. Milk's musical tastes were much more contemporary than his own. Poodle was an old school country boy. And proud of it.

When he first went to college, he got a heavy dose of what he called 'party music' from his dorm mates. Lots of electric guitars and extended jams. The stereo was always cranking. Sometimes it got so loud it ripped the speakers.

Poodle didn't care for that. Or the lifestyle. He was all for having fun, making jokes, and horsing around. But those boys were too wild for his blood. They were always in search of something new. Either to ingest or put on the turn table. Their lives were an endless experiment. What would make your face hit the floor the fastest?

Poodle didn't understand. What was wrong with banjos and a few beers? You'd fall down eventually. But it didn't have to be a race. Why not stay upright long enough to have a few laughs along the way.

Milk glanced down, then held up a cassette case. Poodle read it aloud.

"Numb Chunks." He didn't know if that was the name of the band or the name of the tape. But it didn't matter. Either way, it made him think of vomit.

"Local band." Milk said. "They're pretty good."

"No they ain't." Poodle sneered. "What else you got?"

"You ain't even heard them yet."

Milk was right. Poodle hadn't. Nor did he intend to. As far as he was concerned, Hog Call radio covered all his musical wants or needs. The only exception these days, was that he endured Top 40 in the mornings. That was his big concession to his wife and daughter. But that was it.

"Don't you have something twangy?" Poodle thought he was compromising.

"Yeah, but I hid it." Milk said. "I want you to listen to this."

"You're such a liar."

"Only lying that I hid it." Milk said, reaching below the dash. "I do want you to listen to this. They're good."

He fumbled a bit and found the cassette player he had installed. He pushed the button. Numb Chunks was already in there. And began playing.

Poodle sighed and grabbed the bag.

"It's going to cost you the last of the doughnuts." he said.

"Oh, it wouldn't have otherwise?" Milk said dryly.

"Either way." Poodle answered, tearing the last doughnut in half with his teeth.

Milk watched with amusement as his friend devoured the last of his breakfast. After Poodle licked all his fingers and began crushing up the bag, he spoke.

"I did some homework last night. Guess what I found out?"

"You're ugly? And your mother dresses you funny?"

"We already knew that."

"What?" Poodle asked, somewhat indifferent.

"That Floyd's Stationary got another store in Mumsford."

That got Poodle's attention. Suddenly it made sense. No wonder that guy was such a jerk. He probably got robbed. And thought one of the culprits came back to rub it in his face. Or rob him again.

"How do you know that?" He asked.

"It's in the phone book." Milk answered. "You want to go there?"

"Not without a police escort." Poodle muttered. "That maniac had a gun."

"Gun? Ph-h-h-h." Milk dismissed with a grunt. "We got fishing rods. And live bait. Dumb bastard doesn't stand a chance against our fine casting skills." And just to be annoying, he turned the music up.

Mumsford had grown considerably in the last 20 years. But it was still, primarily, a one industry town. Before Nash Screen and Filter went public, Mumsford was little more than a farm village. And Nash, little more than a tractor repair house.

But all that changed with a single government contract. Whatever it was that Theodore Nash offered the United States Army, back in May of 1958, they went for it in a big way.

Now, with a population approaching 20,000, the blossoming city had shed its rural childhood, entered an urban adolescence, and was aggressively pursuing growth investment.

Theodore Nash and his 2-bay garage, with an apartment above, had been replaced by a board of directors and a 160,000 square foot factory, that ran 2 shifts, 6 days a week.

Neither Milk nor Poodle knew any of that as they pulled into the public parking lot behind Wexel's Shoe store. They just knew Mumsford was growing. And a few of the places had been robbed. And they weren't really sure what to do next.

When they stepped out of the truck, Poodle looked at the backside of the shoe store. Then at the other, surrounding buildings. There was still a small, upstate ambiance to the town. All of the buildings were brick. Nothing he could see was over 6 stories tall. And, because they were viewing the backsides, every one of them had rusty, metal fire escapes running down from the top floor to the ground.

"Easy enough to get inside." He thought.

Milk walked up and brushed away a few glazed crumbs from his friend's shirt. Poodle looked at him.

"No." Milk said, "You ate on the way up here."

Poodle pushed his friend away from him. "Shut up." And they both headed around the side of the store, towards the sidewalk that lined both sides of Main Street.

"Do you know what stores were robbed?" Milk asked, looking up and down the street.

"Nope." Answered Poodle. "But judging by those fire escapes, any one of them might be pretty easy."

Milk pointed up the street and began walking. "Another bit of homework." He said over his shoulder. "Cop station up ahead."

Poodle caught up with him in a single step. They walked in silence for a block or two. Then turned into the newly renovated Mumsford Police Center.

Cops are, by nature, a rather suspicious lot. And SGT. Alvin Green, the semi-retired officer working the front desk that day, was no exception. Since Poodle and Milk weren't filing a complaint or calling in a crime, Officer Green wasn't quite sure what to do with them. And that made him suspicious. They were up to something. He just couldn't figure out what.

He listened to them. Then dismissed them. And tried to send them on their way. When they wouldn't go, he looked at each of their IDs. But he still refused to let them in. Or speak to anyone else. Finally, he threatened them with obstructing his ability to do his job.

That, of course, didn't make any sense to the boys. If he had let them talk to someone, they wouldn't be there being the obstructionists he accused them of being.

In Poodle's mind SGT. Green was obstructing his own job. And should probably give himself a ticket. For being a dumb ass. But he had had his fill of cops the day before. And knew enough to walk away.

Outside, at the bottom of the Police Center stairway, Poodle and Milk regrouped.

"You want to go to Floyd's and see if there is somebody we can talk to?" Milk asked.

"I do… but I don't." Poodle answered.

"What if we got some field glasses and spied on him from across the street? You know, real nonchalant like."

"No one would notice."

"I'm certain they wouldn't." Milk said with confidence.

"I'm certain that would put us one peeping tom phone call away from re-visiting our new best friend SGT. Green." Poodle grumbled.

"Well…" said Milk, scratching his chin.

"Let me guess, you had a second slice of homework pie, last night. Didn't you?"

Milk shrugged. "That first one tasted good." Then he pointed the opposite way down the street. "They got a local rag, comes out

Tuesday, Thursday, and Sunday. Somebody covered the story."

"And how, pray tell, do you know all that?" Poodle was certain he already had the answer. But still he asked.

"Ma Bell's 'knows all-tells all', free to every customer, white pages." Milk replied, as if reading Ad copy. "Don't you own a phone?"

Poodle ignored Milk's question and asked one of his own. "Speaking of 'knows all-tells all'," He said, "Think we should go back and talk to that Moselle lady?"

"Don't you owe her like a hundred pounds of cookies?" Milk asked. Then quickly took a step backwards.

"Shut up." Poodle raised a hand, but his friend was already out of reach. They laughed and pointed at one another. Then headed to the newspaper.

The Mumsford Chronicle began as a weekly swap sheet. If you had an extra car tire, or needed a car tire, or were, in any way, shape, or form, lovesick, you could, for 5 cents a column inch, tell your neighbors all about it. They would swoon. They would giggle. They would peruse every page. And if interested, they would call you.

Car tires sold well. So did almost any car part for that matter. But discreet encounters, or at least the desire for discreet encounters, sold the best. So now, years and years later, with a subscription based of almost 9,000 and a ten cent per copy, street corner value, the Chronicle still reserved the last 3 pages, before the comics, for distraught members of the Lonely-Hearts Club.

It was for the best that Poodle and the Milkman had no understanding of this financial windfall, when they reached the Chronical entryway. If they had, they would have invested a dime in cannon fodder. And spent the afternoon drinking beer and making crank calls to the forlorn. Amusing perhaps. But mean. And unproductive.

As it worked out, they were met in the lobby by Hershel Watts, the middle aged, managing editor of the Chronicle. He was also an adjunct professor of journalism at Sycamore Community College. And just happened to be the reporter that followed the story of the robberies. He was happy to talk with them.

They told him of the mistaken identity fiasco at Floyd's. He appreciated their position and told them what he knew. Which wasn't much. But more than they had known before.

Three businesses were robbed in the same night. From what police believe, the robberies were conducted by the same gang of thieves. One of the thieves, as the boys already knew, was almost seven feet tall. There were a few others. They all wore masks and gloves. And seemed to know exactly what they were doing.

In two of the locations, the thieves successfully stole entire safes. One of them weighing over a 1,000 lbs. The police concluded this couldn't have been done without advanced surveillance of the sites. Upon interviewing each of the store owners, it was revealed that all had been approached by an evangelist named Tucker Fry. He represented the Witnesses to the Apocalypse Congregation.

Reverend Fry was new to town and in search of a meeting place for his expanding congregation. All three victims were practicing Christians and believed Fry to be sincere. They each toured him around their property to evaluate if it would meet his needs. In each case, Fry said he would be back in touch but never returned. And the business card he provided proved to be a dead end.

But Mr. Watts was a journalist to the core. And did a bit of digging on his own. He discovered that some 14 businesses had been approached by Reverend Fry. A total of 5 had given him tours of their property. It was entirely possible that the gang would be back for more, at a later date.

Poodle asked about Floyd's Stationary. And was surprised to find that it was not among the victims. Although its Mumsford location manager had talked to Fry, he had not provided a tour of their business.

They asked a few more questions. Watts was not as helpful as they hoped. He read their expressions and understood their disappointment. He offered advice.

"A couple of things you need to keep in mind," He said. "One, this isn't television. You're not going to uncover some significant clue the cops missed. They are actually pretty good at their jobs."

Both men frowned at being forced to face reality.

"And two, this is an ongoing investigation. You might want to be cautious with where you go. And what you say and do." Watts pointed at Poodle. "Particularly you. Weren't you already the victim of mistaken identity?"

"Yes." Poodle answered.

"Somebody your height is about the only thing people can agree on, that they remember. Even the descriptions of this Reverend Fry are inconsistent."

"He used disguises?" Milk asked. "Seems like a lot of work."

"You're right." Watts answered. "But this guy was clever. He changed his appearance with little things he was sure people would notice. One time he had a gold tooth. In another place he had a monocle." Watts formed a ring around one eye. "One store owner said all they could remember was he had bushy eyebrows, so thick they needed combed."

Poodle grinned, "That's an odd thing to remember."

"Kind of the point." Said Watts. "Another person said he had a bright blue bandage on the bridge of his nose. Told them he just had a wart removed."

"He did that so none of the descriptions match." Milk said.

"Bingo." Said Watts. "Everything the police gathered still doesn't tell us what he looked like."

The boys both looked at their feet, unsure of what to say next. After a long moment of silence, they both thanked Watts, shook hands, and headed back outside.

The sun was out. And it was getting warmer. They didn't talk about it, but both men were glad they were no longer wearing jackets.

They walked somewhat aimlessly down the sidewalk. Each lost in thought. When they reached the intersection, they looked at one another.

"Something doesn't make any sense." Milk said.

"You mean there's something we haven't figured out yet." Poodle corrected, as they started across the street.

"There's plenty of that." Milk said. "But something about that guy changing disguises is eating at me."

"Sounds kind of smart, to me." Poodle said. "People won't have matching descriptions."

"Agreed, but if you go to that trouble," Milk paused as he looked for oncoming traffic. "Why have a guy as tall as you show up? Everybody's going to remember him."

With no traffic coming they crossed the street and kept walking. It didn't matter that there was no specific destination in mind. It's what they both did when they were thinking.

"Maybe he's the head guy." Poodle offered. "Things won't happen without him."

Milk had already considered that. But being in charge didn't obligate the leader to be present at the actual robbery. He could have sent in someone else. Someone of less notable stature. He stopped and faced Poodle.

"If we assume the tall guy was the leader, then we assume the guy posing as Reverend Fry was not the leader." He said.

"Okay." Agreed Poodle. That made sense.

"If you trust a guy to pick the jobs..." Milk began.

Poodle finished the sentence. "Then why wouldn't you find a qualified guy to do your part. And stay home. Or drive the getaway."

Milk nodded. He intended to say 'Exactly'. But stopped. And pointed to the other side of Main Street. They had inadvertently stumbled upon the 'other' Floyd's Stationary store.

"Want to go in?" He asked.

"I don't even want to be seen out here." Poodle said, turning sideways, away from the stationary window front.

"Your profile isn't any shorter, you know that, right?"

Poodle snickered and squatted down until he was Milk's height. Then shuffled behind his friend, as if hiding. Milk grabbed him by the arm.

"There's no hope for you." He said. "Come on." And led him into the first store he saw.

Inside, Poodle straightened up. "That was a close one." He said, pretending to wipe sweat from his brow. Then he looked around.

"What is this place?" He asked.

Chapter 15

Jericho had been to City Hall many times. And each time she went, she had to agree, Raoul was right.

He referred to the entire building as the "In" crowd. Inert, Inept, and Indifferent. There were a few staff that made notable exceptions, but overall, his assessment seemed to capture the culture in a nutshell.

But now, based on what she had read in the newspaper, Jericho knew there was an added element of concern in the mix. The city had recently awarded a bid to a company called DOCU-STORE.

Docu-Store was out of New York City and specialized in transferring paper documents to substantially more compact micro-fiche records. She knew from conversations in her own building, that the archive and records section of the City Hall basement was in turmoil.

True to form, some decision-making bureaucrat had not paid close enough attention to what the bidder had promised. What they agreed to transfer to microfiche was only 85% of the overall volume of city records. The remaining 15% would either have to be overlooked, or required additional funding.

The city was not going to spend any more money. Nor were they going to win in a lawsuit. Somebody had simply screwed up. So, it was decided that all of the records would be reviewed beforehand. The intention being to discard and shred any unnecessary surplus of documents. Thus, getting them back on budget.

How things would really unfold, was a slightly different matter. With little or no regard for what was being handled, documents were taken out of their file cabinet homes and re-stacked somewhere else. Every once in a while, some well-intentioned temp would bother to leave a handwritten note on top of each stack, explaining what it was. But even that effort did little to offset the mess that was made. And how long would it be, before unidentified piles started to overlap one another?

The whole idea made Jericho shutter. She didn't want anything to do with it. And to make matters worse, the nether world of City Hall smelled like the 95-year-old basement it was. There were no windows. And unless someone went down there, the door remained shut. And locked. The air had been stagnant for almost a century.

Jericho had never been in a mausoleum before, but having been in the City Hall basement, she had a good idea of how one would smell.

She parked her bug in her usual spot. With the basement in question, being only 3 blocks away, she decided to walk over. She figured as much fresh air as possible, before her descent, was advantageous.

City Hall didn't open to the public until 9AM. But Jericho was prepared. From attending social events, both she and Carey knew Deloris Fink, one of the afore mentioned exceptions to the City Hall drudgery.

Deloris was 10 to 12 years older than Jericho. It was hard to tell her exact age. She took the utmost care with her appearance. And presenting herself youthfully was a priority.

Twice a month, she made sure her hair was jet black. There was no variation of shade anywhere on her entire head. Not exactly natural, but it made Deloris feel better about her slowly aging, still single self. As did wearing spike heels, unnecessarily tight skirts, and perfectly plucked eyebrows.

Gazing on her professional appearance, Jericho sometimes wondered if the word 'comfortable' was allowed in Deloris's vocabulary. It didn't seem that way.

But beyond that, Deloris was pleasant and competent. She was organized and kept her word. She was one of those uniquely skilled people that knew how to get around the rules without actually breaking them. That carried weight with Jericho. And if the chance ever arose, she would hire Deloris in a heartbeat.

With a phone call from Carey, Delores agreed to meet Jericho early. And to get her set up.

Jericho was about a half an hour ahead of schedule. She waited in the parking lot. It was annoying, but even enduring a 30-minute down time was a far better arrangement than getting proper permission. That required an appointment. Followed by a meeting. Jericho would lose an entire day, possibly more, by following standard proto-call.

Deloris arrived. And once inside, unlocked the thick oak door that led downstairs. She used a skeleton key. Both the lock, and the door, were still original parts of the building.

"You didn't bring a gas mask, did you?" Deloris joked, waving the air in front of her face. "I keep threatening to leave a caged canary down there, just to make a point."

Jericho followed her down the stairs. The air quality had not improved since her last visit. She started to wonder what decaying rats might smell like, but pushed that idea out of her head. She simply had to get through it.

"Over here," Deloris said, pulling on an overhead light string, "They put up an evaluation table. Now you have somewhere to sit and look at the files."

Two florescent bulbs flicked and buzzed to life. Just as Jericho had anticipated, the table was already filing up with stacks of folders piled on top of one another.

"We can push those aside if you need." Deloris offered.

"I think I have enough room." Jericho replied. Then she explained what she was looking for, in the hopes that Deloris could take her right to it. But that, of course, was too much to expect. Deloris wasn't sure where to look. She thought for a second.

"That was really just a one and done." She started walking deeper into the basement. Jericho followed her.

Deloris perused a row of file cabinets. Then opened several of the drawers one at a time. Each was empty.

"I thought so." She murmured to herself. Closing the last of the drawers, she pointed to another table filed with files. It was even more disheveled than the first. Taped to the side of the it, were several 3 x 5 index cards. The same thing was written on each card. DNS. DNC.

"Do not save. Do not copy." Deloris patted the top of one of the heaps. Dust puffed up slightly as she did.

"Let's start here." She said, glancing around for something to wipe off her palm. "Can't promise this is right. But I don't imagine anyone would want to keep those records."

Jericho sighed and thanked her. Then move the stack of files sitting on the chair to an open spot on the table.

"I have a college girl that comes in, a couple days a week. If today is her day, I will send her down, to help." Deloris said, turning to walk away. "And don't forget to come up for air."

It wasn't funny. But Jericho appreciated the attempt. She watched Deloris leave and wished she had brough a transistor radio. And a flashlight. And maybe her father's old revolver. Then she got down to work.

More than two hours passed before Jericho found anything of value. In that time, she made the mental note of adding aspirin to the list of things she should have brought with her. She went upstairs twice in that time, hoping fresh air would sooth her headache.

But, beyond air quality, the absurdity of the task was probably a nausea causing factor as well. City Hall appeared to keep every scrap of paper that passed through the building. She found ancient lunch orders from staff meetings dated June of 1958. Itineraries for visiting political figures that were no longer alive. Endless notes from endless meetings that seemed to serve no purpose beyond scheduling the next meeting. And on and on.

Finally, back at the table of files yet to be gone through, she found correspondence between someone from the mayor's office and a federal bureaucrat. The letter from Washington provided guidelines on how federal grant money should be disbursed.

Jericho's heart sank. Was this going to lead up to a list of people that got paid? That wouldn't work. If they got paid back then, they'd want paid now. She didn't have free government money to hand out. She bit her lip and thought it through.

"*No, that can't be right.*" She looked again. This time reading the entire letter of instructions.

To her relief, it spelled out re-imbursement funding for City expenditures; insurance, police overtime, and the like. But no federal money was being offered to parade participants.

She smirked. That was good news. But, as pleased as she was to dodge a bullet, there was still no list. She kept digging.

The next stack of files didn't offer much. A few things. But nothing of real value.

She found letters between City Hall and eight different retailers. She assumed they had been parade participants and set them aside. She also found an unsigned copy of a parade contract. She thought it might be worth reviewing, and set it aside as well.

But as she continued on, she found more and more files misplaced and mixed into unrelated folders. She assumed it was part of the sloppy process used when pulling them from the file cabinets. But in the back of her mind, she wondered if maybe local government was just that disorganized.

Or maybe deliberately disorganized. She found receipts for out-of-town hotels. And restaurants. They could be legitimate she surmised. But what where they doing in a LITTLE LEAGUE FIELD MAINTENANCE file?

It was from 1969, so it didn't matter anymore. But on the plus side, the overall task of digging around, suddenly got more interesting.

Deloris came down to check on her. She brought iced tea for each of them. Jericho stopped working. They sipped tea and made small talk. Jericho showed her what little she had found. And didn't bother mentioning the 'misplaced' items she had uncovered.

Deloris tapped at her temple. "You know, I didn't think about that part." she said, setting her glass down.

"What part?"

"Correspondence with State and Federal agencies." Deloris answered. "We paperclip what they send us to copies of what we sent them. That way it's all together if someone has a question."

"Makes sense." Jericho said. "Where do you keep those?"

"They got moved." Deloris said, almost to herself.

"Go figure!" Jericho thought. But she held a poker face. She wanted Deloris to find them.

Snapping her fingers, Deloris said, "Give me a second!" And walked towards the far end of the basement.

"Could be pay day!" Jericho sang to herself. She began moving stacks of folders on top of one another, to create more table space.

As she let go of one restacked pile, to grab the next, Jericho elbowed the neighboring peak. Files slid, fell off the table, and onto the floor. As she bent down to scoop them up, Deloris returned.

"This might help." The older woman said, holding out a single folder, over an inch thick. There were maybe a dozen files inside. Jericho stood up and took it from her. She opened the top file.

Someone had created a hand written list of retailers. Some names were crossed out. But next to others were check marks and dates. Some even listed dollar values.

Deloris spoke while Jericho studied what she was holding. "If you look at the top of the page, there is an entry date."

After Jericho glanced at that, Deloris continued. "I only looked real quick, right now, but I think there are a few of those lists inside."

"So, I can see who got on board when." Jericho finished Deloris' explanation.

"Exactly." Then, remembering how putrid the air was, Deloris made a face. "Look, I don't think you should stay down here any longer. You're going to give yourself a disease."

Jericho chuckled. "I'll be fine. This won't take long."

Deloris disagreed. "It's going to take hours. And I don't want to find you dead. How about you take them with you and bring them back in a couple of days?"

"Is that okay?" Jericho hadn't expected that.

"Probably not. But they're all going to get shredded." Deloris held out her hands, in mock frustration. "Just bring them back, so no one's the wiser."

"Thank you! Thank you very much." Jericho smiled at Deloris. "It does stink down here." She agreed. Then she looked down at the spill of paperwork she had created.

"Oh, just leave that." Deloris said with a wave of her hand. "I told you; I have a girl coming in."

Jericho shrugged. "It will only take a second." She bent down and shuffled the folders together.

Deloris began waving her hand in front of her face again. "I don't know how you could stand it down here for so long. Ugh!" She turned and walked away. From over her shoulder, she called back. "I'll be upstairs."

"Right behind you!" Jericho called. She stood up. And as she did, she knocked another, larger stack of folders from the table. They hit the floor and spilled paperwork everywhere.

Jericho groaned.

"*Really*?!" She muttered under her breath. And decided that she would put minimal effort into amending the damage. Everything was getting tossed anyway. She bent down and started sliding the papers together into piles.

Before she stood, with one arm full of papers, she reached over to the chair seat, with her free hand, to balance herself. When she did, she spotted a cardboard box, under the table. UNCLAIMED had been written across the side of it.

And although she knew there was absolutely no way that this box had anything to do with her, she stopped and stared at it. Was it calling to her? Begging to be opened?

Jericho looked to the stairwell. Deloris was upstairs. She was all alone.

Setting her arm full of papers on the table top, she reached for the box. The top flap was loose. She grabbed it and pulled. It wasn't heavy at all. And slid right towards her.

"Got'cha!" She whispered with a grin.

Before she pulled back the other flaps, she looked over, a second time, to the stairwell. She was still on her own.

"It's going to be nothing." She told herself. "Take a peek so you don't drive yourself crazy wondering. Then put it back."

She opened the box. Then frowned. It really was nothing. Just a box of junk. It looked like what you'd have, if someone told you to go clear out your desk. There was a calendar, a stapler, a few pictures with thumb tack holes on top, a very small plastic trophy, and assorted business cards.

"Why did they bother to pack it up, then not take it with them?" She wondered. Then realized they may have already been gone. And the packing had been done by somebody else.

That notion made things a more interesting. It made her gossip glands tingle. She dug around a bit more. Maybe she'd find something interesting.

Off to the side, having slid to the bottom of the box, was an envelope. It was unopened and had been stamped, RETURN TO SENDER.

"What do we have here?" She purred to herself. Then she jumped out of her skin.

"You're going to die down there!" Deloris shouted from the top of the stairs.

"Coming!" Jericho yelled back. She shoved the envelope into the bottom of the box, and pushed it all back under the table.

She stood up. Her face was flush. Getting the daylights scared out of her was exciting stuff. She looked around to make sure she had everything. Then headed up the stairs.

*****

Back at her own desk, in her own office, Jericho was feeling better. Two aspirins and half of the sandwich she brought for lunch helped with that.

She pulled out the folder. And went through all the pages. One at a time.

It was a lot of bother. But Deloris had been right. Jericho separated out fifteen different pages, each with at least a partial listing of participants from the Bicentennial parade.

She found walking groups; some musical, some not. As well as lists of floats, fire trucks, army vehicles, wagons, and horse clubs. She couldn't tell, from what she had, if it captured the entire parade or not. But it didn't matter. She had a starting point.

It took an hour to review, but when she finished, Jericho gave the stack of papers to Carey. And told her to create a single list, on as few pages as possible. Then added that she would also need corresponding phone numbers.

She walked back to her office. Raoul was standing in her doorway, looking into the room.

"What's so intriguing?" she asked, slithering past him. She knew he was hoping they would have reason to break open the bottle.

He winked. "Just daydreaming."

"About my drawers, I suppose. You're so fresh." She smiled, enjoying the double entendre. Then she patted the hidden whiskey cabinet. "But my drawers are off limits."

"Who's the one being fresh?" He asked, pleased that she was in better spirits than he anticipated. He came in and sat down. "Success?" He asked.

"A collection of partial lists. A dozen pages, maybe a few more."

"Which equates to how many participants?"

"Sixty?" She shrugged. "I'm guessing. Carey is drawing up a final list of potentials."

"Oh phew." He said, putting a hand to his ear. "It must be her grumbling I heard. I thought someone had rabies." He smiled and lowered his hand so he could examine his fingernails.

"Oh stop." She said. "There wasn't even twenty pages. And it's only lists."

He ignored her for a moment, then flinched dramatically. "I just heard her swear!"

Jericho was amused at his nonsense. But wasn't going to give him the satisfaction of knowing that. She looked at him sternly.

"Why are you here?" She moved a few objects around on her desk, pretending to be impatient.

"Your budget has been approved."

"The entire thing? In full?" This had dragged out so long that Jericho sometimes forgot it was still an outstanding issue.

Raoul shook his head in agreement. "Yes, in full. But also…"

"Yes?"

"I heard you were back from the netherworld. Just making sure you didn't need oxygen. Or CPR."

"You can do CPR?" She almost wanted to see that.

"Heavens, no!" He shuttered. "I'd assign someone."

"You're too kind."

"Thank you." He said, pretending it was a compliment. "I've been down in that dungeon myself. Never again."

"When were you ever down there?" There was doubt in her voice.

"I really was." He said. "Back before we leased this building, Eric considered buying it. He sent me to town hall for…" He waved his hand. "Something. A copy of the deed maybe. I forget."

"Well, I'm sure it hasn't improved any." Jericho said, waving a hand in front of her face. "Even just thinking about it."

They both gagged. Then laughed that they had done so in unison.

"Synchronized retching." Raoul said. "Certainly, a first."

There was a knock on the office door frame. When they both turned, Carey held up the completed paperwork. Jericho waved her in.

"Thank you. That was quick."

"Could have been quicker." Carey answered. "I spilled the white out."

"I told you I heard her!" Raoul snapped, pleased with the

unexpected coincidence.

"Raoul says you're bi-lingual." Jericho said.

"I did not!" He said, sitting up.

Carey looked at her boss then turned back to Jericho. "Nope. Only men."

The two ladies started giggling. Raoul smoothed his moustache, leaned back, and stayed silent. He wasn't much for risqué humor. And now twice. At work. In mixed company. He wasn't quite sure what to do. His cheeks were flushed.

"What I mean is," Jericho explained, deliberately not looking at her boss, "Raoul thought he heard you speaking sailor."

"Oh that." Carey answered, secretly pleased she had embarrassed the old stick in the mud. "Yes, I told you, I spilled the white out. For a little bottle, it makes a big mess."

Jericho looked over the list. She deliberately took longer than necessary because she enjoyed when Raoul was out of sorts. He wouldn't think twice making others feel awkward. Sometimes the tables turn. And if it creates an awkward silence; well, there you go.

Carey knew what Jericho was doing. And stood by patiently, happy to participate. Finally, Jericho looked up.

"I think we're good. Thank you."

Raoul watched Carey go. But still didn't say anything. He turned and looked at Jericho.

"That's a couple of foul-mouthed broads you hired." She said.

Raoul was up and out of the chair in an instant. "I'll see myself out." He said, in an attempt to sound haughty. Then he left, leaving the door open.

Jericho shook her head. And went back to work.

Chapter 16

The business the boys ducked into was called, Quasars. It was the first personal computer store to open in Mumsford. And only the third store, of that kind, in the entire county.

Computers sold, but were still a high ticket, low volume mover. The owner of Quasars rounded out his inventory with science fiction themed games, books, posters, costumes, and assorted novelty items.

The floor of the big, open showroom was a shimmering white. So lucent the tiles look wet. Posters of battling spacecrafts were pinned up on all the walls. Planets and stars covered a black ceiling. Some were part of a mural. Some hung from strings.

"This place is kind of cool." Milk said, looking around. He was a Star Trek fan. And recognized some of the items on display.

Soft, ethereal music hung in the air. The speakers were hidden and the sound was well balanced. It seemed to manifest out of nowhere. As did the faint scent of patchouli.

"Think this is one of them-there head shops?" Poodle asked, with a deliberate twang. Then made a show of tilting his head back and sniffing.

Milk ignored his pal's antics. "Smells like one. But I think...," he pointed to the item directly in front of them, "I think these things are computers."

Poodle was doubtful. But there was no one else in the room to ask.

"Oh yeah?" He said, spreading his arms apart as wide as possible. "I thought computers were...you know..." And he looked back and forth between his palms.

Milk leaned out of the way. Poodle had made a point of trying to slap him, when he spread his arms.

"Used to be," Milk said, "Back in the ancient, black and white days of Buck Rogers. But not anymore." He pointed at a poster of intergalactic assault vehicles firing on each other. "Everything's going that way."

"Hmmm," Poodle considered that, then asked, "Where is everybody?"

When Milk didn't answer, he continued, "They must have forgot to lock the door last night."

"Yeah, that's it." Milk said. "And left the music playing. And the lights on."

"Hello!" A voice came from behind them. Both men turned to the sound.

A young, thin fellow was closing the door. He had on double knit slacks and penny loafers. And a collared, paisley shirt. His hair was well trimmed and reached his collar in the back.

"I was just next door. He said. "How can I help you?"

"What is that?" Poodle asked, pointing to the same display that Milk had, a moment earlier.

"That's a Commodore PET. You're not familiar with them?"

"I don't know what any of this stuff is." Poodle confessed.

The man bobbed his head like he had heard that response a thousand times. "You fit right in with the rest of the world." He waved his hand, as if introducing the whole room. "These, gentlemen, are all personal computers." He said. "And I'm Gil."

Poodle felt Milk give him a 'told-ya' jab in the ribs. But before he could offer his friend an elbow in return, Milk stepped up and introduced both of them to the shop keeper.

"These things sell very well?" Milk asked.

"It's an up-and-coming market." Gil answered. "People still think of them as science fiction."

Poodle looked around the room. "I'm not sure you're doing anything to help change that."

Gil conceded. "Geeks are my strongest customers." He said. "They are the people that recognize the future of these things. But that will change. Eventually, everyone will have to have at least one. Possibly more."

Have to have at least one? Both of Gil's visitors doubted that. But they were too polite to disagree. They just smiled. Before either one could speak, Gil continued.

"But you're not here for a computer." Gil had focused on Poodle's height and his tone changed. "Right?"

Milk explained who they were. And why they came to Mumsford. It was clear that Gil was suspicious of the mistaken identity explanation.

Poodle was sure he would soon be talking to the police again. This guy thought they were scamming him. So, he put his hands behind his back and tried to look passive, and modestly disinterested. But underneath, he was starting to get annoyed.

Milk bent the truth a bit, as he continued. He said they came into the store with the hopes he might know something that they didn't. He didn't mention skipping past Floyd's Stationary. Then asked if the Reverend Fry had been there.

Gil listened. But he had questions of his own.

"You're promoting a parade?" He asked, without bothering to hide his doubt. "You have any literature? A pamphlet, maybe?"

Milk pulled a business card from his wallet. Gil took it. But looking it over didn't diminish his skepticism.

"I can have this?" Gil put the card in his shirt pocket while still asking.

Milk thought about saying no, just to make him give it back. But he didn't do that.

"That fly by night came in here." Gil continued. "But I'm a science guy." He made a sneer. "There was nothing for us to talk about. I sent him packing."

"*Science guy*." Poodle repeated in his head. He went up and down slightly, on the balls of his feet. Just to burn a little restlessness. Even though Mr. Store Owner was talking about someone else, Poodle couldn't help but feel targeted.

Maybe he was still stinging from the mistaken identity fiasco from the day before. Maybe Moselle Sayer's crack about not paying attention in Church, bothered him more than he wanted to admit.

Maybe a lot of things. But right now, being a passive, good natured chump was beginning to wear thin. This guy wasn't going to help them. He was being snarky. And giving Poodle the stink eye.

And, no matter what, this guy was guaranteed to call the police as soon as they stepped back onto the sidewalk. And all of that was supposed to be okay? Maybe, on a different day.

"Are these things dangerous?" Poodle cut in abruptly. He took a step towards Gil while talking. His intention being to emphasize the word dangerous.

"Dangerous?" Gil looked up. Poodle, standing an obvious head taller, was now less than half an arm's length away.

"Don't these things have like lasers or government secrets packed inside them?" Poodle asked, giving Gil the cold stare. "Dangerous." He repeated, meaning himself, not the computer.

Gil raised an eyebrow and swallowed. "You're right." He finally said. "That's why we sell them empty."

"You sell them empty?" Poodle repeated. It was his turn to express doubt.

"Yes, empty." Gil took a step back and turned to one of the computers on display. He cleared his throat, recomposing himself.

"I suppose if you filled them with government secrets, or lasers," He said 'lasers' with a tone that revealed how moronic he thought that idea was. "That would be dangerous. Most people use them for making lists. Saving recipes. That sort of thing."

"Oh. Oh yeah. Okay." Poodle was still straight faced. "They hold a lot?"

"Yes, they do. Quite a bit." Gil stopped there, without encouraging further conversation. He wanted them to leave. He intended to call the police.

Poodle let out a low whistle. And with a finger, touched the top of the computer. "Right in there?" He asked with an air of innocence.

"Yes." Gil answered curtly. He took out a handkerchief, from his back pocket, and politely waited for Poodle to remove his finger.

Poodle bit his lip and tapped the computer top several times as if another question was on the tip of his tongue. Then he looked at his watch.

"Oh. Look at the time." He said. Then with an insincere smile, he added. "Thank you. You've been most helpful."

The two men walked out.

On the sidewalk, Poodle said, "He's calling the cops, I know it."

"Calm down." Milk said. "Look on the bright side. You've already got a rap sheet. When they arrest me, poor bastards will have to start from scratch."

"Shut up Milk."

Both men laughed. It was time to leave Mumsford. Milk knew where they could load up on sandwiches before heading off to the lake.

*****

On their ride out of town, both men were still chuckling. They had a half dozen sandwiches in the cooler. And a paper basket of hot fries resting between them. There was a fistful of catsup packets scattered next to the fries basket, atop the milk carton of cassettes.

Milk reached in the bag, grabbed a few fries, then started laughing again.

"What?" Poodle asked.

"You asked him if those things were dangerous."

"I did, didn't I?" Poodle smiled. "I don't know why. I guess I was mad."

"Because of the LAY-zers!?!?" Milk said, all bug-eyed.

"Hah-ha! Lasers." Poodle started laughing and shooting imaginary light beams out of his index fingers. "Phew! Phew-phew!" When he stopped his gun play, he said, "I don't really think they're dangerous. I just don't understand them."

"Understand what?"

"Why anyone would want them. They only do what people are already doing. Save recipes? Come on."

"You think it's a fad?" Milk asked.

"I just think that unless they teach them to sing or dance or run errands, they're not worth much." Poodle jammed a few fries in his mouth and chewed. Then said, "If they intend to stick around, they've got to do something to hold people's attention."

"Like television?" Milk asked.

"Yeah, maybe. Something like that." Poodle said, reaching into the bag again. "But whatever it is, unless they figure it out, I don't see where they are worth very much."

"Ya know," Milk started, but then interrupted himself. "Look!" He pointed out the passenger window as they rolled past a hitch hiker.

"What?" Poodle hadn't even noticed there was a person on the side of the road.

Milk slowed down, and eased onto the shoulder. "That's our boy." He hit the horn and started backing up.

"What boy?" Poodle looked out the window. The hitchhiker had already started trotting towards them. He carried a crutch. And had a visibly lopsided gate.

"Oh my God!" Poodle blurted in exasperation. "And he's smoking! He's what? 10? 12?"

"Slide open the door." Milk directed. "Maybe he's green enough to get in before he discovers it's us."

Poodle didn't know if that was a good thing to wish for or not. But having no other plan, he moved the folding chair back, and did what Milk said.

The truck stopped. Rodney jumped on. Poodle pushed the door shut. And Milk immediately started rolling again.

"Hey Rodney. Long time no see." Milk lifted the brim of his cap long enough to nod, then returned to watching the road.

"Oh shit!" Rodney said. Then turned around to jump out the door. But Poodle already had his foot on the slide rail, blocking the door from opening. Rodney started to turn purple with anger. Then stopped. And flopped down on the floor.

"You taking me back?" He mumbled, keeping his eyes down.

"Well, probably eventually..." Milk said without looking over.

"Right now, we're going fishing." Poodle added.

Rodney didn't answer. He just stared at the floor.

Milk pointed at Rodney's crutch. "I see you brought a pole."

For a long, silent minute there was no response. Then Rodney realized he smelled French Fries. He snuck a glance at the bag. But didn't say anything.

Poodle walked back to the cooler and retrieved a sandwich. He dropped it in Rodney's lap.

"Fries in the bag too." He said. "Careful. Still hot." Then he repositioned the folding chair so he could sit down with one foot on the slide rail.

For a few miles, Rodney just sat there with the wrapped sandwich on his lap, as if he was too tough to be hungry. But eventually, the smell of the food got the best of him. He undid the wax paper and ate.

Then, he did something neither man expected. He wadded up the paper and looked over at both of them.

"Thank you." He said. It was a low, mumbled, unappreciative thank you. But a thank you none the less. A good sign.

Milk nodded that he heard him. And kept driving. After another minute, he pointed at the crutch a second time.

"My old man had a cane. About half that tall. When I was a kid, we only had one fishing pole. Couldn't afford two. So we took turns and shared it. And the other guy had to use the walking stick."

Rodney looked over. It was obvious he thought he was getting played. He looked back at Poodle for a reaction.

"Yep." Poodle said. "That's how they invented fish sticks. You know what they are, right?"

That was so dumb, Rodney forgot he was being tough. He started to laugh. "What is wrong with you?" He asked.

"There ain't enough left of your life for him to go through all of what's wrong with him, kid." Milk said. "But hey, we've got extra line. And bait. And if you want," He pointed at the crutch. "I'll show you how it's done. Until I catch one. Then it's your turn to use the fish stick."

Rodney mouthed okay. Not because he agreed. Or thought it was a fair arrangement. He was confused. Why wasn't he in trouble? Or was he? He couldn't tell.

They parked the Mythical Milk Machine at the boat launch. And unloaded their gear. There wasn't much.

Poodle said he'd take charge of the sandwiches. And grabbed the bag, along with the bait, from the cooler. Milk told Rodney to wave 'Bye-bye' to the remaining food. Then handed him one of the poles. They all walked to the dock.

It turned out to be a great day for fishing. But not such a good day for catching fish.

Milk, using the crutch as a pole, caught a catfish right off the end of the dock. He threw it back. And didn't have any luck after that.

Rodney managed to land a few perch. They were all too small to keep. But it was fun watching him forget his obligation of being 'too cool for school' and get all excited when he got a hit.

Poodle got his line stuck in the weeds a few times. Finally went back and got the folding chair out of the truck. He sat down and kept asking the other two if they were hungry yet, just to be annoying.

They all told bad jokes and tall tales. Everyone laughed and took a turn. Rodney told them he was born in Texas. But didn't really remember much of being there.

Milk told Rodney they had done a road trip and seen Texas. Once, a long time ago. He said five guys piled in his truck to go to Dallas. Poodle didn't like the way the other guys drove. So, he wouldn't give up the wheel for whole ride. Kept slapping himself in the head with a shoe to stay awake.

Rodney laughed. "You're making that up." He said.

"I wish I was kid." Milk shook his head at the memory. "That was just a ba-a-a-d idea."

"I had big red marks everywhere." Poodle said, pointing all over his head. "Looked like I got in a fist fight with a bee hive. Then I had to wear a suit."

"Why's that?" Rodney asked.

Both men quieted down. Poodle shrugged and looked at the bag of food.

"Funeral." Milk finally said. "We went to Texas to say good-bye to an old friend."

Rodney looked out at the lake and didn't say anything. He tugged at his line and watched the bobber bounce.

But it didn't take long before Poodle's endless desire to chew changed the mood. They all stopped and sat on the dock for lunch.

About half way through his sandwich, Rodney asked, "Am I in trouble?"

"That's not for us to decide." Milk said. He picked at the last of the French Fries.

"But it is the kind of thing you're likely to get in trouble for." Poodle added. "I don't imagine you bothered to tell anyone you were leaving."

Rodney chewed in silence.

"We all get in trouble." Poodle continued. "Take your medicine and learn from it. That's all you can do."

"I don't want to go back." Rodney said. But his words were listless and defeated.

"Well, maybe talk to father Phil. He seems like a good guy."

"It's not him." Rodney said.

Milk sniffed. And scratched under his nose. "Don't matter where you go kid. There's always going to be something you don't like.

Somebody you don't get along with. Something that ain't fair. Be that way your whole life. It ain't going to change. Don't matter. Here. There. Anywhere."

Rodney looked over at him then back down at his sandwich. He had things he wanted to say. But it was all still too blurry and angry inside his head.

"Besides," Milk added, "You stick around a place for a while, you start making pals." He made a fist and pushed against Rodney's shoulder. "There ain't much in life better than that."

Rodney pushed away at Milk's fist. But it was clear he didn't mind having a friend.

"Speaking of pal's," Poodle said, looking at his watch, "We got guys waiting on this fish fry we promised."

"We ain't got no fish." Rodney said, confused.

Poodle grunted and pulled himself out of his chair.

"We've got no fish, *yet*." He corrected. "That's because we fished all day in the wrong fishing hole." He folded up the chair. "I'm going to show you how we fix that." He headed back to Milk's truck.

Rodney watched him walk away. Then looked at Milk. "He's going to buy some fish, isn't he?"

Milk smiled. "You my friend, have a promising future. Come on." He handed Rodney the tackle box and began picking up their trash.

When they finally reached CAPTAIN FLOUNDER'S FRESH DAILY. Poodle handed Milk cash.

"Get enough for the fam and a few more." He said. "I'm calling Jeri."

Poodle dug through his pocket. He had enough change for two calls. He walked to the phone booth, looked up the CHRISTIAN CHARITY CHILDREN'S CENTER and called Father Phil. It was a quick call. Father Phil thanked him. And said everyone was very relived. Poodle told them where they lived and invited him to dinner. The priest said he would be there. Poodle hung up and looked over at the fish market.

From where he was standing, Poodle could see into the big glass window. Milk had bought Rodney a root beer. And was deliberately taking his time.

The message Poodle left on Jericho's answering machine was short. He filled her in on finding Rodney. He told her they were stopping for fish. And that the priest was coming to the house for dinner. Maybe her mom would like to come over.

Poodle smiled as he hung up. *"That was a nice touch,"* He thought, complimenting himself. *"Invite mom over for dinner with the priest."*

It wasn't like they didn't already have dinner with her 300 days of the year. But it was still a point maker. He had thought of her.

The other two came out of the store. Poodle made a cornball joke about how they suddenly smelled funny. No one laughed. Then they all piled back into the truck. And headed off for dinner.

Chapter 17

When Raoul left, Jericho thought it might be in her own best interest to review the now approved budget. It had been so long since she had submitted it, that she couldn't recall all of the specifics.

"Better late than never." She told herself, as she fished through her files to find it.

The light on her phone began to flash. It was from the front desk downstairs.

"Hello?"

"Hello Jeri," Theresa said, "I've got two people down here, wishing to see… you, I believe."

Jericho pulled out her appointment book. "Hmmm, I'm not seeing anything in my calendar. Hang on." She flipped a page or two ahead, then behind, just to be sure. "Nope. Nothing. They're asking for me?"

"No." Theresa answered. "But they have a satchel, filled with parade literature. They said they would like to speak with the satchel owner's boss."

"Oh no!" Jericho thought. It was that lunatic Floyd. What the hell did he want?

"Bald on top, maybe 45ish?" She tried to remember how Clark had described him.

"Yup. And he brought some woman. I'm guessing it's his wife." Theresa answered.

"Oh?" Jericho wasn't expecting that. "He doesn't have a gun, does he?" She wasn't expecting to be taken seriously.

But Theresa's voice got cold. "Would you like me to find out?"

"No!" That came out louder than intended. Theresa could, and would, disarm the man. Literally. Nobody needed to see flopping forearms on the floor.

"No. No. But thank you." Her voice was calmer but she was already out of her chair. "I'll be right down." She hung up the phone.

When the elevator doors opened, Jericho was surprised. She didn't see Floyd. Or his wife. Or even Theresa. She walked over to the reception desk. Arthur, a post-retirement temp was sitting in the chair. He smiled as Jericho approached.

"Your gal is on top of things." He said, pointing at the hallway, on the far side of the lobby. "Push the alarm button if there's any concerns. Any at all."

Jericho smiled back and said thank you. As she headed across the lobby, she wondered what Arthur would do if she actually had a concern? He was eighty. And couldn't have weighed more than 130 lbs. Unless he had a rabid German shepherd in his car, he wasn't offering much.

Theresa had taken the couple to the former first floor conference suite. It was now used as the security office. A rather plush one, at that. There was a conference sized table in the front room. They had fresh coffee and tea to offer. And it was removed from the general public, in case anyone felt the need to raise a voice or make a threat. Jericho knocked and walked in.

Pete Floyd, and the woman Jericho presumed was his wife, were sitting at the table. Theresa was standing quietly, off to the side, with her hands behind her back, military style.

The woman nudged Floyd in the shoulder. He looked at her, confused. Then, realizing her intent, he stood up. And cleared his throat.

"Hello. I'm Peter Floyd. This is my wife, Carol." He motioned towards the seated woman. His hand was wrapped, as if it had been injured.

Carol Floyd nodded at Jericho. Jericho smiled and introduced herself. Pete Floyd was indifferent. And made no effort to continue.

"How can I help you?" Jericho finally asked. She glanced at Theresa, who gave the tiniest curl of a smile, in response.

Mrs. Floyd looked up at her husband. "Peter." She said flatly.

Floyd continued to stand motionless for several more seconds.

Then, pointing at the satchel, sitting in front of him on the table, he spoke.

"This was left in my store." There was anger in his voice. But it was checked and subdued. It was clear this was not his idea. Whatever he and his wife were doing, she was behind it.

"I recognize it. Thank you." Jericho offered politely. She wasn't sure where this was going.

Floyd remained silent. His wife, obviously annoyed, spoke up.

"One of your salesmen came to our store." She began.

"Yes, my husband Clark."

"Your husband?" Carol Floyd turned her attention momentarily to her own husband. And then continued.

"Well, now it seems my husband chased off your husband. At gunpoint. And we are here to apologize." With that, Carol Floyd poked at her husband again. He grimaced. But didn't speak.

Mrs. Floyd displayed annoyance. Then continued.

"This is not easy for my husband." She said. "Three weeks ago, perhaps slightly longer, our daughter-in-law was robbed. At her store in Mumsford. She was tied up and threatened, by several armed men." Carol Floyd took a deep breath. Then added, "Your husband matched the description of one of her assailants." She brushed a hair from her forehead. "Or so Peter thought, when he came into our store."

Jericho looked at Peter Floyd. The anger had drained from his face. He looked sorrowful.

"The police told us your husband was not the man we mistook him for." Carol Floyd looked at her husband as she emphasized the word 'we'. "And that he was gracious enough to not press charges."

Pete Floyd mumbled something that carried the tone of sarcasm. Jericho couldn't make it out. She glanced at Theresa, who gave a slight shrug of uncertainty.

But Mrs. Floyd heard him. Loud and clear. And her tone soured and her volume spiked.

"Your legal right does not allow for your irresponsibility!" She pointed at his hand. "You damaged yourself, you damaged store property, and thank God Mrs. Canderankle's husband is not as stupid as mine, or you would have shot an innocent man!"

The anger in Pete Floyd's face returned. But he stood perfectly still, saying nothing. After several tense seconds of silence, Mrs. Floyd sighed heavily, and continued.

"I'm sorry for the outburst. I'm sorry that we have to be here, telling you this. We will be leaving, but first…" She lifted her purse from her lap and set it on the table in front of her.

Jericho's heart jumped. Mrs. Floyd was as crackers as her old man. They were all about to eat lead.

As Carol Floyd reached into her bag, Theresa's hands swung around from behind her back, fists clenched. She came around the corner of the table, intending to pounce.

Mrs. Floyd withdrew a checkbook. Theresa stopped in mid-step. Jericho put her hand to the lump in her throat.

The anger and embarrassment Carol Floyd was wrestling with internally, made the immediate circumstances outside her own skull oblivious to her. She continued talking, without realizing she was within a half second of being cold cocked.

"We've decided the only thing we can do," She said, clicking a pen, "Is swallow our pride, apologize, and hope that in some small way, our buying two spots in your parade begins to make amends." She looked up, ready to fill out the check.

Both Jericho and Theresa giggled. The spontaneous shift to and from terror was too much to contain. Mrs. Floyd squinted. She was confused. And looked at her husband.

Pete Floyd was fully aware of what his wife had just missed. And had done nothing. It was as if he intended to stand idly by while Theresa clobbered her. But that hadn't happened. So, he kept his eyes down. And remained silent.

"Two?" Jericho asked, regaining her composure.

"Yes. One for us and one for Millie, our daughter-in-law. We thought under the circumstances, we should be generous."

Pete Floyd gave a subtle snort of rebellion. But again, had nothing further to say. His wife ignored him.

"That would be wonderful." Jericho said, trying to sound matter-of-fact. She calculated a number. Padded it. And offered it to Mrs. Floyd.

Carol Floyd wrote the check without hesitation. She handed it to Jericho and stood up. "If you mail us contracts to sign, we will return them promptly." Then without saying anything further, she turned and left. Her husband obediently followed.

Both women watched the couple go down the hall and across the lobby.

"I thought I was about to take one for the team." Theresa said.

"I thought I was about to piss myself." Jericho replied. Both women giggled a second time. Then went back to their jobs.

When Jericho got back to her office, her message machine was flashing. To her, the recorder was a fairly new contraption. And although it worked well, she wasn't completely comfortable with it.

That was because her mother insisted it wasn't just a recording machine. Pearl claimed it was a listening device. And Lord only knows who was on the other end, sticking their nose in where it didn't belong.

More than once, Jericho had told Pearl that she was ridiculous. But she couldn't help thinking about her mother's conviction every time the little green light blinked.

As it turned out, it was the message Poodle had left her. She listened. Then turned it off and sat back in her chair.

She was sad that Rodney felt he had to run away. She wondered what had happened. And she was glad Clark and Babs had intercepted him before he was gone.

But on the other hand… She leaned back, crossed her arms, and bit her lip. The boys decided it was okay to take a half day and go fishing. Who approved that? Certainly not her. It's not like they were crushing it; setting new sales records. They didn't have any sales at all until Mrs. Floyd walked in. Without her sense of diplomacy, they'd have nothing. Zip. Zero.

Jericho looked over at the check. She had set it on her desk while listening to Clark's message. The number was impressive. And that woman hadn't flinched. Jericho could have recited twice the price and she would have agreed, without hesitation. She must have spoken to a lawyer.

Jericho smirked. And wondered what Clark would think if she could arrange for him to get chased out of every shop at gun point. They'd hit their nut in no time.

She set the check back down. It was a nice start. But it was also a fluke.

And if the boys were fishing, instead of selling, she couldn't even count on that much. She growled like a dog. Then looked around to make sure no one had heard her.

It was going to be hard to focus on the rest of her afternoon. Maybe she shouldn't bother. She had to figure out how to get her sales team back on track.

Back on track? Didn't that imply, that at some point, they had been on track previously? She wasn't sure she could win that argument.

But it didn't matter. Neither getting carted off to the hoosegow nor sneaking out to the fishing hole were acceptable options. They had to do better. And they both knew it.

And just in case they didn't, she'd be addressing it with them. Tonight. She shook her head in agreement with herself.

But not until the priest left. She didn't want him to see it. It was bad enough carrying on like a mad woman behind closed doors. If he saw it, he might think she needed an exorcism.

That would mess up everything. Those boys struggled to focus as it were. If she had sizzling holy water boiling the skin off her face, they wouldn't hear anything she was telling them.

Chapter 18

The ride back from Captain Flounder's, was a quiet one. All three were lost in thought.

Poodle thought about the upcoming consequences of choosing fishing over work. He didn't want to hear about it. But knew it couldn't be avoided.

They all looked like they had been fishing. And probably smelled that way too. Plus, they were bringing home better than 5 pounds of fish with them. Not that they caught it. But that was secondary.

His explanation of what they did that day, would be seen as an excuse to screw off. The whole 'we went to investigate the robberies' notion wasn't going to fly. Not with his wife. Jericho was going to rip into both of them. It was just a matter of when.

"Want me to wreck the truck?" Milk asked. He could read what Poodle was thinking. "I can speed up. Drive into the next ditch. Probably flip it once or twice."

"That might work." Poodle answered.

Rodney looked back and forth between the adults. He had been lost in his own melodrama and was oblivious to theirs. He pointed ahead.

"There's a ditch." He said. "Next to that mailbox."

"Calm down there, Evel Knievel." Milk said, without looking away from the road. They drove past without slowing down.

"What?" Rodney asked. "I thought you wanted a ditch."

"Good thing you ain't driving, kid." Poodle muttered.

"We were just fooling around." Milk said. "Remember we talked about just taking your medicine? When you get in trouble?"

"Yeah."

"Wel-l-l-l-l," Poodle dragged out, "We're trying to avoid taking our own advice."

"You are?" Rodney didn't understand.

"We were playing hooky today." Milk said. "We were supposed to be at work. Not fishing."

Realizing he wasn't the only one in trouble put a grin on the young man's face.

"Geez, that stinks." He said, unable to stop smiling.

Poodle grabbed the top of Rodney's head. His palm covered the entire thing.

"Oh, you think that's funny?" He shook his skull playfully. "How about that? You think that's funny too?"

Rodney laughed. And Poodle let him escape when he pulled away.

"You're in trouble!" Rodney sang, pointing back and forth between the two men.

"We're going to get paddled." Milk agreed.

"And have to stand in the corner." Poodle added.

"And go to bed without supper." Rodney said.

"Hey!" Poodle barked. "Whose side are you on?"

Rodney jumped. And Milk laughed.

"Don't cross the food line, kid." Milk warned. "He'll turn you upside down. Toss you out the window."

Rodney looked at Poodle, who, with crossed arms, tried to look scornful, as he stared straight ahead.

"Messing with my food." He grumbled.

Shortly after that, the sounds of the road overtook them again. And they each drifted back into their own thoughts.

Rodney was somewhat happier that he wasn't the only one in trouble. But he knew it wasn't actually going to improve his situation. They were in adult trouble. And that was probably different.

But on the other hand, it was kind of eye opening to realize that adults could get in trouble. He thought that only happened if you were a criminal. Everyone else got along fine.

After a few more miles, he asked, "What are you really going to do?"

Milk looked over at him. "About being in trouble?"

Rodney nodded.

"Catch hell. Feel bad. Try to do better."

"It doesn't change all that much, when you get older." Poodle added. "Still about the same as when you're a kid."

Well, that was disappointing. Rodney frowned. But he didn't say anything more. He still had a few things to think over.

*****

Jericho started down the hallway three different times before deciding what to do. She wanted to drag her feet and not tell Raoul about the first sale. He knew the contracts were still unapproved; probably better than she did. If she told him they had landed a sale, he'd have questions.

Which meant, she'd have to explain. And given the choice, she'd rather not. The Floyd's were already popping up in her life more than she wanted.

Instead, she'd prefer to let this particular check sit on her desk for another week or two. Hopefully, in that time, contracts would be approved and other sales would come in. Then this one could be submitted unnoticed. And undiscussed.

But she couldn't bring herself to do that. Even thinking about it somehow felt like she was daring fate to make things worse. And that always ended well.

So, on her third try, she made it all the way to his office. And told him.

Raoul, of course, didn't believe her. Until she showed him the check. Looking it over, he recognized Floyd's name immediately. He thought about it. And combed his moustache with his fingers.

"They sign anything?" He asked.

"They weren't happy to be here. And in a bit of a hurry." Jericho answered. "Mrs. Floyd said to mail the contracts, they'd sign and return them."

"They have a lawyer?"

"Waiting in the car."

"In the car?"

"Just kidding. No lawyer."

Raoul shook his head. "Ah-h-h, they spoke to one." He tapped the check against his open palm. "Told them to be proactive. Make nice. And get this behind them."

"So… what are we doing?"

Raoul extended his arm to hand back the check. "So, we're making nice. Send out the paperwork."

"Unapproved?"

"They're not going to fuss. They're not even going to know."

Jericho went to speak but Raoul held up a hand, cutting her off.

"And as far as Mr. Abbott," Raoul cleared his throat and lowered his voice. "Maybe this is just what he needs to… get off the pot."

Jericho smiled, took the check, and headed back down the hall.

Raoul watched her go. Like her, he was a bit torn with the situation. For as much as Raoul was willing, almost eager, to confront his underlings, he was equally reserve when faced with challenging his superiors.

The parade wasn't the only thing Eric was ignoring. Raoul understood the scope of what was going on behind the scenes. Running for office required a lot of work. Eric was often gone now, for days at a time.

And Raoul was pleased to have been entrusted with the responsibility of keeping the business on track. But he didn't have carte blanche. Nor did he want it. Some decisions were simply not his to make. And those decisions were beginning to pile up.

He got up and looked out the window. There was nothing much to see. Parking lot, with a small stretch of sidewalk going around the corner. Maybe someone would slip and fall. He'd enjoy that. But no one came by. And nothing happened. He sighed and sat back down.

He re-arranged a few things on his desk. Then, getting impatient with himself, he got up and walked to the outer office.

"When is Eric back?" He asked Carey.

She looked at her Calander and told him. He instructed her to schedule a lunch meeting. Which she did. Then, feeling rather proud of himself, he gave her another instruction.

"And get Mr. Cowl, the interviewee, on the phone, please."

He closed the door behind himself. He sat back down and after a minute of doing nothing, the phone rang. He picked it up.

"Mr. Cowl on line one." Carey said. Raoul thanked her and changed lines.

"Hello. Mr. Cowl. How are you?" He spoke into the receiver.

They talked for several minutes. Raoul postured for a bit. Then made him an offer.

Bobby was quite pleased, and a little surprised. But he knew better than to question fate. If things were falling into place, then it was meant to be. He listened, smiled, and accepted the proposed terms.

The pay was immaterial. He wouldn't be there that long. He just needed a cover while he took a good look around. See what was achievable.

And the take, if successful, would be ten times what this fellow was offering. Why squabble over loose change? Just seal the deal and get started.

But this guy Raoul enjoyed the sound of his own voice. He wouldn't stop talking. That made Bobby uncomfortable.

For one thing, he knew Raoul assumed he was paying attention. That's what people on the phone did. They listened to one another. And, as best he could, Bobby was paying attention. Sort of. But it was hard. Much harder than drifting into the next phase of their adventure. That was going to be glorious! And that's where his brain wanted to be. He liked the thrill of his own imagination.

'Rob from the rich! Give to the poor!' Was there a greater mantra in all the world? Bobby didn't think so. He pumped his fist. This was his creed. And he was eager to be the hero. Righting wrongs. Aiding those in need. Punishing evil doers. That's what made a life worth living.

And that life was much more interesting than listening to Mr. Blow hard. This guy didn't have a clue what was really happening. And as much as having the upper hand thrilled Bobby, he knew he had to get off the phone. He'd start to drift. And he couldn't afford to screw this up.

Plus, the longer the call, the greater the chances one of the Merry Men would burst in, oblivious to the fact that he was on the phone. That would be worse than screwing it up himself. He didn't want to have to explain them to anyone. Particularly, his new employer.

So, he did his best to be attentive without prolonging the conversation. He made small, non-committal noises, and short affirmations at appropriate times.

Eventually, Raoul ran out of things to say. They exchanged final pleasantries, set a starting date, and Bobby hung up.

When he did, he realized he was sweating. He had been tapping both feet so hard, for so long, trying to stay focused, he was actually perspiring. Who in the world has that much to say?

It didn't matter. He was off the phone. On to the next thing. He headed downstairs to share the good news.

When he got to the ground floor, he saw Billy was sitting on a stool, in front of an almost empty table. He was visibly upset. Bobby stopped and watched.

In his left hand, Billy held a homemade Morse code key pad. Max had made one for each of them. So, they could continue their spy school training. Quietly.

The device consisted of a 12-penny nail suspended over a metal bottle cap. There was a small compression spring under the arm that held the nail in place. The arm, the spring, and the cap were all secured to a scrap of 2 x 4, used as a base. By tapping down on the head of the nail, a clicking sound was created when it hit the cap. This was much gentler on the ears than the wrench and pipe combo Max had originally designed.

Bobby didn't understand why Billy held the pad, rather than setting it on the table. He was making the task harder than it needed to be. That was probably part of his frustration. But Bobby wasn't going to say anything. He had tried to be helpful in the past. It never went as intended.

Billy was attempting to transmit a message he was reading off of a sheet of paper, sitting on the table. Bobby guessed that Max had also created the message. But Billy's progress was dismal. He was slow and erratic.

Suddenly Billy realized he was being watched. He turned and made eye contact with Bobby. It was clear he wasn't happy.

"Is it dot dot, dash? Or dot dash, dash?" Billy asked.

"Is what, dot dot, dash or dot dash, dash?"

Billy frowned. "Not what. IT!"

"You mean the word it?"

"That's what I said."

"I don't know."

"You don't know what IT is?"

"That's what I said."

Billy sat there, processing what he was just told.

"And you don't know what 'what' is either, do ya?" Billy's tone was snarky.

Bobby sighed. He wished he had snuck back upstairs, undetected.

"That's correct." He said. "I don't know any morse code."

"Well, that's a fine how do you do." Billy crossed his arms. Flinched. Then uncrossed them and recrossed them the other way, so the key pad didn't stab him in the bicep.

"What does that mean?" Bobby asked.

"I mean, well, first off, you're supposed to be heading up this spy ring. And you don't know any morse code at all." Billy pointed at him accusingly. "Don't deny it."

"I'm not a spy Billy. And neither are you. Max is the only spy."

"And another thing, if you don't know any morse code at all, why did you ask me what word I was asking about? Seems to me it wouldn't make any difference. 'I don't know' would have covered for all the words in the dictionary. You didn't have to know which particular word I was inquiring about."

Bobby could feel a vein in his temple starting pulse.

"Where's Max?" He asked, as he reached up to rub his head.

"He went to get his prescription filled."

"Prescription? Prescription for what?"

"For himself."

"No. What's his ailment?"

"His what?"

"What's wrong with him?"

Billy scrunched his face in confusion. "You never talked to him before?"

"I mean besides his brain being in sideways."

"Oh. I don't know. Just said he was going."

"And he had a prescription?"

"Said he did."

"What Doctor did he go to?"

"He don't need to go to a doctor. He already got a prescription."

Bobby thought that over, for a second. "So… you're saying this is for a chronic condition?"

"No. It's for a prescription. I already told you that."

"No. Is the prescription for a chronic condition? Like an allergy?

Or migraines?"

"Oh. I don't know. He just said he was going for his prescription. Then he was going to the bamboo store. Then he was coming right back."

"What bamboo store?"

"I don't know which one."

"I don't mean which one. I mean, I don't think there is such a thing as a bamboo store." Bobby's fingers surrounded Bamboo Store with air quotation marks.

"Sure there is."

"Bam. Boo. And Beyond?" Bobby said, with a frown.

Billy bit his lip. And considered the possibility. Then he said, "No, I don't think he was going to that one. Probably the other one."

"There is no other one."

"Oh. They go out of business?"

"What the hell is wrong with you?"

"What? You asked me where he was. I told you!"

"There is no bamboo store!" They glared at one another. Then Bobby took a breath and tried to explain.

"If all your store sold was bamboo, you'd go out of business. Not enough people want it."

"Max does."

"Once!" Bobby held up a single finger. "Then never again. And nobody else wants it."

"Well, somebody does." Billy slapped the table with his free hand. "They got a hundred acres of bamboo growing in Florida alone. Somebody had to buy all that. And where you think they got them seeds?" He smirked, and puffed his chest, proud that he already knew the answer. "A bamboo store." He said with confidence.

"No, no, no." Bobby shook his head and looked at his feet. "That's all backwards."

"Nu-uh! There ain't nothing backwards about it!"

"They don't buy bamboo or bamboo seeds from a store just to throw in a swamp. Hope they grow." Bobby couldn't believe he had to explain this. "If anything, it's the other way around. They would grow bamboo so they could sell it to a store."

"Oh! Oh!" Billy started pounding the table. And kicked up both feet. Bobby thought he was going to go over backwards. Kind of wished he did.

"You mean so they can sell a whole swamp's worth of bamboo to some store you say don't even exist? Is that right?"

"Oh, mother of…" Bobby slapped his forehead in disbelief.

"Seems to me they wouldn't waste their time growing a hundred acres of bamboo if they didn't think they could sell it. Farmer ain't dumb, you know." Billy raised an eyebrow. Then softened his tone. "You sure you know what you're talking about?"

"You know what, Billy?" Bobby threw up his arms, "You're right. Just tell me when Max gets back." He let out a defeated groan. "I'll be upstairs." Then he walked off, shaking his head.

Billy smiled as Bobby walked away. He didn't often get the last word. And even though technically, his weren't the last words spoken, it was plenty close enough. Bobby was the one that retreated. That's what mattered.

But was it really over? Would Bobby think up one more thing to say? Come walking back? Billy sat still and listened.

When the stairs began to squeak, Billy licked his finger and drew a '1' in the air, on an imaginary scoreboard. Then he returned to tapping out his practice message.

Chapter 19

Before Jericho left for the day, Carey told her of Raoul's phone call to Robert Cowl. She left it at that. And let Jericho draw her own conclusion.

But the truth of the matter was that Carey had heard the entire conversation. By placing herself on mute and making it a conference call, rather than a forwarded call, she could eavesdrop. Which she did, rather often, unbeknownst to anyone else.

"A terrible, nasty habit." She would admit, in moments of self-reflection. But it never curbed her behavior. It was too easy to justify.

Raoul's communication skills, at least with her, were lacking. More than once she had been held accountable for things he had sworn he had told her. And she was just as certain that he had never mentioned them.

She knew her own performance capabilities. And she was proud of herself. She was a good secretary. If he actually told her things, she would write them down. And they would be addressed. By discretely listening in where she wasn't invited, she didn't have to depend on him remembering to tell her. She would already know.

Of course, there were other times, when she was simply being nosey. Not that she would ever call it that. In her mind, she was maintaining a trade secret skill set. God forbid she should ever let them get rusty.

And she was quick to pride herself on her restraint. She could have told Jericho much more. And claimed she overheard it through Raoul's open door. But she didn't. Letting it be known that the call had been made was where she felt her responsibilities ended. So, that's where she stopped.

Upon hearing of the call, Jericho was less than pleased. She wished Raoul hadn't done that. She remembered their conversation from the day before. He had made it clear he liked this guy. But she had taken his words with a grain of salt. And assumed she would still get a chance evaluate the candidate for herself. Apparently, that was wrong.

That put her in an odd spot and she wasn't sure what to do. Raoul was the boss. It was his decision to make. And he had stepped in to assist when she needed him.

But it was her project. And her team. She should be overseeing it. All of it.

Carey watched for a reaction, when she told her. But Jericho knew better than to show her hand. She thanked her. And packed up for the day.

On the ride home, she had a dozen different conversations. Most of them heated. At least three with Raoul, a couple with herself, and almost all of the rest with her husband and brother.

It should have been ALL of the rest with husband and brother. But without intending to, she twice found herself fighting with her mother. Just for good measure.

But maybe it was alright that she went at it with mom. One, it would remind her to pick her up. Pearl liked the clergy. She would love to meet Father Phil.

And two, maybe, just maybe, imaginary shouting matches, alone in the car, would blow out enough pent-up steam that Jericho could regather her composure before she arrived. Then she could calmly ask her mother for some advice.

She knew she could get Clark back on the straight and narrow easily enough. But she didn't have much leverage with her brother. Her mother might have an idea or two. She didn't want to break up their little team. She just wanted their little team to work. At least during working hours.

When she turned into her mother's driveway, the garage door was open. That meant mom was hunting for something. She claimed opening the big door brought in enough light for her to see. It didn't matter that Pearl already had four one-hundred-fifty watt bulbs illuminating a single car garage. That wasn't bright enough.

Oh, it was fine if you were just walking to the car. Or taking out the trash. But if you were rummaging the shelves, trying to find something, that was a different matter.

Jericho didn't agree. She thought the light was blinding. And would cover her eyes and squint any time she went in there. What was the point of having too much light?

Pearl thought her daughter was being ridiculous. Jericho thought it was dangerous.

"Ma, it's like looking into the Sun." She would bark at Pearl. "You're going to damage your eyes."

"You're not supposed to look right at the bulb." Her mother would answer, annoyed at having to recite the obvious.

Jericho made sure she shut her door hard enough for her mother to hear. But Pearl didn't turn around. She was on the prowl.

"What are you looking for Ma?" she asked.

There was a delay as her mother, humming to herself, poked and prodded at several different shelves. Finally, without turning towards her daughter, Pearl answered.

"Not sure yet." She said. Then pushed a paint can to one side. And arched up on her toes, so she could peer behind it.

Whatever was supposed to be there, wasn't. Pearl came down off the balls of her feet with a frustrated snort. She crossed her arms and drummed one elbow with her fingers.

"Jarts? Maybe." She said, almost to herself.

"Jarts?" Jericho repeated. "You mean lawn darts?" She pantomimed tossing one. "Do you even own any?"

"Used to. Not sure what your brother did with them."

Well, Jericho wasn't going to be able to help there. She tried a different approach.

"What do you need them for, ma?"

"The kids. The kids will need something to do."

"It's only one kid, ma. And I don't imagine he will be staying that long."

Pearl turned.

"He doesn't like fish?" she asked.

"I have no idea, mother." Jericho chuckled.

"He's just going to stand there while the rest of us eat?" Pearl made a 'tsk' sound as she went back to hunting the shelves.

"No, he's going to gnaw on the jarts. What are you talking about, mother?"

"Here we go!" Pearl reached past folded chairs, deep into a shelf. After a few seconds she pulled out a small, plastic bottle. "That'll work." She said, nodding to herself with satisfaction.

"What's that?" Jericho asked.

"Glycerol." Pearl answered. Then shaking the bottle. "I don't think this stuff can go bad."

"What's glycerol?"

Pearl looked at her daughter. "It's an explosive. Nitroglycerin? It makes dynamite blow up."

"It's what?!" Jericho started to snatch it, then stopped, mid-grab, afraid she'd cause an explosion.

"You're such a sap." Her mother laughed. "You add it to dish soap, so the bubbles don't pop."

Jericho bit her lip. And offered a very forced smile. She wasn't in the mood to play. But this wasn't worth getting annoyed over.

"It's for the kids," Pearl continued. "They can chase bubbles. I don't know what your brother did with the jarts."

"Get in the car, ma."

Jericho and Pearl lived less than 3 blocks from one another. So, when Jericho turned the corner, away from her house, Pearl knew her daughter was taking 'the long way'. Which meant they had something to discuss. She waited.

"We sold two spots today." Jericho said through an over enthusiastic smile. She thought starting on a positive note would be most productive.

"That's great." Her mother answered. "And?" She had been on this ride before.

"And…" Jericho continued, somewhat disappointed her approach was so transparent. "That sale was nothing more than dumb luck."

"One sale bought two spots?" Pearl interrupted. "That's pretty good."

"Uh, yeah. Yeah, you're right." Jericho didn't want to get off track. "But it was a fluke. The boys stumbled into it. They're really having a hard time focusing."

"Hard to focus on sales when you're sitting in the big house."

"Mom!"

"Okay, okay." Pearl fiddled with her purse. And opened it to make sure she remembered her cigarettes, which she was already sure she had. She liked to have a smoke when they were discussing matters. But she knew Jericho's rules about her car.

"I'll speak to him." She said, snapping the purse shut.

"Speak to who?" Jericho asked.

"Your brother. That's what this is about, isn't it?"

"Well… yeah."

Pearl nodded. "Well… You knew it was going to be a challenge when you hired both of them."

Jericho cocked her head in dis-belief. "You're the one that told me to do it!"

"I did." Pearl bounced her purse on her lap. She wanted a smoke. "But my telling you was totally self-serving." She wagged a finger at her daughter. "Don't you dare tell me you didn't know that."

Jericho shifted down hard, into second, causing them both to lurch forward.

"So, it's my fault?" She thought. *"I listened to your bad advice. And now it's my fault?"*

But she knew better than to say any of that out loud. She drove another block in silence. Then coasted the bug to a stop sign, dropped it into neutral and put her foot on the brake. She looked at her mother.

"I need your help, ma."

"I told you I will speak to him."

"And that's going to fix things?" Jericho snapped her fingers. "Just like that?"

"Probably more like two snaps, smart ass. But it will fix things."

Jericho looked out the windshield. She hit the gas enough to rev the engine but didn't attempt to move forward.

"Look," her mother said after a long pause. "Hiring them was the best thing for both of them. You did the right thing."

"Worked out pretty good for you too, didn't it?" Jericho muttered, but didn't take her eyes from the windshield.

"You weren't doing a favor for me when you hired them." Pearl unsnapped her purse. "That was a windfall. Like those two spots that just got sold. Count your blessings."

"My blessings?" Jericho turned her head, ready to start arguing again.

"Yes! Your blessings." Pearl snapped back. She fished around in her bag, for a tissue. She pulled one out.

"When your father died, your brother sold his house and moved back in with me. Nobody asked him to do that." Pearl put the tissue to the corner of her eye. "He took a pay cut too, changing shifts, so he could be on my schedule."

Jericho knew all this. But had never heard her mother speak of it.

"He's a good man. We're both very lucky to have him. He came back from the war, he could have been all screwed up, like them other boys." She dapped the tissue a second time. "Remember Peter Harper? What happened there?"

Jericho shook her head. That was a very sad tale.

"Count your blessings." Pearl sniffled and put the tissue back in her purse. "I'll get your brother on track. He'll listen to his mother. You talk to your husband."

They sat for a few seconds in silence. In the mirror, Jericho saw someone rolling up behind her.

"Okay. Thanks ma."

Pearl nodded.

"You want a smoke?" Jericho asked, shifting into first.

Pearl's eyes lit up. "That would be very nice." She said, and again unsnapped her purse.

"Well, hang on. We'll be at the house in a minute." Jericho smirked, and pulled away.

"Remind me that I hate you." Pearl said, flopping her bag back into her lap. Then she looked over, smiled, and laid her hand on top of her daughter's.

When they pulled in at home, everyone else was there. The milk truck was in the driveway. And a rather tired Rambler station wagon, well past it's prime, sat on the street, in front of the house.

"That your priest friend?" Pearl asked, pointing at the rust bucket.

"Probably." Jericho answered.

Pearl shook her head. "Damn thing squeaks just looking at it."

"Mom."

"I won't say nothing."

They came through the garage. And everyone was in the backyard. Father Phil was sitting at the picnic table, along with Milk and Rodney and Anna. They were all watching Roberto, standing at the table's end, as he demonstrated his developing magic skills.

Poodle, beer in hand, was keeping himself busy at the grill. He was wearing a bar-b-que apron, with a bright yellow smiley face on the bib. It was too small for him, but because it was a birthday gift from one of the kids, he wore it at every cook out.

Elizabeth was already home from school. Which again reminded Jericho to 'count her blessings'. Not that she was going to mention it to her mother. But her daughter was the only other family member that had the wherewithal to take action.

She had foil-wrapped potatoes. And with the kids, husked corn on the cob. Everything Poodle intended to cook, except a small pot of baked beans, had been provided to him, on a tray off to the side. The beans were already simmering in the corner of the grill, as they waited for the flames to die into cooking embers. Jericho assumed Elizabeth had seen to that as well.

After a round of introductions, Pearl handed the bottle of glycerol to her son. He understood. And, getting up, told Rodney to come with him. They walked back into the garage.

Pearl sat down next to the priest. They watched Roberto do his one trick, yet again. Then Pearl pointed, and asked Anna about the deck of cards she was holding.

Anna assumed Pearl was asking to play. she started dealing out cards to everyone at the table.

"Sister explained the game of fish." Father Phil said as he picked up his cards. He nodded towards Anna. "It's now an obsession."

After smearing the remaining cards into the 'fish pond', Anna smiled and picked up her own hand. She thought for a minute, then said, "Padre" and showed a 5 of diamonds.

"We're still working on the names of all the cards." Father Phil explained. Then told Anna to 'go fish'. Anna reached into the pond and pulled out a card. She didn't get what she wanted. And sliding the new card into her hand, shook her head no.

"That means it's your turn." Father Phil said to Pearl.

Pearl was still organizing her cards. It was proving to be a more challenging activity that it should have been. That was because her mind was elsewhere.

Walking in, she had had the intention of meeting the social

minimum. Shaking hands, exchanging names and then excusing herself, to go off to the side yard, and have a smoke.

That would still happen. Eventually. But she had been planning on it happening right now. And fish? Fish could go on for another twenty minutes. She could be having nicotine spasms by then. She folded all her cards together then reopened her hand.

"You need help, ma?" Jericho asked, knowing full well what was going through her mother's head.

"Yeah." Her mother answered. "You got a ten of clubs?" Their eyes met. Jericho smiled. Her mother glared.

"Sure do." Jericho said, sounding as sickeningly sweet as she could. She pulled a card from her hand and gave it to her mother.

Pearl took it without saying anything.

"Oh, you're welcome." Jericho said. "Still your turn."

Milk and Rodney came back from the garage. Rodney was carrying a metal bucket. Milk had a tennis racket and a plastic bottle of dish detergent. When they stepped into the yard, Milk glanced around. Seeing the garden hose off to the side, he motioned for Rodney to follow him.

"Hey, that's my racket." Elizabeth called over.

"It's filthy!" Milk yelled back. And kept walking.

"It is not." Elizabeth said in a lower tone. But made no attempt to get it from her uncle.

Pearl saw the opportunity for what it was. She pointed.

"Oh, my word." She said, trying to sound captivated. "Whatever is going on over there?"

As she knew would happen, both youngsters looked over. Roberto quickly turned back to the priest. His eyes asked if he could join Rodney.

"Take your sister." Father Phil said. Both kids ran off to investigate.

Pearl made an audible sigh. And put down her cards.

"You're a life saver." She said to the priest. And started to get up.

When he noticed Pearl was taking her purse with her, Father Phil put two fingers to his lips, as if dragging off a cigarette. His way of inviting himself to the smoke break. Pearl smiled. And waved her hand, telling him to follow her.

Jericho watched them both walk off towards the side yard.

"Isn't that like a sin, or something?" She asked herself. She didn't know. She didn't really care. But if asked, she would have assumed that priests and nuns abstained from everything under the sun.

She knew that was silly. But it was still odd, to her, to see a priest wander off for a puff. It was like finding out your teachers smoked, when you were a kid.

"Think I should wait?" Poodle called over from the grill. When Jericho looked, he was holding up the platter of fillets.

"I think they're about to start playing something." Poodle nodded towards Milk and the kids. "These things take 5 minutes. Tops."

Jericho got up and walked over to her husband. She sized up the food situation. The potatoes and corn were on the grill. And the beans were bubbling. She pointed at the pot.

"Thank you." Poodle said, using his spatula as a spoon, and giving them a stir.

"Let's wait on the fish." Jericho said.

Poodle set down the platter. "How was your day?" He asked. And took a swig of his beer. He was hoping the meat of the matter could wait until their company was gone.

"Interesting." Jericho answered.

Poodle didn't like the sounds of that. "Oh yeah?" He said, cautiously.

"You made two sales today."

"Who did?"

"You did."

That was not at all what he had expected.

"I think you're confusing me with one of your other husbands." He said, and swirled the last of his beer around the bottom of the can.

"No. It was you." Jericho smiled because she knew he would never guess in a million years. "Mister and Mrs. Floyd came in this afternoon." She waited for his rection. "They apologized. Returned your satchel. And bought two spots in the parade."

"Really?"

"Yes. Really."

"I always liked that guy." Poodle said. And drank the last of his beer.

Jericho waited for him to finish. She smiled again. But it wasn't a welcoming smile.

"Think how many more sales you could have by now if you weren't taking afternoons off to go fishing."

Poodle frowned and crushed the can in his hand.

"Aw, Jer, come on." He pointed into the yard. "We've got people here."

With that, the two younger kids squealed. Both Poodle and Jericho looked over. Milk had put dish soap and glycerol in the bucket. Then filled it with water from the garden hose.

By dipping the tennis racket into the suds and then swirling it through the air, he released a thousand soap bubbles over everyone's heads. Some of the bubbles stretched and were over a foot long.

All three of the kids laughed chased around the yard trying to pop them. Milk created a second cloud of suspended soap suds. Then called to Rodney.

"You try it." He said, handing the boy the racket. "But... make sure you have room before you swing. Don't be decapitating your sister."

"She's not my sister." Rodney said, taking the racket.

"Oh. Well then just swing away." Milk said with a frown.

Rodney laughed. "I'll be careful."

"Why don't you tell them that they need to be careful too."

Rodney agreed. And made a generic statement in Spanish. The two younger kids listened. Then shook their heads.

"Look." Jericho said, still watching the bubble-fest. "I already ripped into you on the ride home." Her eyes narrowed. "Be glad you weren't there."

"Okay."

"The point is, Raoul hired another salesman. He's going to be starting... I'm not sure yet."

"Wait. He can't just do that."

"He's the boss Clark. He can do whatever he wants."

Poodle wanted to continue protesting. But Jericho cut him off.

"We have to set a standard. A standard of excellence. This guy sees you two talking each other into kick ball games and fishing trips, he's not going to work. He's going to join the party."

Poodle was all for inviting him along. But this was not the time to be clever. He looked down at his feet and waited. Jericho continued.

"You two distract each other. We can't have that."

"Maybe we shouldn't be a team." Poodle shrugged.

"You weren't really a team Clark. You were supposed to be working opposite sides of the same street. The main drag. The road with the highest potential."

Something Poodle missed earlier, suddenly occurred to him.

"We were working the same street because you thought I'd get lost."

Jericho put her hands on her hips. "Did you get lost Clark?"

"Hell yeah! I even ended up in jail. Did I happen to mention that?"

"Clark!"

"Sorry." Then to himself. "But I did."

"You don't need to mention that to anyone."

"Speaking of mentioning... You going to have a talk with your brother?"

"Speaking of my brother, you're getting off way easier than he will be."

That didn't seem possible. Until Poodle saw Pearl and Father Phil coming around the corner of the house. Then the lightbulb overhead lit up. He smiled, pleased that he was himself rather than his best friend.

"What's so amusing?" Jericho's hands were still on her hips.

"I... I can see the future!" Poodle said. He put his palm up to his mouth, pretending to hide his grin. "Hee-hee-he!"

"Clark!"

"Gonna get a whoopin-n-n!!" He started to dance in place.

"Clark!"

"Okay, okay." Poodle stopped dancing and stood up straight. He looked down at his wife. She had stepped into his personal space, to challenge him. He thought for a second to pick her up and continue dancing. But that would have been a serious mistake. He slumped his shoulders.

"Look," He said, trying to sound defeated. "We're still figuring it out. Trying to get things started. We already got two sales. By accident! Imagine how good we'll be when you get us whipped into shape?"

Jericho' jaw stayed stern as she stared up at her husband. She could hear the chatter between her mother and the priest growing closer.

"We'll talk more." She said with finality. Then turned away with a ready-made grin, and motioned for their guests to have a seat.

Poodle let out a soft, low whistle as his wife walked away. He knew she wasn't done. And he was in for it. Then he looked over at his brother-in-law playing with the kids. He started to dance in place again.

"Whoopin-n-n…" He sang to himself.

When the potatoes were done, Poodle put the fish on the grill. The coals, still hot, had cooled enough that the fillets were spared being instantly flash fried. He was relieved. More than once, before, he had done it wrong.

Elizabeth came out with paper plates and utensils. She had the kids follow her inside for condiments and cups. They all sat down. Father Phil said a prayer. And everyone ate. And ate.

At the time of purchase, Milk had been certain that they bought too much fish. But he was mistaken. All of them dug in.

Particularly Anna. She had two ears of corn and a whole potato. And she went after the fillets like she was a dues-paying member of the fish-eating union. By the time everyone else stopped, she was still eating. They all watched her.

While they were staring, Rodney leaned over and whispered to Poodle.

"You get in trouble yet?"

Poodle nodded that he did. And then glanced sideways, back at the boy, as if asking the same question.

Rodney shook him off. "Father will wait till them two fall asleep on the ride home."

Picking up his plate, Poodle held out a hand for Rodney to give him his. Which the young man did. Then he stood up, with the intention of gathering everyone else's. But before he walked away, Poodle leaned in, over Rodney.

"Think about sticking around a while, kid. We still got a whole summer of fishing to get to." Then he winked. And began clearing the table.

Rodney grinned. He liked that idea.

As Poodle moved around the table, Pearl took the opportunity to change seats and sit next to her son. She nudged him, to make sure he noticed. Milk slid sideways, closer to Roberto, to make room.

Then his mother elbowed him.

"What?" Milk asked.

"You got plans after this?" Pearl asked.

Milk didn't understand. That wasn't something his mother would ask him.

"I do now." He answered back.

"Good. We need to talk."

"Ugh!" Milk dropped his head. "No, we don't ma. We don't need to talk."

"Oh, have a little chat, cellmate." Poodle chirped from the other side of the table.

When Milk looked at him, Poodle jerked an imaginary hangman's noose and pantomimed being hung. Milk frowned.

Father Phil didn't understand. But got enough of the message that he figured they should probably get going. He got up and instructed the kids to help before they left.

Elizabth quickly asked Rodney how to say 'dessert' in Spanish. When he told her, she repeated it several times, making sure the young ones heard her. Then she waved for them to follow her back into the kitchen.

The priest sat back down.

A minute later, Elizabeth returned with a chocolate cake, in hand. And the kids, caring fresh plates and utensils, right behind her.

Setting it on the table, Elizabeth used the same line that both her mother and grandmother recited whenever they presented a store-bought dessert.

"I was up all-night baking it." She said.

The kids couldn't have cared less. And the adults over complemented her, as a way of playing along.

They ate three-quarters of the cake. Then Jericho insisted Father Phil take the rest of it with him. He politely refused. But was glad when no one took him seriously.

As Elizabeth set the last of the cake, wrapped in plastic, in front of him, Father Phil stood up. And offered a bless.

He thanked the Lord for their new found friends. And he thanked each of them for sacrificing two full work days to share their time and lives to improve the quality of life for the children. He wished more people were that way.

Father Phil gave such thanks and gratitude that Jericho began to wonder if perhaps her husband had slipped the priest a note. She gave

Poodle the inquiring eye.

Poodle knew what she was thinking. And was glad that he could be truthful when he would say that he hadn't said anything. But he also liked the idea of having a favor to call in. And made a mental note to remember it.

When the priest was done, everyone helped clean up. Then went out to the driveway for good-byes. The kids climbed in the car, waved, and the Rambler rolled off.

Pearl, standing next to Poodle finished waving and said, "You didn't find your 7-foot nemeses in Mumsford?"

"No. Not even close." Poodle answered.

"He must have come from out of town." Elizabeth said.

"Yeah, good chance." Milk said.

"But even so," Jericho said, "Unless he came to town in the back of a truck, somebody had to see him. Stopping for gas. Or at the bus station. Something like that."

"People would notice." Elizabeth agreed. "How many 7-foot people can you name?"

"Wilt Chamberlain." Pearl said. "Probably it."

Milk laughed. "Ma, you think Wilt Chamberlain came to Mumsford and robbed these people?"

"Your father and I seen him rob the Knicks of their dignity in Hershey when he put up a hundred points single handed."

"Come on, ma." Milk said.

"He did. It's in the books."

Poodle gawked at his mother-in-law. "Wait. You were at that game?"

"We went to a lot of them." Pearl answered. "Your father-in-law loved the Knicks."

Elizabeth put her hand to her chin, to signify her grandfather's height. "Grampa loved basketball?" She asked.

Milk grabbed Elizabeth by the elbow, tugging her towards him. "Ma got lots of pictures." He guided his niece around himself, to right in front of his mother. "They went all kinds of places. Didn't you, ma?" He attempted to step away.

"Babylon…" Pearl said without looking at him.

"I'm just saying it would be good for her. It's a side of pops she doesn't know."

"It will be even better for her tomorrow." Jericho said, putting an end to the debate.

"See?" Pearl said. "What I say?"

Milk rolled his eyes. "Last thing I remember you saying was you wanted to walk home tonight."

"Tsk," Pearl shook her head. "Talk to your mother that way." Then she walked over to the Mythical Milk Machine and slid open the door.

Chapter 20

Later that night, the moon rose just before midnight. And when it did, Bobby Cowl had one ear pressed against his AM-FM clock radio. With safe cracking precision, he was listening intently and edging the dial across the radio band, hoping to lock onto a big city station.

His room put him 4 stories in the air, in a ghost town between farm fields. With no obstructions, and a little patience, he could, on a clear night, pick up WNBC in New York. Or KDKA in Pittsburgh. He had found a few others as well. But he liked those two the best.

The radio was a cracked plastic rectangle with a long cigarette burn across the top. It had a non-working, oversized clock face in the center, surrounded by a pair of two-inch tweeters. One on each side. It wasn't much to look at. And didn't tell time worth a damn. But with a 30-foot home made antennae running out the window and down the side of the building, its long-distance reception was impressive.

Bobby bought it at the Rescue Mission on South Lexington, when he and Billy first came North. It was the first, and almost the only, money they spent from the heist they pulled on J.T.

The rest of that loot was safely hidden, in a place only he knew, waiting on… Bobby wasn't even sure what. He just knew there was something about that money he didn't like. He didn't want to touch it any more than absolutely necessary. And so far, that had been minimal.

Maybe it was cursed, like the other two thought. Or blood stained. He wasn't sure.

When Max first saw the cash, he took one look and threw himself on the ground, convulsing.

"Devil dollars!" He yelled. Repeatedly. Until Bobby finally closed the lid on the trunk and carted it away. As he did, Max sat up and recited some mystic mumbo jumbo, waving his arms and contorting his fingers.

Billy watched all that in shocked horror. He had never seen anyone attempt to exorcise money before. If his cousin was tossing hex fingers at it, he wanted it gone. He told Bobby they should burn it all. Max agreed.

Bobby thought they were both nuts. He might concede there was something that left him feeling creepy about the stash. But to actually burn money? Even he knew better than to do that. And he had spent time in three separate psych centers.

So, looking as sincere as possible, he told them both that he would. If the money was evil, he would take it out and burn it all, that very night. And he did. Or so they thought.

That little lie turned out to be a mixed blessing. With his two partners thinking the loot had been purified and returned to the almighty, via smoke signal, he had no worries about them double crossing him.

But in order to convince them, he had to actually start a fire. Which he did, in the middle of the night. And the other two watched, from a safe distance. But so did all the neighbors.

They weren't in the abandoned bank, in the middle of nowhere, back then. They had just hit town. And were illegally squatting in the house Max's mother had rented, before she died.

The neighbors saw the fire and called Sylvester, the landlord. He got phone calls starting at 11:30 PM, telling him some pyros were trying to torch his property. He showed up with a shot gun and two rottweilers.

The money had already been buried, behind the garage, by that time. All the unwelcome guests had to do was hop a fence and run away. Billy took some rock salt to the back of one leg, as he was climbing over. It made him scream. And limp. And he was certain he was about to die as canine fodder.

But Sylvester didn't want them dead. He just wanted them gone. He already had too many run ins with the law to do anything more than terrify them. So, after he was sure they were scared shitless, he called back the dogs and let everyone escape. He assumed they were merely kids. Stupid ones.

Bobby snuck back before dawn, on his own, and recovered the trunk. Then he went back inside and took his radio. He called a cab from a phone booth down the street. They took him to the bus station. And he put the trunk in a locker.

He let the other two think he was willing to risk his life for the radio. Which he wouldn't have bothered to do, if there wasn't a small fortune involved. But there was. So, he did.

That left his merry men thinking he was the bravest. Or at least the craziest. Either way, it cemented his authority position in the group.

And that authority was about to get exercised. On the sly. As soon as he found a radio station that he liked, he was going downstairs to check on them.

Bobby assumed they would be knee deep in whatever secret bamboo activity Max had dreamed up. He just had to make sure, before he took care of business.

Max really did come home with bamboo. Quite a bit of it. Bobby couldn't get a straight answer out of either where he got it, or why he had to have it. And Max was even more evasive about his alleged prescription.

But Bobby knew he'd be sneaking out later. So, maybe it was best to let Max have his way, and let them pre-occupy themselves for a few hours. They'd be less inclined to notice his coming and going.

There was going to be another fire. A small one, this time. And it was best if no one else saw it. Bobby was going to burn the painter stilts Billy had worn during the heists. The ones that made him appear 7 feet tall.

He wouldn't need to do it, if they had left the damn things alone, as instructed. But those two clowns didn't have that kind of self-restraint.

When he came back from his interview at Abbott, Bobby found the two of them in a parking lot, down the street, jousting. They were each hopping around on one stilt, trying to stab the other guy with a broom handle.

As far as Bobby could tell, no one besides himself, had witnessed any of that. But it was foolish to take chances. Ghost town or not, the parking lot was adjacent to the county highway, which served as the town's main street. Plenty of people, including the County Sheriff's department, still travelled it.

It was time to dispose of all incriminating evidence. The stilts had served their purpose.

You see, in the midst of a hold up, even though people are afraid, they are still going to remember things. So, a good trick of the trade is to give them something worth remembering.

Everyone notices a 7-foot-tall person. They couldn't not notice if they tried. Throw in masked men waving pistols, and it becomes too surreal for most people. It's weird. And they're afraid. They can't think clearly. All they remember is Goliath, looming overhead.

Bobby was banking on that. He knew the police would eventually figure out what they did. But in the meantime, a consistent description of a person that didn't exist, was a useful delay tactic. Now, with all the loot fenced, he just had to finish cleaning up.

The speakers came alive with sound. He leaned back. The dial was somewhere around 1100 AM. He didn't recognize the station setting. And he didn't care for the music. Maybe it was a good time to check on the boys and eliminate some evidence. If the tunes didn't improve, he'd move on when he got back.

He put on his shoes. And walked out, leaving the radio playing. After another minute of instrumental bravado, the song ended. There was a slight pause, for effect, before the DJ came on.

"It's 11:02. And time for the news at K-K-G-Y, 1070 AM, here in Little Rock. Tonight's head line; convicted racketeer Jebediah Morris is still at large. In a daring escape earlier today, a three car police motorcade was ambushed in broad daylight. A spokesman for the police department said Morris was being relocated to St. Anthony's hospital for an undisclosed ailment, when the attack occurred. Road blocks have been established throughout the state. Morris is considered armed and dangerous. No further details have been released. A press conference with State Attorney General, Adam Wicksley, has been scheduled for tomorrow morning at 8 AM. In other news…"

End Part I.

ACKNOWLEDGEMENT

The cover art for The Sycamore Centennial Parade was designed and created by **Stella Blue Porzongolo.**

Stella Blue is an architect working in the restoration of NYC's historic buildings. In her free time, she likes playing softball and making up creative recipes for dinner.

We hope you enjoyed **The Sycamore Centennial Parade Part I**. Thank you.

Part II (and final portion) of the story will be available soon.

Join our mailing list at https://fintanandturtle.com